the further adventures of

SHERLOCK HOLMES

THE ALBINO'S TREASURE

AVAILABLE NOW FROM TITAN BOOKS
THE FURTHER ADVENTURES OF SHERLOCK HOLMES SERIES:

THE COUNTERFEIT DETECTIVE (November 2016)
Stuart Douglas

THE RIPPER LEGACY (August 2016)
David Stuart Davies

THE WHITE WORM (February 2016)
Sam Siciliano

MURDER AT SORROW'S CROWN (November 2015)
Steven Savile & Robert Greenberger

THE VEILED DETECTIVE
David Stuart Davies

THE SCROLL OF THE DEAD
David Stuart Davies

THE ANGEL OF THE OPERA
Sam Siciliano

THE WEB WEAVER
Sam Siciliano

THE GRIMSWELL CURSE
Sam Siciliano

DR JEKYLL AND MR HOLMES
Loren D. Estleman

SHERLOCK HOLMES VS. DRACULA
Loren D. Estleman

THE ECTOPLASMIC MAN
Daniel Stashower

THE WAR OF THE WORLDS
Manly Wade Wellman & Wade Wellman

THE WHITECHAPEL HORRORS
Edward B. Hanna

THE SEVENTH BULLET
Daniel D. Victor

THE TITANIC TRAGEDY
William Seil

the further adventures of SHERLOCK HOLMES

THE ALBINO'S TREASURE

STUART DOUGLAS

TITAN BOOKS

THE FURTHER ADVENTURES OF SHERLOCK HOLMES:
THE ALBINO'S TREASURE
Print edition ISBN: 9781783293124
E-book edition ISBN: 9781783293131

Published by Titan Books
A division of Titan Publishing Group Ltd
144 Southwark Street, London SE1 0UP

First edition: May 2015
10 9 8 7 6 5 4 3 2 1

A CIP catalogue record for this title is available from the British Library.

Printed in the USA.

What did you think of this book? We love to hear from our readers.
Please email us at: readerfeedback@titanemail.com,
or write to Reader Feedback at the above address.

To receive advance information, news, competitions, and exclusive offers
online, please sign up for the Titan newsletter on our website:
www.titanbooks.com

For Julie, without whom I'd never even have started

Prologue

Throughout my long acquaintance with Sherlock Holmes, it was my practice to present to my friend a copy of my notes on any case of particular sensitivity. Generally, Holmes would glance over the freshly written adventure with barely concealed irritation, mutter some unflattering remark, and indicate that I could do with it as I wished. Occasionally, however, he would frown and, showing a sudden interest, quickly read the entire manuscript. 'I think,' he would say, in due course, 'that this particular case would be best kept between ourselves for the moment.' And with that he would disappear into his room, my piece for *The Strand* in his hand – and it would be consigned to the tin box he kept there, never to be seen again.

Now, however, with everyone involved – bar myself – long since deceased I find myself often sitting in my favourite bay window in the weak winter sunlight, with the same tin box open on my lap. I read the collection of notes and asides, summaries and complete manuscripts, and am transported back to my younger days, when Holmes tackled any mystery that came his way, and I stood at his side, his faithful chronicler to the end.

But the world has changed immeasurably during my long life, and matters that seemed scandalous to us in the old century appear commonplace as we navigate the second third of the new. If a king may abdicate his throne and choose love over duty – and be applauded for doing so – then perhaps the time is right to bring these last few cases of Sherlock Holmes into the light? At the very least, the case I find recorded in my notes as 'The Albino's Treasure' has surely lost all power to rock the nation, and yet several elements contained therein may prove to be of interest to a modern readership.

The tale which follows occurred in the year 1896, when the new National Portrait Gallery had just opened its doors, and I was back in Baker Street, sharing rooms with my old friend.

One

It was never the habit of my friend, Sherlock Holmes, to rise early in the morning. Though he was more than capable of remaining awake and alert for days on end if the need arose, his preference was always to breakfast late if he possibly could. As I was by no means an early bird myself, this suited us both admirably, and Mrs Hudson knew better than to allow anyone to call before a reasonable hour of the morning. A heavy knocking at the door to my room, therefore, and Holmes's voice calling gruffly for me to rouse myself came as something of a surprise.

Responding to the urgency in his voice, I barely took the time to pull on my dressing gown before moving through to the sitting room we shared, and was already asking questions of Holmes before I took one step into the room.

'What on earth is going on, Holmes?' I asked. 'And what time is it?'

In reply, Holmes – who I saw was as poorly dressed for company as I – gestured first to the mantel clock, which stood at a little after five a.m., and then to the long figure of Inspector Lestrade of Scotland Yard, who stood just inside the door, directly in front of us.

The Inspector at least had the grace to appear momentarily embarrassed, before the obvious seriousness of his mission overcame whatever reticence he felt. He laid his hat on the table beside him and, as Holmes waved an irritated hand in his direction, began to speak, evidently continuing a discussion curtailed by my arrival.

'Yes, Mr Holmes,' he said firmly, 'anarchists it is.' From his tone it was apparent that Lestrade was as impatient to progress with matters as Holmes, though it remained to be seen if their motivations were equally well matched. Holmes said nothing and, after a small pause, Lestrade continued. 'Now, before you say another word, complaining about politics and the like, I should tell you that we have reason to suspect an anarchist plot aimed at the very top of English society – possibly even threatening the safety of Her Majesty, the Queen.'

As he spoke these last few words, Lestrade favoured first Holmes then myself with a look; his small eyes narrowed even further than usual, stressing the importance of this last statement, as though that were at all necessary.

Holmes – who had until that point remained slumped in his chair – sat forward as the Inspector named our sovereign, suddenly as alert as a man well rested rather than one roused from sleep in the early hours. 'Her Majesty, you say, Lestrade?' he asked, eagerly. 'You are certain of this?'

Lestrade nodded once, sharply. 'I'd hardly be standing here at five in the morning otherwise,' he said, straightening his shoulders and letting his fingers rap on the crown of his bowler.

Holmes was suddenly all energy, gesturing for the Inspector to sit as he reached for his favourite pipe and the Persian slipper in which he kept his shag tobacco. Standing in front of the empty fire, he filled the bowl and applied a match to it. 'Begin at the beginning,' he said, 'and be sure to miss nothing out.'

Lestrade shifted himself forward in his seat and pulled a small notebook from his pocket. Flipping through its pages, he seemed unsure where to begin but, after a brief interval, he evidently satisfied himself and began to speak.

'Are you aware, Mr Holmes, of a group calling itself the Brotherhood of Ireland?' he asked first, glancing from Holmes to myself.

Holmes nodded. 'The name is familiar,' he replied. 'I would need to consult my notes before going any further than that, but they are, if I recall correctly, a political group dedicated to the cause of Home Rule in Ireland?'

'Indeed,' said Lestrade. 'And until recently that's all they appeared to be. However, we have been hearing rumours of a growing militancy amongst their membership, and last evening those rumours bore a most unfortunate fruit. At a little after two o'clock this morning, we were alerted to a disturbance at the newly built National Portrait Gallery at St Martin's Place. The night guard at the Gallery discovered a man in the section devoted to political portraits, engaged in an act of vandalism on the painting of Lord Salisbury—'

'Vandalism?' Holmes interrupted, his tone making it clear that a vandalised painting, no matter how august its subject, was not, in his opinion, of sufficient import to warrant an interruption of his rest.

'Yes, Mr Holmes. Slashed with a knife, right across, and the letters "BOI" daubed on the wall beside it in red paint. The guard intervened, of course, and a chase ensued before a colleague, alerted by the noise, arrived and the two of them managed to subdue the intruder.'

Lestrade paused in his narrative for a moment, allowing Holmes once again to interrupt. 'This is all very interesting, Lestrade, but

I confess I remain at something of a loss. That a likeness of the former Prime Minister has been so egregiously attacked is certainly disturbing, but I fail to see either what you believe I might do to help in the matter, or the link between this crime and the safety of Her Majesty.'

I admit that I too found myself confused by Lestrade's obvious urgency. It was, granted, not yet a decade since the disturbances dubbed 'Bloody Sunday' by the press, in which a mob, thousands strong, led by socialists and republicans had marched on Trafalgar Square and been rebuffed only by the intervention of some two thousand policemen. Irish Home Rule was a subject seemingly designed to foster strong opinions, but it was hardly a new problem, nor did the attack on Lord Salisbury's portrait seem to be anything more than the sort of grand gesture so beloved of republican agitators. I was on the verge of making this very point to the Inspector, when he held up a hand to forestall me.

'Nothing on the surface, I admit,' he said. 'But when the man was brought in for questioning, he refused to say anything beyond a single statement. "Next time it won't just be a painting," he said, and then clammed up, refusing to say another word. It may be nothing, Mr Holmes, but my superiors fear that this is the start of something bigger – the first salvo in a new campaign of terror, as it were.'

With that, the Inspector sat back in his chair and allowed his notebook to fall shut. 'We'd be grateful, Mr Holmes, if you'd speak to the man, see if you can't discover something useful from him. Even his name would be a start. All we know for certain is that he entered the Gallery in the late afternoon, spent some time admiring the royal portraits on the top floor, and must have secreted himself somewhere before closing, only to emerge in the early hours bent on destruction.'

While Lestrade had been speaking, Holmes had finished his pipe.

He laid it down and rose from his seat. 'I am not entirely convinced that this matter is one which requires my presence, but I am awake now, and it would be churlish to refuse, I suppose. What do you say, Watson – shall we take an early morning trip to Scotland Yard?'

I held my hands out in agreement. 'I think we should, Holmes. Perhaps the threat is a hollow one, but perhaps not. And if anyone can discover this man's secrets, it is certainly you.'

Holmes turned to Lestrade. 'We will need to dress, Inspector. If you would care to go on ahead, we shall be with you within the hour.'

Lestrade stood and replaced the bowler on his head. 'Thank you, Mr Holmes, Dr Watson,' he said as he opened the door to leave. 'I'll expect you then.'

After he left, Holmes pulled a volume of newspaper clippings from a bookcase, and stood for some time in contemplation. 'I had hoped for something more challenging from the good Inspector,' he said, finally. 'Perhaps some interest can be garnered from this gentleman and his unwholesome activities, but somehow I doubt it.' He ran a hand through his sleep-tousled hair. 'In any case we must first make ourselves presentable for Scotland Yard's finest!'

I watched him disappear into his room and repaired to mine. For all Holmes's dissatisfaction, I was keen to witness his interrogation of the suspected anarchist. The man might believe that there was safety in silence, but I knew of old that my friend rarely required a dialogue in order to draw his conclusions.

I had never had cause to visit the Inspector in his office on the new Victoria Embankment, to which the entire Metropolitan Police force had decamped some five years previously. I was impressed, as Holmes appeared to be, by this re-born Scotland Yard, which loomed out of the morning fog like a minor European castle, studded with turrets and topped with large chimneys in stripes of red and white brick. The building combined an air of modernity with an aura of impregnability which, when seen close up, I found strangely reassuring.

Even so, Lestrade's office, into which we were shown by a helpful constable, was cold with the early morning chill in spite of the close-fitting windows. Lestrade rose from his desk as we entered and indicated two wooden chairs.

'If you'd care to sit, gentlemen, I'll have Constable Mann bring the suspect up.' He nodded to the constable, who disappeared back into the corridor, closing the office door softly behind him. 'The man has said nothing since I spoke to you earlier, Mr Holmes, but we're hoping you can use your trickery on him, and give us something to work with.'

I could feel Holmes bristle at this talk of trickery and to forestall an indignant reply, I asked Lestrade what he could tell us of the recent activities of the Brotherhood of Ireland.

'To be frank, Dr Watson, there's not a great deal that I can tell you. The Brotherhood are known to the police, but, until tonight, they seemed content to agitate peacefully in England. Pamphlets handed out in the streets, evening meetings with republican speakers, that sort of thing. Enough for us to have them under observation, but compared with certain other groups, harmless enough.'

'Or so you thought,' interjected Holmes with a frown. 'Has there been any change in the behaviour of this Brotherhood recently? Has there been any indication that they have chosen to change their mode of operation, abandoning their peaceful campaigning for a fresh approach more akin to the current case?'

'Nothing, Mr Holmes,' Lestrade replied immediately. 'That's

partly why I've brought you in tonight, in fact. My superiors are concerned that we've missed some vital element. They're worried that this attack isn't an isolated incident, but more by way of a first step. A marker, if you take my meaning.'

'It would not be the first time that such a group moved from lawful protest to unlawful, that is certainly true. I am reminded of the case of the kidnapped Spanish diplomat last year in Madrid. The faction who took – and eventually murdered – him were believed to be a political reading club until that terrible incident, and the bombings that followed. Thirty-five dead in total, unless I am mistaken, and the ringleaders never captured.' Holmes paused for a moment, as though assuring himself that he had his figures correct. 'No,' he concluded as there was a sharp knock on the door behind him, 'your superiors are not wrong to be concerned.'

Lestrade did not seem reassured by Holmes's words. He barked for whomever had knocked to come inside. As the door swung open, Holmes and I turned to examine the newcomer who shuffled in at a nudge from our helpful constable.

The man was aged somewhere between thirty and fifty, and stared straight ahead as the constable ordered him to stop, giving no indication that he was aware of anyone else in the room. He was tall and spare, with a small round face dominated by a thick moustache, which curled down past the corners of his mouth. A thin scar on one cheek ran from beneath his left eye to a point just above his jawline, but other than that he was unremarkable. He was dressed in what I presumed were the clothes he had been wearing when apprehended: dark working man's trousers and a loose shirt, ripped at the collar. There were no shoes on his feet, causing the chains which ran from his wrists to his ankles to rest on the top of each foot, rubbing them painfully red as he hobbled forward.

'You can wait outside, constable,' Lestrade ordered, then, turning to Holmes, announced, 'This is the man.'

'I had surmised as much,' Holmes replied with barely concealed irritation. 'An Irishman from one of the northern counties, who has lived in England for some years now, and who was, for a time at least, a member of our own armed forces. Any name he gives you will almost certainly be false.'

'Oh come now, Mr Holmes, how can you possibly know that?' Lestrade was on his feet, annoyance and incredulity plain on his face.

'Trickery, Inspector,' said Holmes with a tight smile. 'Isn't that the very thing you suggested, after all?'

'Holmes...' I warned, knowing his low opinion of Scotland Yard and its inspectors. He looked at me with a raised eyebrow, inviting me to share his amusement, but this was not the time for such games. If there were even the most remote chance that this man was involved in a plot against the Crown and its ministers, every second could prove vital.

My interjection evidently reminded Holmes of his responsibilities, for he cleared his throat and addressed Lestrade more usefully, if not markedly with any more cordiality. 'It is really quite straight-forward, Lestrade. Observe the man. He is not merely standing upright; he is at attention. His arms are held straight down each leg, in spite of his manacles, with his hands bunched and his thumbs to the fore, a stance one might almost describe as the hallmark of the British soldier on display.

'Additionally, I see the edges of a tattoo on his chest, usually hidden by his shirt, but currently partially visible due to his torn collar. The section I can make out contains the Latin word "*caritatem*", or "charity" in English, which I would hazard is the end of the motto of the county of Donegal, "*Mutuam habeatis caritatem*" –

"Maintain amongst yourselves, mutual charity".

'Finally, it is implausible, in these turbulent times, that an Irish Catholic from Donegal would be able to move straight from home to a position in the British Army. Hence, he spent some time in this country, softening his accent and Anglifying his manners. The man's voice is faintly flavoured with the Irish brogue, I'll warrant. He also, most probably, joined up under an assumed name.'

I could not be sure but it seemed to me that the man stiffened slightly beside us as Holmes spoke. Holmes obviously thought the same, for he turned round in his chair to stare at our prisoner. Before he could say a word, however, Lestrade laughed and slapped a hand against his desk.

'I should know better than to doubt you, Mr Holmes,' he said. 'Hear that, young Paddy? Mr Holmes here has the measure of you already!' He turned back to Holmes, with a more serious expression on his face. 'Of course, we had already guessed that he was really an Irishman, for all his English talk. But knowing which part of that blasted country he calls home is a small additional help, Mr Holmes.'

I admit that I bridled a little at Lestrade's words. Scotland Yard, while seemingly happy to make use of Holmes's remarkable brain, were also jealous of their own reputation and had, on more than one occasion, purloined credit that rightfully belonged to my friend. That this rarely concerned Holmes himself was scant consolation. I said nothing, however, for I knew that he would not thank me for the intervention.

In fact, he appeared utterly sanguine about the matter, and continued in his observation of the prisoner. After a minute or more of silent contemplation – while Lestrade fidgeted at his desk and seemed, on more than one occasion, about to speak – Holmes steepled his fingers in front of his chin and came to a decision.

'Can you please leave us alone now, Inspector?' he asked. 'I believe your presence – as a representative of the Crown – is making this man uncomfortable in the extreme.' He gestured with one hand to the door. 'I should like to come to know him better, and to discuss his grievances more fully, but, I fear, that is unlikely to happen while you remain in the room.'

Again, Lestrade seemed on the verge of protest, but Holmes's half-smile and unmistakable tone of command rendered him mute and, without another word, he rose and left the office to Holmes, the prisoner and myself. Throughout this exchange, he too had remained utterly silent, but as before I was aware of a subtle shifting of his body, a slight relaxing of his shoulders and softening of his face as Lestrade closed the door behind him.

'Now,' Holmes said without preamble, 'perhaps you and I can talk.' He rose from his chair and indicated that the prisoner might be seated in his place. The man made no move at first then, hesitantly, as though expecting a blow, and without taking his eyes from Holmes, sat down in the vacated chair. Holmes moved round Lestrade's desk and pulled the Inspector's chair towards himself, before sitting down so close to the prisoner as to be almost touching.

'My name is Sherlock Holmes,' he began. 'I am a private citizen–'

The man, whose eyes had remained fixed on Holmes throughout the exchange, suddenly flicked forward, and his shoulders squared and lifted as he sat at attention once more.

The next hour was a peculiar one. Holmes addressed the prisoner constantly, unceasingly, beginning with one train of thought, then moving to the next without pause, trying out first this conversational gambit, then that, and all the while scrutinising his silent audience with unblinking eyes. Holmes spoke of towns and rivers in Donegal, of great political leaders and popular journalists, of religion, and science and philosophy. For one who claimed to know little beyond that necessary for his detective work, Holmes, in that hour, exhibited a breadth of knowledge that would not have disgraced a university tutor.

Finally, he laid his hands on his thighs and pushed himself to his feet with a heavy sigh. Still, the prisoner sat unmoving, only an occasional slow blink betraying the fact that he was still awake.

'I think,' Holmes said slowly, 'that now would be an opportune moment for you to explain what you meant when you told Lestrade that "next time it won't just be a painting".' He cocked an eyebrow quizzically, as though expecting a response, then continued, more forcefully, 'Don't you agree, Corporal Charles O'Donnell?'

The reaction from our prisoner was dramatic.

He leapt to his feet and swung himself round to face Holmes. Their faces were mere inches apart as he grabbed a handful of my friend's jacket. Of course, I immediately moved to intervene but I need not have concerned myself. With a twist of his body and a flick of his wrist, Holmes easily reversed positions with his assailant, driving the man to his knees with no apparent effort.

'Thank you,' Holmes said, 'for the confirmation. Now,' he continued in a harder, colder voice, 'will you resume your seat and answer my questions, or must I break your wrist?'

Though Holmes was no shrinking violet, this was a side to him that I had not often seen. I admit that I had never heard of Charles O'Donnell, but Holmes evidently knew exactly who he was.

O'Donnell was no coward, at least, and though the pain must have been excruciating, he gave no sign of discomfort as Holmes bent his wrist unnaturally then – with a grunt – pushed him back into his seat.

He sat, rubbing his wrist and staring up at Holmes with undisguised loathing. Holmes, for his part, walked across to the door, pulled it open, and spoke a few words to the constable standing outside. He had barely crossed back to Lestrade's desk before the Inspector appeared in the doorway, puffing as though he had run some distance.

'My apologies, Mr Holmes,' he said between exhalations. 'I was having a cup of tea downstairs in the canteen. I didn't expect you to discover anything quite so quickly.' As Holmes was already sitting in his chair, Lestrade perched himself uncomfortably on the edge of the desk. 'You *have* discovered something, haven't you?' he asked.

Holmes allowed himself a small smile as he replied. 'That depends on your definition of *discovered*, Inspector. I now know this gentleman's name, and his former rank and regiment in the British Army. I can tell you that he has been resident in England for more than ten years but fewer than twenty. Finally, I can tell you that, though no common foot soldier in the struggle, neither is he currently high in the confidences of the Brotherhood of Ireland leadership and that, therefore, any threats he makes beyond the immediate should be treated with caution.'

For the second time in an hour, Lestrade stood, nonplussed, before Sherlock Holmes. I was conscious of a certain pleasurable anticipation running through me as I prepared to hear an explanation for this collection of facts plucked, it seemed to the Inspector at least, from thin air.

Holmes, as was often his way, allowed himself a small expression of impatience before any such explanation was forthcoming. After a moment, though, he murmured, 'Oh, very well, if you have failed to observe *anything...*' and settling himself more comfortably in Lestrade's chair, explained his reasoning.

'I have had occasion in the past to mention the need for thorough preparation, have I not? The current case is an ideal example of the efficacy of such preparation. Why, even before leaving Baker Street I knew that the prisoner held by the Inspector was likely to be Irish and Catholic. Who else, after all, would have so vehement an objection to Lord Salisbury and the question of Home Rule? So far, so good; the most fresh-faced of police constables could hardly fail to have reached the same conclusions.

'But then there is the fact that the man strolled into the Gallery some time before he strictly needed to. Confidence is required to look over the location of the crime in advance, especially in so public a place. An Irishman recently arrived in this country would lack such confidence, while one who had lived here for two decades or more would not, I suggest, have quite the same revolutionary fire in his belly as he once had. These few, simple facts I was able to surmise while we yet sat in front of the fire in Baker Street.'

As Holmes paused to take a sip of water, O'Donnell's face took on a peculiar aspect, of fear mixed with what could almost have been respect, which surprised me, for the man had until that point appeared to be made of granite. But I had seen the same look before, on the faces of other men brought before Sherlock Holmes: men secure in their own secrets until that great mind began to winkle them out. Lestrade took the opportunity of the brief pause to open the office door and speak quickly to a uniformed police officer standing in the corridor. This constable hurried off, returning just as Holmes re-commenced his narrative. He handed Lestrade a thin brown folder and closed the door behind him on his way out.

'Knowing these several facts as I did, I was therefore able to examine my own personal files this morning, before Watson and I made our way to Scotland Yard. As you are possibly aware, Inspector, I have an extensive library of newspaper clippings relating to criminal activities included in my records, and it was a relatively simple matter therefore to scan those reports specifically linked to republican crimes in Ireland between ten and twenty years ago and, from there, check on the known whereabouts of all suspected parties in the period immediately afterwards. Of eleven such incidents – bombings, assassination attempts and the like – the vast majority of the culprits were either killed in the commission of their crimes or later by the process of law. On two occasions, however, the most strongly suspected individual, though named, was never caught, and in one such occurrence was never heard from again.

'That individual, Charles O'Donnell of Clonmany in County Donegal, was responsible for the destruction of a Protestant church and the murder of its minister nine years ago. His likeness was circulated to newspapers in both Ireland and England, though to no avail, and he was believed by the authorities in Ireland to have fled to the United States. Before coming here, Inspector, I refreshed my memory from just such an image. This man is Charles O'Donnell.'

At this point Lestrade, impatient as ever to demonstrate his own utility, flipped open the folder he carried, and held it out for Holmes's inspection. Holmes examined the few pages within for a minute, and no more, before handing the file to me.

The photograph on top of a slew of handwritten documents clearly showed the man sitting in front of me. He was now a little older and a little heavier, but the scar on his face was unmistakable, and the look of hatred in his eyes identical. I quickly examined the pages beneath, but they held little which Holmes had not already expounded on. Our prisoner was a dangerous and merciless man, of that there was no doubt.

'That's all very well, Mr Holmes,' Lestrade said, rising from his desk to take the folder which I now held out to him. 'But you claimed to know the man's rank and regiment. How can that possibly be?

Unless... did he speak to you after all?'

'After a fashion yes, he did,' Holmes replied. 'A man may say not a single word aloud, and yet his face will betray him every time, if his interrogator knows what to look for. The eyes in particular are not called the windows to the soul for nothing, Lestrade. Every movement tells its own story. And as I spoke to Mr O'Donnell of this and that I read the story in his eyes, and can tell you that – under an assumed name which, I regret, I do not know – your prisoner has spent the better part of the past decade in the South Staffordshire Regiment, rising, I believe, to the rank of corporal. In that time, I have no doubt that he has remained in occasional contact with his former revolutionary compatriots, but it seems highly unlikely that he will have maintained a sufficiently regular degree of communication to be aware of more than the Brotherhood's most immediate plans. A small fish, at best, Inspector.'

Lulled by O'Donnell's long silence and stillness, I was not prepared for the reaction that this parting line evoked in the prisoner. No sooner had the words left Holmes's lips than the man threw himself forward with a hideous snarl on his face. Lestrade and I barely moved, so swift and unexpected was the attack, but Holmes had obviously been expecting it and took two steps backwards as O'Donnell's lunge was brought short by the manacles at his ankles and wrists. The very act of stretching his arms towards Holmes caused the connecting chains to snatch at his feet and brought him tumbling to the ground. He lay there, groaning quietly, until Lestrade pulled him roughly to his feet and thrust him back into his seat.

'Enough!' the Inspector barked. 'One more trick like that and–'

Whatever consequence Lestrade intended to convey was lost, however, as O'Donnell pushed himself to his feet and, with his eyes locked on Holmes, snarled in his direction, 'I tell you this, who thinks he's so clever. I tell you this. Next time it'll be flesh being cut, not canvas and paint.' With that, he was evidently satisfied that he had spat his defiance well enough, for he sat back down carefully, smiling, as though taking tea with a friend rather than facing an uncertain future in custody, and refused to say another word.

Try as he might, Lestrade failed to pierce this wall of silence and eventually, after twenty minutes or more, he called for the attentive constable to take O'Donnell back to his cell.

'Perhaps we might have been better to stick with our own methods,' said Lestrade once we were all settled again. I thought this more than a little unfair, given the progress Holmes had made, and said so, making no attempt to keep the annoyance out of my voice.

Holmes though was sanguine and shook his head as he murmured, 'No, Watson. I thank you for the defence, but the Inspector is quite correct. I miscalculated the manner in which our erstwhile companion would react, if his importance to the "movement" was cruelly downplayed. I had imagined, I admit, that he could be manipulated into boasting of his position within the Brotherhood, even perhaps brought to the point of confession regarding his recent activities. And yet, apart from identifying the prisoner, all I managed to extract from him was the very same threat that inspired Scotland Yard to ask me to consult on the matter.'

'No,' repeated Holmes with a frown, as he stood and reached for his hat and gloves. 'This meeting has not been the success I had hoped for. The few snippets of information I was able to glean do not, in truth, advance our case overmuch. We now know who the man is, I grant you, but, in every other important respect, we are in an identical position to that of several hours ago.'

Lestrade, too, was frowning as he stood to show us out of his office. 'What can we do then, Mr Holmes? We've kept the whole affair as quiet as we can, with no word to the newspapers, and I've arranged for an extra police presence at the Gallery for the next few nights, in case O'Donnell's confederates try again. But I can't ignore the specific threats the man has made, even if my superiors were willing to do so – which they are not. And I have to tell you, this business could not have come at a worse moment.'

'In what sense?' I asked.

'Just that we already have enough on our plates here at the Yard, dealing with proper criminal types, without having to waste time on the likes of O'Donnell and his friends.'

'Anything of particular interest?' asked Holmes, never one to miss the opportunity to expand his knowledge of crime.

'Oh, nothing to trouble you, Mr Holmes. Just that we've had reports of an odd sort of foreigner in town. The Albino, they call him.' He chuckled. 'Can you believe that, Dr Watson? The *Albino*. Foolish foreign sort of name, if you ask me. Apparently he gets up to his criminal activity all over Europe. Turns up in some city or other, with a plan and not much else. Recruits locally, they say, a different gang every time, oftentimes borrowed from the local mobs. Another Moriarty, eh?' Holmes did not return Lestrade's smile, so he hurried to a conclusion. 'Anyway, rumour has it that he's in London to steal… well, something or other. Nobody knows what, exactly, but "England's Treasure" they call it, so obviously something very valuable.'

I expected Holmes to react to this fascinating speech, but he seemed barely to be aware that Lestrade had spoken. '"England's Treasure"?' I said, with interest. 'What do you think, Holmes?'

'The Crown Jewels, perhaps,' he drawled, though evincing little sign of interest in the subject. Indeed, beyond that, he would not be drawn. 'I think,' he said, 'that the time has come for more direct action. I will,' he concluded as he stepped through the office door, 'need to get to know these republicans far better than I do now.'

With an apologetic nod to Lestrade, I hurried after my friend as he strode down the outer corridor.

Two

Once outside, we quickly hailed a cab. The morning promised to be pleasant, with the early sun already warming the air, and the promise of clement weather to come. Holmes, as was usual when his interest was roused, was impatient of any delay. He began to speak before we were even properly settled in our seats; plainly that keen mind had already formulated a plan of action.

Sure enough, he began without preamble to lay out his intentions. 'I think it clear enough that the threat posed by O'Donnell's faction is not one that can safely be ignored, even though the specifics of the threat thus far elude us. That the Brotherhood of Ireland wish to keep the identity of their target secret is unsurprising, but I believe that O'Donnell's last words had the ring of truth to them. *Someone* is in grave danger.' He fell silent as he turned the problem over in his mind. I took the opportunity to make a suggestion of my own.

'Could Scotland Yard not effect the simple solution of arresting everyone in the Brotherhood? Some kind of dawn raid of the sort the newspapers so love?'

I thought at first that Holmes had not heard me, for he continued to sit in silent contemplation while the hansom cab passed through the rapidly filling streets. Finally, he looked up with a half-amused expression on his face. 'And if Lestrade and his colleagues fail to capture everyone? If one or other of the ringleaders slips the net? What then? We do not know the identity of the target O'Donnell mentioned, nor who will carry out any attack that may come. No, Watson,' he said decisively, 'that will not do at all.'

He resumed his pensive brooding for several minutes then, with a sudden jerk, rapped on the roof of the cab. The driver pulled the vehicle to the side of the road and Holmes threw open the door and leapt out onto the pavement. 'I have an errand or two to run,' he said with a smile. 'And then I think I shall pay a visit to certain public houses I know. The Earl of Dublin does a splendid pint of porter, I'm told.'

Used as I was to this type of swift mood change in my friend, I simply nodded my understanding, and asked if there was anything I could be doing while he was occupied elsewhere.

'Perhaps you could take a trip to the National Portrait Gallery, Watson? I admit that it may well be something of a wild goose chase, but I would be interested nonetheless in discovering whether anyone saw O'Donnell earlier in the day and, if so, whether they could provide a description of any company he might have been in. If you could make a reservation at Peele's for, say, eight this evening, I will be sure to rejoin you then.'

With that, he turned on his heel and, with a characteristic turn of speed, strode down a side street and disappeared from view. I wondered for a moment if I should go after him – this was not the most salubrious area of the city after all – but there was no chance I could catch him even if I wanted to. Besides, I really was in need of some breakfast, a wash and shave, and a change of clothes. After that, I knew I would be more usefully employed at the Gallery than in providing an unwanted chaperone for Sherlock Holmes. I shouted to the driver to take me to Baker Street and settled myself back in my seat.

Later that morning, therefore, I found myself in St Martin's Place, standing before the entrance to the National Portrait Gallery just as its doors were opened for the day. I made enquiries within and discovered that the gallery in which the painting of Lord Salisbury had been hung was in fact no gallery at all, but the main corridor along the centre of the first floor of the building, from which each gallery room abutted. Because of this, it had not been possible to close off the area, which had the particular benefit from my perspective of allowing me a preliminary inspection of the scene of the crime without having to make myself formally known to any Gallery staff.

I made my way up the main staircase to the first floor. The corridor was wide and long, stretching nearly the entire length of the building, though there were not, in fact, many portraits on the walls. I passed one of the late Mr Disraeli and another of Lord Russell, before coming to a patch of very slightly lighter wall upon which, I assumed, the damaged painting of Lord Salisbury had, until recently, hung. The area round the missing portrait – the entire corridor, in fact – had obviously been thoroughly cleaned before opening, so that the minor variation in colour on the wall was the only sign that anything had ever been amiss.

I was, I admit, at something of a loss as to my next move. Having found the spot where the portrait had once been, I was struck by the fact that its complete absence did rather hinder any investigation I might have hoped to make in Holmes's absence.

Far from desiring to avoid making myself known to the Gallery staff, as I had previously intended, I was now keen to speak to someone in authority. But as is so often the case, as soon as I wanted to speak to a member of staff, none were to be found. The Gallery was not busy at this early hour, and I wondered if perhaps the bulk of the staff did not start work until later in the day. In any case, I knew that the administrative offices in the building were to be found on the ground floor. I took the stairs back the way I had come, then walked along the main hallway, passing doors marked BOARD ROOM and WAITING ROOM – both of which were empty – before coming to one with a small gold plaque on it which read SECRETARY'S ROOM. I knocked and, a voice inside bidding me do so, opened the door and entered.

The Secretary was a small, balding man with a neat grey moustache and appeared to be the ideal example of the office administrator. He was rising from his desk as I entered the room and stood with a puzzled look on his face as I approached him.

'How do you do?' he said, his eyes never leaving my face. 'My name is Donald Petrie and I am the Secretary of the Gallery. Please forgive me for staring, sir, but are you not Dr John Watson? The colleague of the detective, Mr Sherlock Holmes?'

I owned that this was indeed the case. The effect on Mr Petrie was astonishing. On first sight, I had taken him for the very epitome of the solid, unimaginative office manager, for whom the rulebook is the highest of literature and nothing else is of any consequence. Yet my name – or, to be more precise, the proximity of my name to that of Holmes – was enough to transform the man. He was, it transpired, a great enthusiast for Holmes's work and, to a lesser extent, my own writings.

'In what way may I be of assistance?' Petrie asked, eagerly, and I explained that Scotland Yard had asked Holmes and myself to involve ourselves in the case.

'Mr Holmes is currently working undercover,' I concluded, 'so I thought I might pay the Gallery a visit in his absence.'

Petrie could not have been more helpful. He explained that he had been called into the Gallery at a quarter past five that morning, and had immediately begun arranging to have the upper corridor thoroughly cleaned.

'It was impossible to tell that there had ever been a disturbance on the first floor corridor by nine o'clock,' he announced proudly. 'I might even go so far as to say that it would be impossible to tell that *anything* untoward had taken place, were it not for the unfortunate gaps in the display.'

'It's not as noticeable as all that,' I said in reassurance. 'I doubt that many of your patrons will notice a single missing portrait amongst so large and distinguished a collection.' A thought occurred to me. 'Could you not borrow another suitable portrait from elsewhere and hang it in place of the damaged one?'

If I had expected fulsome thanks from Mr Petrie for my suggestion, I was to go unrewarded, for he was shaking his head before I had even finished speaking. Indeed, I think he might even have let out a small sigh as he did so.

'Were it but one painting that would, of course, be exactly the plan of action I would have undertaken, Dr Watson.' He shrugged apologetically. 'But with so many paintings damaged, I fear that the gaps will be too frequent to be overlooked by our patrons.'

I felt sure that Holmes would immediately have grasped the import of Mr Petrie's words, but I confess that, for all my desire to put my friend's methods to use whenever possible, I would have been reduced to staring at the man in incomprehension, had not a knock come at the door behind me, and a hesitant female voice spoken.

'Excuse my intrusion, Secretary, but the restorers are here to collect the damaged works,' the voice said. Petrie beckoned the voice's owner inside with a nod of apology in my direction. I indicated with a small hand movement of my own that no such apology was required, then stood as the young lady entered the room.

The appearance of the newcomer came as something of a surprise. Where I had expected the type of timid young lady most often encountered in museums and galleries, wearing pince-nez, a disapproving frown, and with her hair in a tight bun, the woman who stood before us was altogether different.

She was small in stature, and slight of build, with large brown eyes and a small nose and mouth, but what was most striking was her hair, which was almost, but not quite, scarlet in colour. I admit that even as Mr Petrie introduced the lady, I was unable to take my eyes from that shock of red hair. Fortunately, I came to my senses before making a complete fool of myself, and retained enough good manners to murmur 'Pleased to meet you, Miss Rhodes,' in response to Petrie's introductions.

Her voice was melodious as she apologised to the Secretary for the intrusion, and handed him a sheet of paper. 'The complete breakdown of damages which you requested for the restorers,' she said quietly. He examined it in some detail before thanking Miss Rhodes, then turned his attention back to me as she left the room, with a shy smile of farewell in my direction.

'It appears, Dr Watson, that you and Mr Holmes have been misinformed regarding the full extent of the disturbance in the Gallery. As you know, Solomon's portrait of Lord Salisbury was attacked by a madman in the early hours of this morning, at around two a.m., but as you are seemingly not aware, several other paintings were subsequently damaged – some quite badly – in the chase and struggle which ensued, as our guards laid hands upon the miscreant and delivered him, eventually, up to justice.'

I inwardly cursed Lestrade. He must have known of the other damaged paintings, but he had been too focused on the potential threat from the republicans to mention such comparative trifles to Holmes or myself.

Thankfully, Petrie was eager to provide the missing details. He scurried over to a large cupboard and extracted a floor plan of the Gallery, which he spread out on the desk before us.

'The scoundrel first knocked down Walton's portrait of Joseph Hume from its hanger on the corridor wall, here,' he said, pointing to a line on the plan. 'Then it seems that a guard blocked the stairwell, forcing him upwards where – if you can believe the perfidy of the man – he attempted to use a particularly fine bust of Cromwell as a weapon. In doing so he damaged several portraits which, ironically, were scheduled to be taken down later today, preparatory to being lent to the Royal Household. Finally, he was cornered amongst the larger portraits and subdued by two members of staff, though not before he was responsible for a significant tear in the canvas of the First Earl of Mansfield.'

This was new information, indeed, but not, I thought, the sort of thing that Holmes had sent me to the Gallery to find out. I wondered again why Lestrade had failed to mention this additional damage, but perhaps he himself had not known about it at the time and, besides, it was at best tangential to the question of the republican threat which, justly, was the Inspector's primary concern.

'Will you be able to repair the damaged artworks?' I asked, though more for politeness' sake than from any genuine desire for information.

I am as fond of art as the next man, but only because I have found that the next man, generally, is not terribly fond of it either.

A frown crossed Mr Petrie's face. 'That is what I intend these restorers should ascertain, Doctor. From a very cursory examination this morning, I would hazard a guess that yes, each work of art can and will be saved, though the Cromwellian bust in particular will require a good deal of care and attention. But as to the portraits? Yes, I believe all will be well.'

Mention of the bust of the erstwhile Lord Protector gave me an idea, which I quickly tested. 'Could there have been a specific reason for the choice of artwork the intruder damaged? I ask simply because—' I hesitated then, as it crossed my mind that the identity of O'Donnell – and more particularly his Irish background – might be something best kept secret for the moment. 'Cromwell is not the most popular of characters from English history, is he? Were the other portraits of similarly controversial figures?'

I was concerned that my hesitation had been noticed, but Petrie gave no sign of interest, never mind suspicion, as he shook his head. 'No, Dr Watson, I'm afraid not. The subjects are varied both in terms of their era and their politics, including, for instance, both Samuel Johnson and Pitt the Elder. A purely random collection of those portraits closest at hand, I would say.'

I decided that there was nothing else to be learned at the Gallery, and rose to my feet, preparatory to taking my leave. I would have been away, and thus missed the important news which was shortly to arrive, in fact, had it not been for the enthusiasm with which Petrie pumped my hand as I made my farewells. It seemed that he had a wealth of observations to make regarding Holmes's cases, in addition to literary ambitions of his own. An image of Holmes in a similar predicament came to mind, and was enough to bring a smile to my face, which only encouraged Mr Petrie to continue his fascinated interrogation for several minutes further.

Due to Petrie insisting I sign my name upon the cover of an issue of the periodical, therefore, I was still present when the office door suddenly flew open with enough force to bang hard against the stopper. In the doorway stood Miss Rhodes, again holding a piece of paper, but this time anything but the shy and timid young lady of our earlier meeting. Instead, her face was flushed and ruddy. Her hair had come undone above her left ear, allowing a coil of red to fall across her cheek as she breathlessly announced the news that had led her to storm into her superior's office so unexpectedly.

'The portrait of Charles the First – the one damaged last night – it's a forgery!'

In a hansom that evening, on the way to the restaurant at which I was to meet Holmes, the forged painting remained on my mind. On the face of it, it seemed implausible that O'Donnell could be involved. Why, after all, would he draw attention to the forgery in such a foolish manner, if it was part of some Brotherhood scheme? Adding a further layer of confusion was the fact, helpfully explained by Miss Rhodes, that the forgery was of such poor quality that it had been spotted even before the painting had been loaded into the restorers' transport. In situ, it might have passed muster for a day or two, but no longer than that – and removed from its usual position and taken outside into natural light, the deficiencies were immediately evident. What could be the purpose of such an inferior counterfeit?

Thoughts such as these swirled about in my head as the hansom made its way to Fleet Street, and I admit that my full attention had wandered as the cab pulled up at the restaurant. I stepped onto the pavement and handed the driver his fare, paying no great deal of attention to my immediate surroundings, so lost was I in inner speculation. It was this, perhaps, which caused me to miss Holmes arriving in a second hansom, just behind my own. There is no denying, at any rate, that a mind more focused on the task at hand might have been able to prevent the terrible occurrence which took place a moment after our joint arrival.

'Watson!' Holmes shouted through the window of his cab. I turned quickly at the sound of the familiar voice, sure that I heard something – some note or key – which indicated haste and perhaps danger. Too late did my distracted mind come to its senses, however. Even as I turned and saw my friend's face at the cab window, a figure stepped between us, and, in the half shadows of the gas-lit street, raised a hand in which flashed a wickedly long knife. The arm descended and I heard a muffled and pain-filled cry as the assassin's blade struck home, sliding into my friend's chest almost to the hilt.

A woman screamed, and somewhere in the distance two dogs barked furiously, but other than that the world was entirely still as the knife-wielding attacker pushed a passing couple out of his way and ran towards a nearby alley. I watched in horror as Holmes fell backwards into the cab, with his blood-soaked hands clasped tight but ineffectually to his wound. Even at a distance I could see that it was a mortal one, and I felt my heart stutter within my chest at the thought.

Nobody else moved and all sound faded away... and then Holmes's driver leaped down and threw open the cab door a second before my heart began to beat once more and, with what I fear was a shout of animal rage, I threw myself forward in pursuit of the fleeing killer.

I have read in *The Lancet* of cases of mothers lifting fully laden carts with their bare hands in order to save their trapped child, and I have no doubt now of the truth of such claims, for horror and fear lent my legs a turn of speed I would not have previously believed possible. Even though the man had a lead of several seconds, he had barely entered the alleyway before I was immediately behind him then, with an improbable leap, I brought him crashing to the ground.

I pulled my fist back and matters would have gone very badly for the fellow, had he not hurriedly uttered the one phrase guaranteed to save him.

'Watson, my dear fellow, do let me up before you completely destroy this suit!'

Three

The next few minutes were as harried and emotional a period as I have ever known. Far from being a murderous Irishman as I'd expected, the would-be assassin I'd chased through the back streets had been Sherlock Holmes himself, heavily disguised.

My natural reaction upon making this discovery was to apologise for bringing my friend crashing to the ground. I was actually on the verge of doing so when I realised the absurdity of such an action, and a swelling feeling of indignation replaced that of apology in an instant.

'What on earth are you doing, Holmes? And if you are the assassin, then who did you just attack?' I asked, angrily, even as he took my proffered hand and pulled himself to his feet. I confess that I was as confused as I was angry at this sudden and unexpected turn of events, and it may be that the mixture of the two caused me to be less prudent than I might otherwise have been.

Whatever the cause, Holmes thrust a hand over my mouth as soon as he was standing upright, then hissed, 'Will you please stop shouting fit to wake the dead, Watson?' in my ear. 'My own anonymity is vital at this point,' he continued, 'which – if you will forgive me saying so – is a difficult trick to carry off if you insist on bawling my name to the heavens in that manner!'

As a speech it was hardly one designed to mollify me, but I did take his point. Whatever Holmes was doing, I owed him my trust. If he said silence was essential, then I could do nothing else but be silent. 'Go back to the hansom as quickly as you can, and I'll meet up with you by St Clements,' he said quietly and, without another word, turned and loped further down the alley at a deceptively swift pace. I stood for a moment, still stunned by the speed at which recent events had occurred, then, remembering his admonition to be as quick as possible, hurried back to the cab, around which a crowd had now gathered.

'Dr Watson! Dr Watson!' a voice called out. Above the heads of the assembled mass of people I could just make out the cab driver waving a hand in my direction. I pushed my way towards him, ignoring a flurry of questions from the onlookers and gawpers, each of whom wished to know what had become of the knifeman. Only once I reached the hansom and pulled myself inside did I take a moment to announce to the crowd in general and to no one in particular that I had lost him in the dim alleyway, and that I would now take Mr Sherlock Holmes back to our lodgings, where I could better tend to his injuries. The driver flicked his whip and we moved off. Within a few minutes we passed the Courts of Justice, where a dark shape slipped from the shadows, grabbed hold of the door of the cab, and swung inside.

I have had cause before to note that for all his many excellent qualities, Sherlock Holmes was, in some respects, an exasperating individual, with sundry eccentric habits that appeared designed to irritate his friends and colleagues alike. The willingness with which he fell back into the easy embrace of cocaine was, of course, the most troublesome of these, but in my opinion the manner in which he kept his plans a secret known only to himself ran that a close second. When pressed, his various defences – that his was a naturally secretive nature, that caution must be his watch word, that the fewer people involved the less chance of failure – were convincing enough, but even so there were times when I found my role as ill-informed stooge a trying one. It was this, and perhaps the natural release of tension generated by finding Holmes to be safe and well, which prompted me to declare, with some asperity, that I would not in future act as a prop in his machinations if he did not have a very good explanation for his recent behaviour.

Holmes had the grace to seem abashed in the face of my anger. He held out his hands placatingly, then pulled himself onto the seat beside me. 'My profoundest apologies, my dear fellow,' he began, with every appearance of contrition on his long face. 'But before I explain further, may I take this opportunity to introduce Jamie Ewing, one time Baker Street Irregular, now turned to an honest life – of sorts – on the London stage. Jamie is a contortionist with the Lees Circus, to be precise.' He reached down and helped the blood-soaked 'corpse' from the floor to his feet, then onto the seat opposite, where I could finally get a decent look at the man I had thought to be a mortally wounded Sherlock Holmes.

Up close, the resemblance was not, in fact, particularly striking. Ewing was a little shorter than Holmes (not that that mattered when he would only be glimpsed inside a cab, of course), and somewhat heavier, particularly in the face. But the general shape of the two men's faces were similar enough and the hair and eyes the same colour so that, seen only fleetingly and dressed in Holmes's clothes, it was unsurprising that he would pass muster as London's foremost consulting detective.

'How do you do?' I said politely, unsure of the etiquette when meeting a man pretending to be a dead friend.

In reply, Ewing continued to wipe the blood from his hands and, looking up from underneath heavy brows, nodded in my general direction.

'Ewing is a friendly soul,' Holmes interjected, 'but like many creative types he can be… intense… immediately after a performance. It makes him disinclined to talk. But,' he rubbed his hands together enthusiastically, 'I can certainly take up the conversational slack and provide an acceptable justification for my recent activities. You will, I think, be interested to discover the manner in which Jamie and I so convincingly carried off our recent charade.

'You will have noticed that the "injury" Jamie suffered is low on the left side of his chest, with copious amounts of blood soaking the entirety of that section of his clothing. A balloon, filled with goat's blood and taped beneath the shirt, of course. Childishly simple, but effective. The puncturing of the balloon, though… now that is far less pedestrian. Perhaps you would care to test your observational skills, Watson?' He gestured to our companion. 'Jamie, if you will?'

Ewing shrugged indifferently as Holmes beckoned him over, but leaned forward nonetheless, in order, it seemed, that I might better view the rent in his shirt and the area immediately beneath. I studied the torn fabric, the sticky, deflated balloon and the man's untouched skin, but I could see nothing which would indicate how Ewing had survived the attack unhurt.

'Some form of trick knife, I suppose,' I said, knowing even as I spoke the words that they were a poor guess.

So it proved as Holmes pulled the knife from his coat pocket and rapped the hard metal of its blade against the door of the cab. 'I'm afraid not, Watson. This knife is as real and deadly as any other. Look more closely.'

I did as he suggested, but a minute or more of careful study offered up no fresh knowledge and I was forced to admit defeat.

Holmes smiled with pleasure. 'I grant you that it is an unusual problem, but the information you require *is* in plain sight. Observe the blood balloon, to begin with.' He traced a finger along the length of the long cut in the thin rubber. 'It was not punctured, but sliced. Do you imagine I involved a contortionist, rather than an actor, for no reason, Watson? You know me better than that, I hope.'

'Ewing twisted his body as you stabbed down!' I exclaimed, pleased to come to the answer before Holmes could tell the entire story. 'By some miracle of his contortionist arts, he was able to position himself such that the blade cut along the balloon, rather than entering it directly!'

'Bravo, Watson!' Holmes agreed with delight. 'After years of training, Jamie is able to contract his rib cage as he desires, and in doing so can create as much as two inches of space where one might reasonably expect his flesh to be. It took hours of practice, but as you saw, we managed a decent facsimile of a murderous knife attack when it was required. The knife slid along the length of the balloon, releasing the goat's blood and giving every appearance of having been fully thrust into the victim, without inflicting any actual physical injury.'

As was often the case when Holmes revealed his secrets, I was caught between a desire to applaud his genius, and a temptation to lambast him for the risks he took. It was all very well to admire the aftermath of his fakery, but as a doctor I knew how easily things could have gone wrong. I had no chance to do either, however, for Holmes resumed his narrative with an altogether more sombre look on his face.

'But I have begun my tale at the end and it is the period before that which is of most importance in our investigations. As you will recall, I left you this morning with the intention of infiltrating the fellowship of which our Mr O'Donnell is a member. Moving from the general to the specific, when we parted this morning I made my way to a little place I keep not far from Covent Garden, where I changed into clothes more fitting an itinerant labourer, freshly arrived from Ireland. Thus attired, I took a stroll down into St Giles, bound for the Earl of Dublin public house. It is, as you know, one of the very roughest and most dangerous areas of London, but the efforts of philanthropists have elevated it in recent years to something closer to a place fit for human habitation. Even so, I confess that I was not entirely prepared for the degree of squalor I experienced as I left the fashionable shops of Oxford Street behind and turned into what remains of the old rookeries. Stop here, driver!'

This last was directed upwards, and had the effect of swiftly bringing the cab to a stop. As soon as it did so, Holmes clapped Ewing on the shoulder and flung open the door. 'On your way now, Jamie, and thank you once more. You have been more than helpful.' Ewing quickly slipped outside and within moments had faded into the light fog, which hung in the evening air. Holmes closed the door behind him, rapping on the roof to signal the driver to move on.

'You have done rather well to find a hansom driver willing to have murder seen to be done in his vehicle,' I wondered aloud.

Holmes let out a short barking laugh. 'My dear fellow, while the London cabbie has many sterling qualities, a willingness to aid a complete stranger in the faking of a murder is not one of them. No, the driver is our old friend, Wiggins. This night has been quite the Irregular reunion.' And with another laugh he resumed his story.

'There is no need to go into detail regarding my passage through the rookeries. Suffice to say that the tattered, dirt-matted and glowering figure I presented was a perfect match for the other unfortunate souls I encountered as I navigated my way down a series of tiny alleyways running with filth, until I eventually found myself outside the unmarked entranceway to the Earl of Dublin public house. It is little more than a one-room gin shop, in truth, and the men who frequent the place exactly the sort you would expect in such a hovel. But, as I had hoped, in one corner sat a group whose appearance was unmistakably superior to that of their fellow customers. Their clothes, their speech, their very bearing marked them as something out of the norm in that place, though not sufficiently so as to cause suspicion or alarm. This was the meeting of the Brotherhood I was looking for.'

By now, the cab had arrived at Baker Street. Wiggins jumped down from his perch and opened the door for us. I made to leave, but he held out a hand to stop me, then quickly informed Holmes that we had not been followed, nor did he think anybody was watching us now. Clearly, Holmes was leaving nothing to chance. With a final thank you to the driver, Holmes leaped to the pavement and led the way into our lodgings.

I was glad to be inside in the warmth, and lost no time in pointing out to Holmes that thus far he had not touched upon the reason for the astonishing scene at the restaurant.

'I hope,' I said with some sharpness, 'that though a long story, there is a satisfactory conclusion?' It had been quite an eventful evening and I was in no mood to be told only half a story, as was Holmes's usual practice.

Holmes, for his part, threw himself down in his favourite chair with a tired sigh. 'I am coming to that, I assure you, Watson,' he said as he settled himself. 'Let us get comfortable, and I will move my story on a little.'

I took my own seat and lit a cigarette. As soon as Holmes was satisfied I was ready, he continued his tale.

'As I said, one small group caught my particular attention as I entered the Earl of Dublin. Knowing that it would be the worst of possible mistakes to approach them directly, I ordered a glass of porter and took myself to a seat close enough to them to overhear, but not so close as to raise suspicion. Once in place, I simply sat back and waited, listening in on their discussions about freedom committees and fundraising and the like, and sipping what was in truth an excellent glass of beer.

'As I suspected, I did not have long to wait. Even the most politically astute Irishman is a foolish creature when he has been drinking, Watson. Where the Scotsman will fight his own shadow when drunk, and the English become gay and merry, the Irish descend into a melancholy of the most pitiable sort when strong drink has been taken to excess. Terrible tales of the Famine are brought out, dusted down and retold for the thousandth time; lamentation and sorrow fill the air; and, in due course, there is a particularly Irish form of communal singing, in which everyone within reach is embraced like a long-lost brother, so long as he too is an Irishman far from home.

'That was the moment I had been waiting for. It took another two glasses of porter on my part, but with the whiskey flowing freely at the table beside me, it took no more than half an hour for the political talk to fade away and the strains of "Carrickfergus" to replace it. Rest assured, I lost no time in inserting myself into the company and was soon on good terms with several of them, and accepted by the rest as exactly what I seemed to be – Edmund Brady, a fellow republican and Irish nationalist, homesick for the Emerald Isle.'

I smiled a little at the thought of Sherlock Holmes in such company. He grimaced in acknowledgement. 'It was, I admit, an unusual situation, but a fruitful one nonetheless. I quickly struck up a particularly amicable acquaintance with one of the younger men of the company, by the name of Peter Keane. A baker by profession, he said, but one unable to make a living in his own country due to the restrictive laws imposed by the English oppressor. I, of course, was appropriately sympathetic and alluded to my own similar misfortunes as a tenant farmer in the north of the country.

'My new friend soon introduced me to his compatriots. Chief amongst these was the quietest fellow around the table, a slim, clean-shaven gentleman with a high forehead and dark, almost violet eyes. While the rest were exactly the sentimental, drunken fools which they appeared to be, he was something else entirely, something difficult to categorise.'

Holmes stopped to tap the embers of his pipe out and, I think, to give further consideration to his next words. Whoever this quiet, dark-eyed Irishman was, he had impressed Holmes in some way.

'He was younger than I expected, for one thing. It is a fallacy much beloved of the lesser sort of Scotland Yard man to claim that a criminal may be known by sight, so ingrained in their features is the infamy of his acts, but it is undoubtedly true that the longer one is steeped in crime, the more it lends a flavour to one's appearance. This man – more boy than man, in fact – had none of the criminal indicators I would have expected. Smooth skinned and clear of vision, his eyes shone with something I can only call contentment as I made the slightest of nods towards him. Had this young man ever visited your surgery, Watson, you would not raise an eyebrow, nor have any concern as to his character.

'And yet I should say, Watson, that this youngster is as dangerous in his own way as the late, unlamented Professor Moriarty was in his prime. Incredible as it may seem, when comparing two men so different in age and education, but I believe him to be almost the equal of Moriarty intellectually, and his superior in physical strength, charisma and moral integrity – but most worryingly for those of us who oppose him, this young Irishman is driven not by simple avarice, nor by a desire for power, but by a Cause.'

Even in conversation I could hear the capital letter with which Holmes began that last word, and I knew well what he meant. The average criminal is, by nature, a selfish and solitary creature, with little thought in his head but his own advancement and profit. In need – or, for that matter, when need is slight, but desire strong – he will betray his colleagues in order to save himself and give the matter little thought. But give that same criminal a Cause, provide him with a higher purpose, and his previous predilections will disappear at once. Such a man will defy the authorities even into the shadow of the noose itself, and his followers will do the same.

'He had presence,' Holmes said eventually, confirming my suspicions. 'That is the only way I can describe it. Even without speaking, he dominated those around him. I was not given his real name – even in their cups, the Brotherhood are not so reckless – but I was introduced to him in due course. Major Conway, they called him, but with a laugh as though the title had some element of mockery in it. Affectionate mockery, I should add, for there was no doubt of the respect those men had for him.

'"And who might you be?" were the first words this Major spoke to me, after looking me up and down for a solid minute. Then, "You are not exactly who you appear to be, I think," and I knew it was not a question but a statement of fact. "Perhaps not exactly, at that," I replied, with a smile which I did not mean.'

My friend laughed. 'That was a sticky moment, I admit, Watson. The Major was looking at me steadily, without rancour or threat, but requiring an answer for all that. I had at most ten seconds to make some plausible, yet unthreatening, addition to my story. It may have been my imagination, but it seemed to me that the entire room had fallen silent and every eye in the place was on me. "I am a man with a grievance, Major," I said and hoped that would be enough to whet his appetite.'

'And was it?' I asked breathlessly, caught up in Holmes's narrative.

'Once I had elaborated, yes, but it was touch and go for a while. The Major raised a hand, and the conversation restarted around me. He indicated that I should sit, and when I had he poured me a drink from the bottle in front of him. It's strong stuff these Irishmen drink, Watson! Pure potheen, distilled in the area around Cavan in Ulster, I'd hazard. I have considered writing a monograph on the distinctive nature of these regional "moonshine" variants, in fact, as an aid to the Irish constabulary… but never mind that. I digress.

'I drank the glass of spirits in a single draught, which in some way appeared to comfort Major Conway, for I felt a definite lessening of tension. "What manner of grievance would it be, Mr Brady?" he asked. "Something which warrants blood being shed, I'd guess."

'I had thought that I would be days, perhaps weeks, in establishing myself, but as the Major looked at me across the table, I saw an opportunity to more quickly achieve my goal. You must bear in mind, Watson, that the primary motivation of these revolutionaries is not, as they claim, to provide freedom and succour for their fellow countrymen, but rather to spread terror and destruction across the mainland. Murder and dynamitism are the means by which they advance their cause, and it would be through murder that I would gain their trust!'

I must have given some involuntary indication of my shock at Holmes's words, for he swiftly moved to reassure me.

'There is no need to look so alarmed, Watson! Of course, I had no intention of killing anyone, but at the same time I knew that without some impressively wanton act of criminality I could never hope to inveigle myself deeper into their plotting, and so discover the gravity and seriousness of O'Donnell's boasts. Hesitantly, as befitted a stranger in the company, unsure of the reception he might receive, I let him tease elements of my so-called grievance from me. I told him of my brother, arrested without cause by the London police for the crime of being an Irishman, and imprisoned on suspicion of republicanism. I told him more: how my brother had died in the cells, the victim of a savage beating when he refused to divulge the names of his fellow conspirators. Conspirators which he did not have, I said, with tears in my eyes. An innocent man, I groaned, murdered by the English.

'You would have been proud of me, Watson. Though I say it myself, my performance was of the highest quality. Grown men openly wept as I described my poor widowed mother back in Ulster, waiting for the return of a son whom she would never see again. The Major, too, was evidently an emotional man for he grasped my hand as my words trailed off and promised that his people would help me gain my revenge. "No son of Ireland could refuse to do otherwise," he said. "But," he went on, "do you know who did the killing? Have you a name which we might attach to this vile slaughter?"

'"The only name I have," I said, "is Sherlock Holmes."'

* * *

While he had been speaking, Holmes had remained in his disguise, bearded and unkempt as any vagrant. Now, he peeled off his false whiskers with a grimace. He rubbed a hand across the genuine stubble which remained and pinched the bridge of his nose between two long fingers. His tiredness was palpable.

'What did he say to that?' I asked. 'Does he trust you now?'

In reply, Holmes stood and shrugged off the tattered jacket he was wearing. 'Sure and I can tell you nothing,' he said in an exaggerated and comic Irish brogue, 'for have I not sworn to preserve our secrets inviolable?' He laughed and tossed the jacket over the back of a chair, then reached for his pipe and a fingerful of shag tobacco. Only after he had the two combined to his satisfaction did he touch a glowing cinder to the bowl and continue in his normal voice.

'I am now a full member of the Brotherhood of Ireland, Watson. I have taken their oath, I have spoken to such of their leadership as is available at present, and I have pledged myself to the overthrow of the British Parliament and Crown. I am–' he concluded proudly, '–a Fenian through and through!'

The sudden change in Holmes's mood was infectious. I found myself laughing along with him, all irritation at his recent high-handed behaviour dissipated. 'But how did you achieve that happy state, Holmes?' I asked. 'How did this Major react to the name Sherlock Holmes?'

'He was delighted, would you believe? Mine is a name known to the Brotherhood, it seems. "Sherlock Holmes, is it?" he said. "Now there's a man we'd be content to see in the grave."

'Mention was made of the Kilkenny business last year and of the capture of the man Marsh in New York. More than one republican plan was derailed by *that* arrest. "It would seem that our interests coincide, Mr Brady," the Major concluded. "Now tell me of his involvement in your brother's tragic demise."'

Comfortable in his chair, wreathed in blue pipe smoke, and warmed by the fire, it was difficult to believe that Holmes had recently been in conference with one of the leaders of a secret society bent on widespread slaughter and then faked his own murder. And yet, there he was, and there he had been, and as I listened to him sketch in the details of the story he had told to the Major, I was impressed once more by the ingenuity and courage of my friend.

'My tale was not enough in itself to convince him,' Holmes concluded, 'but it was sufficient to prevent my throat being cut there and then. When I suggested that I kill Holmes myself, though, that tipped the balance in my favour, and I was engulfed in drunken back-slapping from the other men round the table.'

'And what of Major Conway?' I interrupted.

Holmes frowned. 'He was still not entirely content, but a good leader knows when to give the mob its head, and when to push back, and this was undoubtedly an occasion for the former approach. So he let me explain that I had been following Holmes ever since he betrayed my brother so unfairly, and had overheard him arrange to meet a friend – you, Watson – for dinner this evening. It would be then that I would have my vengeance!

'I will not say that I was wholly unconcerned as I left the Earl of Dublin. For all the hands slapping my back and gripping my arms in congratulation, I was keenly aware that it would take but one slip on my part, one glimmer of recognition from any of the motley crew which surrounded me, for the mood of celebration to turn to one of retribution. Bear in mind, Watson, that "Revolutionary" is not a full-time position, and that much of the mob through which I now passed was composed of the dregs of the criminal world, with all that sorry type's tendency to suspicion and paranoia. Exactly the sort of person who might, in fact, see a resemblance between Edmund Brady, hero of the struggle, and Sherlock Holmes, lackey of the English oppressor.

'Fortunately, though I had thought it unlikely that I would be accepted so quickly by the Brotherhood, I had made certain contingency plans just in case, and Ewing had been primed to impersonate me if the occasion demanded. The rest you witnessed outside the restaurant. You will forgive me, I hope, for not telling you beforehand, but there really was no time and, besides, it was important that your reactions were as natural as possible, else the whole charade might have been for nothing. I had not,' he concluded ruefully, 'allowed for the speed with which you pursued and apprehended me. Really, Watson, you have an unexpected turn of pace when the occasion demands it.'

I laughed with pleasure at this good-humoured jibe. 'I concede that I am more sedentary now than I was in my youth, Holmes, but I was a gifted runner as a youngster, you know. And besides, I thought you dead. My blood was up!' Remembering the body in the cab sobered me in an instant, however. 'So, where do this evening's events leave you, Holmes?' I asked.

Holmes, equally serious now, considered the question carefully before answering. 'It was a test, but an important one. The attack on Sherlock Holmes will have reached the newspaper offices by now, and there were one or two observers from the Brotherhood amongst the crowd at the restaurant.' He nodded once, sharply, to himself as he leant forward and knocked the detritus from his pipe onto the hearth. 'Yes, having passed the necessary assessment, I envisage a warm welcome for the conquering hero when I return to the Earl of Dublin later tonight.'

'Later tonight?' I was incredulous, and made no attempt to hide that fact. Holmes had been up and busy since dawn and was obviously exhausted; that he intended to go out again, without rest, was madness, and I said as much. Holmes, however, tutted his lack of interest in my opinion, and calmly began reapplying his whiskers in front of the mirror, which hung over the fireplace.

Within minutes, the suave consulting detective had disappeared, and a sullen, grimy Irish navvy stood in his place. Only when he was satisfied with his appearance did Holmes deign to reply.

'Yes, tonight, I'm afraid, Watson. At the moment I have a certain standing with the Brotherhood, which I hope to barter for information about the threat to Her Majesty. That standing will not last forever – indeed it will evaporate completely once it becomes known, as it shall, that Sherlock Holmes is very much alive – and the safety of the Queen requires me to strike while the iron is hot.' He shrugged on his filthy jacket, pulled an equally disreputable cap down on his head, and took one final look in the mirror.

'Yes, that will do,' he said in his familiar tone then, 'Another time, Englishman!' in a soft Irish brogue, and he was through the door and away before I could respond.

It was only half an hour later that I realised I had failed to mention the peculiar forged painting.

Four

e ʃ

The next few days were uneventful. Scotland Yard had announced that Sherlock Holmes, though injured, yet lived, but otherwise the case was moribund, and Holmes himself had not been in touch. I busied myself as much as I could with my practice, but in truth it too was quiet, and by the third morning I found myself at a loose end. The weather being unseasonably mild, I was loath to spend the days indoors but with Holmes absent there was nothing I could do to aid with the current case. But perhaps there was another associated problem to which I might apply myself. Though not formally a case as yet, I was sure Holmes would be interested in the forged painting upon his return.

Within the hour, therefore, I found myself pushing open the entrance of the National Portrait Gallery. A combination of a brisk walk through London's sunlit streets and, I admit, the possibility of renewing my acquaintance with Miss Rhodes, had put me in an excellent mood, such that I bounded up the steps two at a time. I may even have been whistling as I strode down the corridor to the office of Donald Petrie, the Secretary.

The door was ajar, so I knocked and entered. To my surprise, sitting across the desk from Petrie with his back to me was the unmistakable figure of Sherlock Holmes. He was dressed not in the near rags in which I had last seen him, but in his more usual gentleman's attire. Without turning in his seat, he said 'Good morning, Watson.'

'Holmes! What are you doing here?'

'I came to find you, of course. I am delighted that your walk here has done you such good.'

I admit to a degree of pique at Holmes's airy greeting, and decided to avoid giving him the satisfaction of explaining how he could have known that I had walked from Baker Street to the Gallery. My intention was rendered moot, however, as Petrie eagerly asked Holmes that very question. 'Dr Watson's good humour is evidenced by his whistling in the corridor just now, of course,' the Secretary allowed, with a small smile of self-satisfaction, 'but how did you deduce that he walked here, rather than taking a hansom? I have long followed your career in the newspapers, Mr Holmes, and am always astonished at your perspicacity.' He suddenly frowned in my direction. 'You did walk, I take it, Dr Watson?'

Such good humour as I had heretofore displayed was in grave danger of leaking away as Petrie addressed himself to me, but I had the grace at least to nod in the affirmative. I availed myself of a chair alongside Holmes, who now turned and gave me his full attention before answering.

'I cannot in faith take any credit whatsoever in the matter of Watson's perambulations, I am afraid, Mr Petrie. No real deduction was involved, you see. I had hoped to meet up with the good Doctor at Baker Street, but upon my arrival there at a little after the hour, Mrs Hudson informed me that he had left for the Gallery some ten minutes previously. Since I took a cab here and arrived a good half hour since, it is plain as day that Watson must have walked, hence his somewhat delayed arrival.' He shrugged. 'Had I known that was his intention I would have hurried to catch up with him on foot; it is an excellent day for a stroll through town with a friend.'

My good humour was entirely restored by this closing remark, for Holmes was not a man given to even such slight declarations of affection. Thus, it was with genuine concern that I enquired if all was well with his current investigation. I knew that he would not discuss the matter specifically in front of Petrie, but hoped that he might give me some indication of his progress.

I was not surprised, therefore, when Holmes murmured 'All is well, Watson, I assure you,' and said no more. Mr Petrie, however, evidently retained his devotion to Holmes and his methods, for he recognised at once that we had something private to discuss and, with the excuse that he had to check on a delivery, left us alone in his office.

'Well?' I asked, the moment the door closed behind him. 'Where have you been, Holmes? What have you learned? Do those scoundrels trust you now?'

Perhaps I imagined it, but it seemed to me that Holmes's reply had an air of disappointment about it. 'Oh, they trust me completely now – for all that that matters!'

I knew that tone of voice well from previous occasions when a promising case had turned out, in Holmes's opinion, to be of less interest than he had initially hoped. 'There was nothing there to learn, Watson!' he continued, and now he made no attempt to disguise the bitterness in his voice. 'I returned to that filthy drinking den as the conquering hero, but to no real purpose. We drank gallons of the cheapest of rot-gut whiskey, and toasted Emmet and Wolfe

Tone – and my own assault on the inestimable Sherlock Holmes, of course – but that was the sum of our revolutionary fervour. Even the slashing of the former Prime Minister's portrait turns out to be nothing more than the result of an evening of hard drinking and a bet taken ill-advisedly.

'No, Watson, what at first I took to be a genuine armed rebellion in the making turned out to be nothing of the kind. Merely a collection of paper revolutionaries, youthful hotheads and misguided patriots whose "best" days were half a century ago. The slashing of the painting is as far as they are likely to go, now or ever. It is all rather dispiriting,' he concluded.

'But what of the Major?' I asked, half perplexed by this unexpected news, and half amused by Holmes's irritation at the absence of a genuine threat.

Holmes shook his head. 'Perhaps he will amount to something of note, but I did not see him again after our first meeting, and my activities over the past few days have achieved very little, other than a certainty that without him the Brotherhood amounts to nothing but hot air and drinking songs.' He brightened as a thought struck him. 'My feeling is that the Major was not part of the Brotherhood at all, but rather he was weighing them up, judging their usefulness to the cause – and finding them lacking, he has departed. I thought that he would contact me – Mr Brady, that is – but there has been no word.' Once more, his long face fell. 'Perhaps he knew who I was from the beginning, and he was toying with me, as a cat would with an inconsequential mouse.'

'Or perhaps he was scared off by the facility with which you subdued Sherlock Holmes? Might he perhaps contact you in the near future, once any furore has died down?'

Holmes shrugged his shoulders, without interest. I have already mentioned Holmes's self-poisoning attraction to cocaine, and as he sat opposite me, mired in dejection, I feared his return to that insidious vice. Desperate to focus his mind on some new puzzle, I cast about for anything that might rouse his interest – and was delighted to recall my reason for being at the Gallery at all.

'Did Petrie explain about the forged painting?' I asked, and was rewarded by a raise of the head and a quizzical look from my friend.

'I have only just made that gentleman's acquaintance, Watson. He scarcely had time to tell me his name and babble some overly fulsome praise of your scribblings for the popular papers before you arrived.'

I decided to allow the insult to pass, so pleased was I to see a glimmer of interest in Holmes's eye.

'Well, don't keep me on tenterhooks, Watson! To what painting do you refer? Certainly not the Salisbury. I would have had news of that, at least.'

'No, not the portrait of Lord Salisbury, Holmes. Another from the collection. King Charles the First, if I recall correctly. That's actually why I came here this morning, to check whether any progress had been made. From the manner in which Miss Rhodes – one of the Gallery employees – spoke, it would have been child's play for anyone with eyes in his head to spot the deception, once the painting was down from the wall.'

'Down from the wall? And why – but no, let us call Mr Petrie back inside and discover what has been happening while I was wasting my time amongst the bog Irish.'

As was often the case, Holmes had switched from torpor to action in moments. He leapt to his feet and pulled open the office door with a sharp tug, then called to Petrie, who was evidently only a few yards down the corridor. That done, he paced impatiently across the carpet until the Secretary had explained the events of the past few days.

'An unexpected development,' Holmes remarked when he had finished. 'You will not object if I ask you a few questions, Mr Petrie? It may be that I cannot shine any new light on the issue, but after your earlier flattering remarks about Dr Watson's jottings and my own work, it would be remiss of me not to make the attempt.'

Mr Petrie smiled up at Holmes's tall figure with obvious enthusiasm and pleasure. 'Why, Mr Holmes, of course, of course! It would be a great honour – and pleasure – to hear your opinion!' He reached into a desk drawer and pulled out a thin folder which, when opened, revealed a single sheet of typewritten paper. 'A portrait of Charles the First by Sir Horace Hamblin,' he read, 'dated to the mid to late 1640s, purchased for the collection in June. The frame was badly cracked during the apprehension of the intruder, as you know, Dr Watson, and upon being removed for repair the painting within was discovered to be a forgery. Not a terribly good one, either! Our fellows spotted it straight away!'

Holmes leaned back in his chair and steepled his fingers beneath his chin in his customary manner. 'A poor-quality forgery, you say?' he said with a frown.

'Apparently so, Mr Holmes. I am no expert myself, but I am told that nobody who is could possibly have mistaken this for a seventeenth-century work.'

'Could the painting always have been so?' Holmes asked. 'Could the forgery have been purchased in good faith and not been noticed as such until now?'

I rather fear that Petrie's professional pride was stung by Holmes's suggestion, and he hurried to reassure us that several prominent members of the Gallery staff had examined and vouchsafed the authenticity of the piece upon its arrival. 'There is no possibility of that sort of error, Mr Holmes!' he announced with some vehemence.

'Very well, then. We must accept that a genuine painting arrived at the Gallery. Was it hung immediately? I am aware that a gallery of this size, particularly a relatively new one, will have more artworks than display space. Was this particular portrait placed in storage for any time?'

I immediately grasped Holmes's meaning and – keen, I must admit, to demonstrate to Mr Petrie that I was more than a mere scribe for another man's genius – I took the opportunity to interject. 'You think that perhaps the original painting was removed whilst in storage, and replaced with this counterfeit?'

'It is a possibility,' Holmes replied, looking across at Petrie.

He, however, shook his head emphatically. 'An excellent thought, Mr Holmes, but I'm afraid not. We do of course have something approaching one thousand portraits in total, which we intend to display in turn, but the Hamblin has hung in place since the opening of the Gallery.'

'Approaching a thousand, you say? And yet of the handful of items to be damaged during the recent disturbance, this one happened to be the sole forgery in the entire Gallery? That seems improbable. Come!'

Holmes strode into the corridor without waiting for Petrie and me to follow, and made his way up to the first floor.

At first, I was unsure what he intended to do. He caught the attention of a young man, evidently a member of staff, then stood impatiently while Petrie and I caught up with him.

'Do you keep a list of each artwork on display?' he asked Petrie as soon as we were within earshot. 'I assume you have some way of tracking whether a painting is in storage or not?'

The little Secretary beamed with pleasure, obviously delighted to play a part in Holmes's investigations, no matter how small. 'Why of course we do, Mr Holmes,' he said, turning to the underling Holmes had just accosted. 'Hoskin, go to my office and fetch the master art list, which you will find in the top right side drawer of my desk.'

Hoskin hurried off, leaving Petrie and me to make conversation, while Holmes glared at the paintings nearby, as though accusing them of having committed some crime.

Presently, Hoskin reappeared, clutching a sheet of paper in his hand. Holmes at once invited the man to accompany him, then began walking slowly down the centre of the corridor, pausing briefly in front of each painting in turn. His examination complete, he said either 'yes' or 'no' to his new assistant, who recorded Holmes's words by means of a tick or cross against the name of each painting on the list he held in his hand. In this manner, he traversed the entire Gallery over the next hour, ignoring both other visitors and myself.

Finally, he came to a stop in the furthest most room. Petrie and I, exchanging baffled looks, stood beside him as he gave one final instruction to the young man who had dutifully followed him round the Gallery.

'What on earth have you been doing for the past hour, Holmes?' I asked, though with my irritation at his high-handedness tempered somewhat by the knowledge that Sherlock Holmes rarely wasted his time, no matter how peculiar his actions appeared to be.

In reply, Holmes waved a hand around the room, indicating the paintings on display. 'Come now, Watson, you are slow today! I told you exactly what needed to be checked before we left Mr Petrie's office. There is every chance that a single forgery might have slipped through the Gallery's net, especially when there are many hundreds of similar artworks in the collection – but the odds of that same dubious portrait happening by chance to be the one damaged during a break-in? No, that stretches the bounds of credibility to the extreme. Far more likely that there are a number of forgeries present – and so I have been noting down the likeliest contenders.'

Though it was, as ever, difficult to fault Holmes's logic, still I had one concern about this explanation. Holmes – for all his undoubted genius and exhaustive understanding of crime and criminals – is curiously deficient in most other areas of knowledge. I have had cause before to remark on his astonishing indifference towards matters of astronomy, but he is equally deficient in the field of the visual arts. In short, I had no more confidence in Holmes's ability to tell a genuine Vermeer from a fake than I would in that of Mrs Hudson. I said as much to Holmes – generating a glare from Mr Petrie – but he was in no way abashed by the accusation.

'Quite right, Watson,' he said, with a mischievous grin. 'But between the Gallery itself and its storage spaces, we could be waiting *weeks* for a formal identification of potential forgeries to be completed, if at all. So, instead, I have chosen a cross-section of those on display, with a mild preference for those of a similar type to the King Charles portrait. Royalty and Civil War generals primarily, but with a small random selection taken from the remainder. Taken as a whole, I imagine I have identified one-tenth of the entirety, and would like each of them examined by an expert, Mr Petrie. I will be very surprised if at least one of them does not also turn out to be a copy of a missing original.'

I wondered if perhaps Petrie would object to Holmes's plan, but on the contrary the man was all but clapping his hands with pleasure at the thought of becoming intimately involved in one of Sherlock Holmes's cases. He took the list of potential forgeries and was already directing his staff to take down various paintings. Once everything was under way to his satisfaction, he excused himself in order to make arrangements to transfer the paintings to the restoration company who were working on the already damaged artworks. 'They employ several well-known art experts in order to check the authenticity of new arrivals and will be able to verify those you have chosen by this time tomorrow. If you will step this way, Mr Holmes, I can give you their card.'

We followed him back down the stairs, with labouring Gallery workers already moving all around us, covering portraits with large cloths and lifting them down from the walls. Holmes's definition of 'a similar type' was obviously wider than my own, for as well as portraits of the Royal family, I saw paintings of the fall of Carthage, of a country squire posed by a lake set in some hills, and of a group of five horses standing round a single, unsmiling gentleman. Other portraiture of equally wide variety swiftly followed these into the group to be taken away and evaluated.

Tomorrow, I thought, promised to be an interesting day.

Five

The weather the following morning was far more typical of the time of year. Cold and grey, with fog obscuring every street corner and tiny drops of rain hanging in the air like points of silk, the world outside was unappealing enough to curtail even Holmes's eagerness to be off.

Consequently, it was nearly eleven o'clock by the time we roused ourselves sufficiently to make our way to the offices of the art restoration company. We stood on the pavement outside the address Petrie had given us, while our hansom faded back into the mist, and shivered in the cold, damp air. The street was dim in the poor light, but a large front window before us declared this to be the offices of YOUNG, MURRAY AND NOBLE, RESTORATION EXPERTS. Black velvet curtains hid the interior from view and gave the entire enterprise a luxurious, if slightly sepulchral, aspect.

In fact, once inside, it was clear that this was more a workshop than an office. The high, narrow interior, illuminated by the slanting light of numerous skylights which brightened the room without reaching below the top half of the walls, was plainly furnished, and dominated by a series of long tables on which lay paintings in various stages of repair. Other artworks were propped against the whitewashed walls, or sat on deep shelves, which stretched the length of one side of the building. The reason for the heavy curtains on the main window was clear now; it prevented the deleterious rays of direct sunlight falling on precious works of art.

Several restorers were hard at work as we entered. One man wielded a paintbrush no thicker than an eyelash, making tiny strokes on a triptych of the Holy Family, while another bent low over a cup made of the thinnest and most delicate china, a large magnifying glass held close to his eye as he worked. I would have waited for either one to finish, but Holmes had no such qualms and impatiently tapped the second man on the shoulder, causing him to jump and almost knock the cup to the floor. Before any unpleasantness could ensue I stepped forward and handed him my card, quickly explaining who we were and the nature of our errand. He considered the card for a moment then, with a final irritated glance at Holmes, indicated that we should follow him.

He led us through an unmarked wooden door and into the more clerical section of the business. A corridor ran parallel to the work area, with evenly spaced doors visible in the opposite wall. Our guide led us to one such, upon which was etched MR NOBLE, and, having knocked, left us to show ourselves inside.

Mr Noble was of less than average height but stockily built, about fifty years old, with a full beard, and beginning to show the first signs of losing his hair. He was dressed as one would expect, in a smart frock coat and trousers, and politely rose to greet us as we entered.

'Good morning, gentlemen. I am Christopher Noble, one of the proprietors of the company. How may I be of service to you?'

'I believe,' said Holmes, 'that you are expecting us? I am Sherlock Holmes, and this is my colleague Dr Watson. Mr Petrie from the National Portrait Gallery sent over a large collection of portraiture yesterday evening, and suggested we pay a visit today to check on progress.'

For once, the name Sherlock Holmes had little effect, but Mr Noble was undoubtedly a shrewd businessman, and mention of Petrie, presumably a major client, was enough to stir him immediately into action.

'Of course, of course!' he said, jumping back to his feet and shaking our hands again. 'I had no idea that you were Mr Petrie's associates. Please, follow me.'

With that, he shot past us and marched purposefully down the long corridor outside, his arms and legs moving in a blur of motion. Holmes glanced at me with a raised eyebrow and, I admit, I had some difficulty in preventing myself from laughing as the little man strode away from us down the hallway like some high-tempo marionette.

'I think perhaps we should follow,' said Holmes with a smile. 'Otherwise he may soon be out of sight.'

Fortunately, the corridor was not long enough for that to be a problem and, in fact, Noble stopped in front of the third door along. He pulled a set of keys from his coat pocket, selected one, and unlocked the door. Pushing it open, he invited us to enter.

Art restoration requires a great deal of space to be carried out correctly, and the firm of Young, Murray and Noble had solved the problem of acquiring a premises sufficiently large for the purpose by purchasing the building behind their own, and knocking through the walls to create an entirely enclosed and secure storage area. In front of us lay a magnificently proportioned room, perhaps sixty feet long and almost as wide, entirely whitewashed and, as with the main building, lit by large skylights.

The portraits we had come to see were arrayed on dozens of slanting easels which criss-crossed the available space, almost touching at points and creating a bewildering pathway which reminded me of a maze more than anything else.

'Gentlemen,' said the excitable Mr Noble. 'Here are the artworks supplied by Mr Petrie, all in perfect condition.'

He led us through the artificial aisles, pointing out one or other artwork as being of particular quality or value, until we reached the far wall, where a small desk stood, from which Noble picked up a large sheet of paper.

'A list of everything we are working on for the National Portrait Gallery, with a record of the progress of the restoration.' He quickly inspected the list. 'Well this is excellent! Mr Petrie will be delighted to learn that as yet not a single one of the items delivered to us yesterday has proven to be less than authentic! My staff have checked–' he ran a finger down one column of figures on the paper, '–one hundred and thirty-four items so far, and expect to complete the remainder within the hour.'

He beamed up at us, clearly of the opinion that he was the bearer of glad tidings, but one look at Holmes's face convinced me that he was mistaken in that belief. Holmes was plainly disappointed that – at best – this investigation would be into nothing more exciting to his peculiar brain than a lone forgery. He said nothing, however, other than to enquire after the portrait of King Charles.

Noble pointed to the nearest easel. 'Ah yes,' he said. 'That is the Hamblin portrait over there.'

The painting was, as Petrie had said, undamaged, though the frame was currently being held together by two clamps and, I assumed, a quantity of wood glue. The portrait itself showed His Majesty in a reflective pose, standing next to a tonsured priest, the pair of them reading from an open Bible. The setting was presumably the King's rooms, for a bed could be seen reflected in the mirror in front of which the two men stood. Though, like Holmes, I make no claim to any great expertise in artistic matters, there was a life-like quality to the two men's images that I found somehow disquieting. I turned to mention this to Holmes, but his nose was by now so close to the canvas that he could not have commented usefully on the subject at all.

Perhaps aware that I was observing him, he straightened up wearily and began to speak – but whatever he intended to say was forgotten as the door was flung noisily open and Inspector Lestrade was framed in the doorway.

'Mr Holmes!' he shouted. 'So there you are! The little chap at the Gallery said you'd be here this morning. I must have a word with you!'

With that, the doughty Inspector began to make his way across the room, initially striding forcefully between the tight-packed easels, then slowly tempering his pace as he passed the same painting for a second and then a third time. From our vantage point at the other side of the room, all we could see was the top of his bowler hat where it cleared the tall wooden frames, bobbing up and down as it doubled and even trebled back on itself. Now and again, Lestrade would shout, 'Am I any closer, Dr Watson?' but in truth he never was. After several minutes, I finally thought to ask Mr Noble if he might go and bring him to us.

The Inspector, following Noble as dutifully as any dog follows its master, was flushed and perspiring by the time he had successfully navigated the maze. Even so, he wasted no time in giving Holmes the details of an incident, which he rightly categorised as 'very queer indeed'.

'The thing is, Mr Holmes, that it's not even definite that a crime has been committed. You recall the forged portrait of King Charles... ah yes, sir, that's the very one there... well, it seems that whoever stole the original version and replaced it with a fake thought better of their actions. By which I mean that last night, under cover of darkness, the villain slipped back into the Gallery, genuine article tucked under his arm, and attempted to swap it for the forgery.

'Of course, on account of the possible threat to the Royal family, we've kept this entire affair hush-hush, with no coverage in the press, so the beggar stumbled into more than he bargained for.'

Up until this point, Lestrade had been extemporising his tale from memory, but at this juncture that imperfect mechanism broke down again, and he was forced to consult his notebook.

He pulled it from his pocket and consulted it briefly. 'It appears that he entered the building at round about two thirty-five this morning, by breaking a window on the ground floor, and then made his way up the main staircase, where he was spotted by one of the constables we've had stationed there for this past week. The lad raised the alarm and the intruder was chased back down the stairs and cornered in the basement. Once there, rather than allow himself to be arrested, he took poison and died on the spot.'

Lestrade closed his notebook and returned it to his pocket. Throughout his speech, I had been observing Holmes, watching his face become more animated as his enthusiasm waxed in light of this new development in the situation.

'Poisoned himself, you say, Lestrade? You are quite certain? Now that *is* unusual. He was not English, I presume?' Before Lestrade could interject, Holmes quickly explained, 'No English criminal that I have heard of – and I have heard of them all – would commit suicide rather than be arrested. That type of behaviour rather smacks of the East, I think. An Indian, perhaps, Inspector?'

'Chinese, apparently. I've not been to see the body yet, Mr Holmes, but my information is that the dead man was a Chinese, or something of that sort.'

'That would have been my next suggestion, of course. Both the Indian and Chinese native is raised with a strong sense that his own life is of little consequence. Suicide, in their cultures, is not the sin it is in our own.'

As it turned out, this was an area where my army service allowed me to contribute an example. 'In Afghanistan, I knew a native soldier who took his own life after failing to obtain a fairly minor promotion. He'd brought shame upon his family, it seems, and this was thought a suitable way by which to expiate that shame.' I shook my head, as saddened by the thought now as I had been then. 'And that was a not uncommon occurrence, I remember being told by one or two of the older hands.'

'Is that so, Dr Watson?' Lestrade muttered morosely. 'Be that as it may, this native wasn't in danger of being overlooked for a new job, was he? And like I said, even now we're not sure that any crime has been committed – other than his own suicide, of course.'

Holmes had stood in silent contemplation throughout this brief exchange. Now, he refocused his attention on Lestrade. 'Oh, I think we can safely say that more than one crime has been committed. Why would this man try to return the original painting, if not to cover the fact that it had ever been removed? Why, for that matter, would he so fear capture that suicide would seem the better option? No, Lestrade, there is certainly a crime here. The trick is to discover on whose behalf that crime was committed.'

During this exchange, Mr Noble had been shuffling from foot to foot, either keen to get back to work, or made uncomfortable by the talk of dead thieves. Now he interrupted to ask if we would like to be guided back across the room and – by unspoken extension – be on our way. Holmes appeared not to hear him, but Lestrade agreed that there was nothing else to be found at the restorers.

I touched Holmes on the arm, and he started as he returned from wherever his mind had been. 'We must take a trip, Watson!' he announced. 'A short cab ride to Limehouse and a visit to the Lord of Strange Deaths; that is the order of the day, I think.'

Lestrade, at least, had some inkling of whom Holmes was speaking, and he was not best pleased. 'The Lord of–! You can't possibly be serious, Mr Holmes!' He glanced at me in appeal, but with no knowledge of this oddly named figure I could only shrug and ask him for an explanation.

'The Lord of Strange Deaths is a savage, one of the most dangerous people in London, Dr Watson,' the Inspector replied. 'He's the leader of the Chinese underworld, for one thing, and strongly believed to be responsible for the murders of as many as ten British agents back in China.' He rounded on Holmes. 'I strongly recommend you stay away from him, Mr Holmes. The most treacherous Chinaman on this side of the Great Wall, they call him, and they're not wrong!'

Such was Lestrade's strength of feeling with regard to this criminal mastermind that he was all but shouting. His face was red and flushed as he punctuated each sentence with a wind-milling arm and a pointed finger. For his part, Holmes remained utterly calm and ignored Lestrade altogether. Instead, he bade Mr Noble good day and, making his way back into the street outside, cast around for a cab. 'Would you care to take a trip, Watson?' he asked as he signalled to a passing hansom.

Short of leaving him to continue the investigation alone, there was nothing I could do but reply in the affirmative. As I pulled myself up into the cab, and looked back at Lestrade's still-scarlet face, I hoped that this was not a grave mistake.

Six

To enter Limehouse is to step into another world.

This was not my first visit to that most insalubrious area, but even so I was surprised and revolted afresh by the horrors which surrounded us as our cab made its way along the side of the Thames, then turned into the lee of a boarded-up and abandoned building, and there stopped.

We had been prepared for this, and Holmes merely shrugged as I opened the cab door and carefully stepped out. The hansom driver had made it clear that he would take us to the outskirts of the area, but no further. We would have to walk from this point on.

I knew that many thousands of people made their permanent home in the slum terraces which took up a large proportion of the interior of the district, but here on the fringes, where the river met the city streets, the buildings were of a more commercial aspect. Disreputable lodging-houses and uninviting beer shops alternated with timber yards, shipping offices, and tiny open-fronted workshops.

The proximity of the docks means that the streets of Limehouse are always crowded. Sailors of every nationality mixed with the mass of natives, or sat, slumped in the street, befuddled with drink or opium. Unfortunate women congregated at corners, and smiled toothlessly at any passer-by who looked to have a few coins to spend, while their unemployed menfolk fought and cursed at one another outside the dingy public houses, which dominated the streets away from the riverfront.

I would have felt more comfortable with my revolver, but Holmes had warned me not to bring it with me. 'The Lord of Strange Deaths might take that amiss, Watson,' he had said, and though his tone was light, the tense look that crossed his face told another, more serious tale.

'Just who is he, Holmes? Lestrade may not be a master detective by your lights, but neither is he a fool. Could this Lord of Strange Deaths not be the mastermind behind everything that has occurred so far?'

'Lestrade is a dullard, Watson. A prattling child of little wit but much noise, whose most useful trait is to serve as a barometer by which more intelligent men may judge what is most incorrect or wrong-headed.

'As for the Lord of Strange Deaths... yes, he is a dangerous man, and yes, he controls the Chinese in London with a rod of iron. He has ordered more men killed than any other man in the city, including the ten British agents Lestrade mentioned – and more, I shouldn't wonder – but for all that, he is a man with a very personal code of honour, which he will break for nothing. Lestrade is too simple a soul to understand that, I fear.

'More specifically, the Lord would consider any activity which took place purely in pursuit of material gain as reprehensible. He is akin to an Oriental version of my brother, Mycroft, you see, Watson.

His every waking moment is spent working for the benefit of his own country, and while he would not hesitate to steal, cheat and murder if there were advantage to be gained for China, neither stolen paintings nor treasure would tempt him, I assure you. He is a political creature alone and would sooner cut his own throat than dishonour himself by scrabbling for mere wealth.

'No, we need not worry about the Lord of Strange Deaths today, though it would be wise always to fear him just a little on general grounds.'

I cannot say I felt completely mollified by Holmes's words, but any immediate fear that we were walking into a trap dissipated a little. 'So, what now, Holmes?' I asked. 'Where do we go next?'

Holmes said nothing, but pointed across the street. A figure detached itself from the shadow of a building and walked towards us slowly. He stopped directly in front of us, so close that I could have touched his face without extending my arm, and bowed from the waist. I was unsurprised to see he was an Oriental. He murmured, 'Follow me,' and without waiting for a response, walked into the heart of Limehouse.

Some twenty minutes later, we found ourselves following our guide along a dark and fetid alleyway, where indistinct shapes moaned in the shadows and women of the vilest sort beckoned from open doorways. Though it was only early afternoon, a combination of the season, the ever-present fog and the manner in which the buildings around us leaned in on one another at their topmost extremities meant that we walked in an artificial twilight, which perversely magnified every horror, while at the same time rendering everything about us indistinct and grey. At one point, a large rat boldly ran across the top of my boot until I instinctively flicked it away in disgust. I turned to Holmes to protest, but he held a long finger to his lips and gave a tiny shake of his head. He at least had some idea of where we were going and who we should meet there, and clearly thought the journey worthwhile.

Just as I had resigned myself to tramping through unlit streets forever, we passed round a bend and a soft yellow light appeared in an opening ahead. Our guide beckoned that we should follow him and quickly moved forward into this opening, which turned out to be an archway leading to the river's edge. A smattering of gaslights illuminated the top of a set of stone steps directly in front of us, down which the little Chinaman clambered, with Holmes and I hard on his heels.

At the bottom of these steps a wide path stretched into the darkness, with the river on one side and a row of derelict buildings on the other. It was part of the peculiar flavour of the area that each of these edifices was raised into the air by pillars, on which the buildings themselves were balanced. The idea was, presumably, to avoid flooding when the Thames was high. A tall ladder at the front of each building provided access to a form of porch, beyond which was a more conventional front door. To move between buildings, however, required descending one ladder and then ascending the next, there being no aerial path connecting any two structures.

I gave a start as a pile of dirty rags lying at the base of one ladder stirred and was revealed to be a sleeping beggar. Holmes glanced down with a thoughtful expression on his face, but gave no other indication of interest. Instead, he lightly touched my arm and gestured at our guide, who stood, unmoving, before us.

In his hands he held a pair of blindfolds. He handed one to each of us and mimed our putting them over our eyes, which we did, though not without trepidation, on my part at least. An unfamiliar hand on my shoulder and a guttural 'Move now!' in my ear did little to assuage my concerns, but nonetheless I responded to a firm push against my shoulder and shuffled hesitantly forward.

I could not say how long we walked or whether we followed a single path; perhaps we doubled or even trebled back on ourselves, but I counted my steps until I reached two thousand, at which point I recognised the pointlessness of the exercise and ceased. What I *can* say is that when the hand on my shoulder pressed down and the same guttural voice said 'Stop now,' I was tired both of walking and of the ever-present stench of decay which permeated the area. The thought that we had only a ladder to climb in order to reach our destination was a relief. I hauled myself upwards, aware that Holmes preceded me by the sound of his breathing above me. Once at the summit, unseen hands reached up and removed my blindfold, and I took a moment to examine my surroundings.

Holmes was standing just inside an open doorway, his eyes flicking quickly from one side to the other as his exceptional brain filed away details that might later turn out to be vital to our understanding of the case – or at least I hoped so. Over his shoulder I could make out a long, dimly lit room, with small square windows spaced out along each wall, and crowds of silent people standing on either side of a carpeted central aisle. It was impossible to make out much of the décor in the room, even after our guide had prodded us inside, for a sweet-smelling smoke pervaded the space and hung in soft clouds from the ceiling, tinting everything it touched a dirty yellowish-brown. I had spent enough time in Afghanistan to recognise the sickly odour of opium.

A nudge in the back from a large, grim-faced Chinese propelled me forward. Perhaps it was the effects of the drug hanging in the air, or maybe it was simple tiredness, but as I followed Holmes down the length of the room, I could have sworn that I heard a voice behind me quietly exclaim 'Sherlock Holmes!' I tried to turn to see who had spoken, but my granite-faced guard gave me a hearty shove that all but sent me crashing into Holmes's back and it was all I could do to remain upright.

By the time I had completely regained my balance, we were approaching the end of the room. Directly in front of us stood an ornately carved oak chair, decorated with arcane symbols and glittering gemstones, and framed by two antique swords, which curved above and around it. Other ancient weaponry hung from the walls. I heard Holmes give the smallest of sighs as a curtain to one side was twitched open and an elderly Chinese man in traditional costume shuffled painfully forward. To my English eyes, the man appeared the very exemplar of the mysterious Oriental, with thin, dark eyes, long, sharp fingernails and a white moustache that reached down past his chin. As he settled himself, two giant guards took up position on either side of him, glaring down at Holmes and myself with implacable hostility.

Holmes, at least, felt confident enough to speak. He took a step forward and gave a low bow, causing a general stiffening amongst our captors. Both of the old man's guards laid a hand on the curved sword at his waist, and around us a rumble of discontent was plainly audible, but Holmes was utterly unfazed. He simply stood, a little in front of me and within touching distance of the Chinese leader, until that luminary waved a languid hand in the air and, to my great relief, everyone relaxed.

'Great Lord,' said Holmes unexpectedly, 'I come to ask a single question, which I believe it would be in both our interests for you to answer. Last evening, a gentleman of Oriental aspect attempted to return a missing painting to the Gallery from which it was stolen.

Given your… management… of your people in London, I wondered if perhaps you had knowledge of this man?'

I admit that I feared at first that the elderly Chinese was in some distress. As Holmes fell silent, he let out a choking, wheezing sound, as though in the worst stages of an asthmatic attack, and thumped one hand on the arm of his chair. I glanced over at Holmes and was reassured to see a slight smile evident on his lips.

'You find the question amusing?' he asked.

As suddenly as it had begun, the wheezing laughter stopped. The old man beckoned to one of his guards, who bent down and listened to his master's whispered commands.

'The Lord of Strange Deaths asks what crime has been committed if the item has been returned.'

'Even a theft reconsidered remains a theft, my Lord.'

The old man nodded to himself, and rubbed the palms of his hands together as he considered Holmes's remark. He conversed again with his bodyguard, then sat back in his chair as the giant turned to Holmes.

'The Lord of Strange Deaths asks why you do not speak to this criminal of his motivations, rather than coming to his own humble dwelling place. The Lord knows nothing of *paintings.*'

I was certain from the look on Holmes's face that this was not the response he had expected. 'The man is dead,' he said finally. 'Poisoned by his own hand, in fact.'

At this, the old man gave out a harsh bark, though whether of surprise or amusement I could not say. He clapped his hands loudly together, and in response the nearest guard bowed low while the Lord whispered in his ear, then turned and spoke to several nearby figures, who detached themselves from the crowd and ran from the room. I glanced at Holmes, who signalled with the slightest shake of his head that all we could do was wait. Ten minutes passed in this manner, with Holmes and I standing silently before the Lord of Strange Deaths, who appeared to be asleep.

The silence was finally broken by a sound behind us, as the men returned and made whispered reports to the Lord. Once complete, he waved them away, then clapped his thin hands once more. Before the sound had finished echoing around the long room, a door I had failed to observe earlier opened in the wall to our right, and three men entered, carrying between them a large wicker basket, which they placed on the floor in front of the Lord of Strange Deaths. Each man then bowed low and left without a word, closing the door silently behind them.

Holmes indicated the basket. 'May I?' he asked. In reply, our host crooked a finger in our direction, inviting us to approach. I made to follow Holmes as he stepped forward, but a soft 'Not this time, Watson,' caused me to come to a halt, so that I was unable to see inside the basket as Holmes carefully lifted the lid.

Whatever hellish sight Holmes exposed within, it was enough to make him recoil violently and hurriedly thrust the lid back atop the basket. Though I knew he was in no way a squeamish man, Holmes's face had paled noticeably, and I, who knew him so well, could tell that his voice was not entirely steady when next he spoke.

'What is this–?' he managed to say before the Lord of Strange Deaths beckoned him to approach, in order that he might murmur directly into my friend's ear.

No sooner had he done so – and Holmes had stepped back with a look of pure revulsion etched on his face – than the elderly Lord took his leave, shuffling back through the curtains while the same guide who had led us to this place silently held blindfolds out to Holmes and me.

* * *

Holmes would not be drawn into conversation in the cab back
to Baker Street. His face remained strained and sombre through
the entire journey, his eyes staring blankly ahead, blinking only
occasionally and slowly. Whatever had been in the basket, it had
affected him greatly.

When we arrived home, he headed straight upstairs, leaving me
to pay the fare. I followed a minute or so behind, to discover him
already slumped in his chair, with a pipe about to be lit. He sat and
smoked the entire pipe in silence, and I sat opposite him, smoking a
cigarette and watching him from the corner of my eye.

Finally, he laid his pipe aside. He ran a hand through his hair
and gave out a heavy sigh, like a man coming to a painful, but
unavoidable, decision.

'"England's Treasure", Watson,' he said, in the end. 'That name
crops up again, and I begin to wonder if I have not perhaps made an
error of judgement in ignoring it thus far.'

'Is that what the Lord of Strange Deaths said?' I asked.

He closed his eyes but remained silent. Fearing that he would
lapse back into silent contemplation, I quickly asked the question
uppermost in my mind since leaving Limehouse.

'What was in the basket, Holmes?'

His eyes flicked open again. He stared at me, unblinking, for
several heartbeats before speaking. 'That is as unpleasant a sight
as I have encountered in many a long year, Watson. It is one that I
suspect you will not care to describe to your readers in *The Strand*,
my friend, even if that august periodical agreed to print the details.

'I am certain that it comes as no surprise to you to learn that the
Lord of Strange Deaths is a cruel man in most respects – but as I said

earlier, he is also an honourable one, by his own lights. He told me that the dead man once worked for him – and by extension for China – but had recently defected, exchanging his proper employment as a spy for that of a common thief. This defection the Lord views as a gross betrayal of his country.'

He rested his neck against the back of his chair and stared up at the ceiling. 'The basket contained the punishment for that betrayal. Three heads, very recently cut from their respective bodies. A young woman, an older woman and an elderly man. The defector's wife, mother and father, according to the Lord of Strange Deaths.

'"In China," he whispered to me, "they say that treason and corpse are brothers, and thus a relative must also pay the price of treachery. We have sought the man you describe, in order to punish him, but if he has escaped justice, it is fitting that his family take his place."'

There was nothing to be said in the face of such barbarity, and so we sat in silence for at least half an hour, as the light outside turned from a dark grey to a bluish-black, and fog descended and hung in dense clouds around the chimney pots on the roofs opposite. I crossed to the window and pulled it shut. As though reacting to a signal, Holmes sat upright as I resumed my seat, smoothed his hair down and, in as normal a voice as I could have hoped for, asked whether I wished to hear the remainder of his story.

'The Lord of Strange Deaths had one more thing to say to me. The dead man, he said, had pledged his loyalty to a new villain, one Lestrade mentioned a few days ago. The Albino seeks a treasure beyond price, according to the Lord of Strange Deaths, something that would make its owner the richest man in England, perhaps even the entire Empire. "Find England's Treasure," he said, "before it falls into the hands of this Albino. He is not an honourable man."'

'Did you believe him?' I asked.

Holmes was uncharacteristically indecisive. 'Wealth breeds power, and it is in nobody's interests for one man to gain such power. I do not necessarily believe the Lord, but nor am I convinced that he is lying. Riches do not interest him, nor personal power, but he might well intervene if he believes this Albino is a danger to China. I fail to see how that could be the case, but at the very least it appears that this forged painting is a far more interesting puzzle than I would ever have guessed.'

He fell silent once more, but I could tell from the tight way he held his shoulders that he was thinking about the Albino, and about England's Treasure, and wondering what each might be.

Seven

The following morning dawned wet and blustery. When I came through to our sitting room Holmes had already finished his breakfast and was standing at the window, watching the rain thrum against the glass. He remained thus for the entire time I was eating, a silent presence at the edge of my vision, then, as I pushed back my chair and lit a cigarette, he said, without turning, 'We are at an impasse, Watson. No further forgeries at the Gallery, and nothing to show for our visit to Limehouse but an unpleasant memory, and a dead end. I was sure that the King Charles could not be the only forged portrait! I remain of that opinion, but having failed with one sample, are we any more likely to succeed with a second? And not only are we no nearer untangling the knot which surrounds the one forgery that we *do* know about, but now we have two new questions without answers: who is the Albino, and what is England's Treasure?'

'Undoubtedly something immensely valuable,' I ventured, aware even as I spoke that such a wide generalisation would not impress

Holmes. In an attempt to be more precise, I continued, 'Or a weapon of some sort, perhaps? To take control of England, never mind the Empire, one would need either enormous wealth or a weapon of terrifying potency.'

'A weapon? Perhaps. The Germans have been doing some… worrying… experiments with gases, I believe. Such a thing *could* be used to blackmail the authorities. But how could our nameless villain hope to maintain his threat? Sooner or later, his weapon would be removed from him, or nullified in some other manner. An antidote or an assassin would put paid to his plans either way. No, Watson, the treasure this Albino seeks is far more likely to be gold than guns or gas. Far easier to buy a kingdom, after all, than win one in war.'

I could see no flaw in Holmes's reasoning regarding either the nature of the Treasure or our own lack of progress. It was thus in a spirit of desperation that I suggested we return to the National Portrait Gallery, and check whether anything new had been discovered. I remained concerned that, in the absence of a new case, Holmes's less welcome enthusiasms would raise their ugly heads again, and he would resort to the needle for stimulation. I need not have worried, however, for while I was still speaking, he whipped round with sudden energy and agreed heartily that this should indeed be our next destination.

'And after that to the Scotland Yard mortuary, Watson. Perhaps the thief's body will yield some indication of where we should be looking – and for what.'

I followed him out of our lodgings, hastily snatching my hat and gloves on the way out the door, and wrapping my scarf tight around my neck as I prepared for the foul weather outside.

* * *

It was beginning to feel as though the National Portrait Gallery was never at peace. When we gratefully ducked inside out of the rain, we were greeted by an untidy mess of ladders and scaffolding. White cloths were draped over several of the items on display, and the first two rooms on the right-hand side were tight shut, with a sign on each door apologising for the inconvenience during essential maintenance work.

We had no difficulty in finding Mr Petrie, who bustled up while we stood, dripping, in the corridor. 'Mr Holmes. Dr Watson. This is a surprise. As you can see, we are in the midst of restoring the Gallery to something approaching its state prior to the recent disturbance.'

Perhaps it was my imagination, but I felt that his voice had lost some of the keen enthusiasm which he had displayed at our earlier meetings and, particularly, upon making the acquaintance of Sherlock Holmes. Evidently the fruitless transfer of dozens of paintings to the restorers for checking, and then their passage back again, had caused a great deal of confusion and upheaval at the Gallery.

Holmes, though, could be charming when he put his mind to it. Sensing that we were not entirely welcome, he took a step forward and warmly shook Petrie's hand. 'A pleasant one, for our part, I assure you,' he began with a wide smile. 'I was just saying to Watson that, before we ask you any more questions, we should check with you, to ensure that any pseudonym he uses when writing up this case is acceptable to you, and does not in any way prove personally embarrassing or inappropriate.'

Holmes smiled effusively again, but he need not have concerned himself. I could tell from one look at Petrie's stunned face that his exalted opinion of Holmes had been restored. 'Writing up the case?' he stammered with a glazed look of delight in his eyes. 'I am to be in one of your cases, Mr Holmes?'

'Why, of course! Isn't that right, Watson?'

I could only nod my agreement, though I cannot say that I felt completely comfortable with Holmes's deception. I reassured myself with the thought that, should the case come to a successful conclusion, I would certainly write it up and would be sure to give Petrie a sizeable role. He had, after all, been of *some* assistance.

For the moment, though, the Secretary was extremely apologetic. 'I would be delighted to provide any possible service, of course, gentlemen,' he was saying to Holmes, 'but unfortunately I am just about to leave London for a few days. I intend to return on Tuesday, but I assume that your questions will not wait until then?'

Holmes assured him that haste was vital. Petrie's face fell, then brightened as Holmes went on to remark that, on this particular occasion, all he really needed was to speak to whomever would know most about the provenance of the forged painting of King Charles.

'That would be our Miss Rhodes,' Petrie cried. 'Dr Watson, I think you met her briefly on your first visit? She will happily put herself at your disposal, and can answer any questions you might have. By happy chance, it was she, in fact, who initially purchased the painting for the Gallery.'

I cannot deny that the prospect of speaking to Miss Rhodes was an appealing one. Holmes, of course, cared neither one way nor the other who helped us, but the combination of intelligence and beauty was one that I have always admired. Consequently, it was with a definite spring in my step that I followed Petrie and Holmes upstairs.

Miss Rhodes was directing two Gallery staff who were in the process of hanging a painting as we entered the room in which she was working. Such was her absorption in her task that she remained unaware of our arrival until Mr Petrie had twice coughed in a marked manner and then finally called her name loudly. She turned with a frown on her face that was quickly replaced with a smile of greeting as she recognised both her immediate superior and, I like to think, myself and Holmes.

In any case, she gave the workmen one last instruction and, leaving them to their task, hurried over to greet us.

Petrie briefly explained to Miss Rhodes that we were hoping to speak to her regarding the recently uncovered forgery, before making his excuses and taking his leave. Holmes, meanwhile, indicated a nearby bench and invited Miss Rhodes to take a seat.

'I am hopeful, Miss Rhodes, that you might be able to provide some detail regarding the history of the King Charles painting? I believe that you were the person who identified and purchased it for the Gallery?'

'Yes, last summer,' she replied. 'I was on a walking holiday in Surrey, travelling across the county in the company of a friend. It was a day much like this one, with the rain hammering down in sheets and a wind which chilled us to the bone, and I may tell you that as we crested what felt like the twentieth rain-sodden hill of the day and caught a glimpse of Hamblin Hall through the trees, it was as though our prayers had been answered. My friend does not keep in the best of health – our holiday was on the instruction of her doctor, who suggested exercise and fresh air as the best cure for her ailments – and I was keen to get her indoors as soon as possible. So we followed the drive up to the house and made ourselves known to the current occupant of the Hall. He was kindness itself and good enough to invite us in. While my poor companion warmed herself by the fire, he showed me round the Hall, taking as keen an interest in our comfort as any host could. In return, I explained the nature of my employment to him, and he was so courteous as to allow me free access to the various galleries.'

'Where you discovered and, I assume, admired the portrait of the late monarch?'

'Exactly, Mr Holmes. It was hanging all alone on the main staircase, and I actually almost walked past it.' She laughed gaily. 'It had not been well maintained, but I must say that that was true of the Hall in general.'

'Hamblin Hall has seen better days?'

'I'm afraid so, Mr Holmes. Willoughby – Mr Frogmorton, that is, the current occupant – does his best to maintain standards, but I believe that... well, it is an expensive business, they say, the upkeep of a house and lands.'

Holmes nodded gravely in agreement. 'That is undoubtedly true, Miss Rhodes. But you were describing the painting of King Charles?'

'Yes. It had been hung halfway up the main staircase, as I said, in a position of prominence in spite of its air of neglect. Its placement alone would have inclined me to stop and examine it, for all that its coating of dust meant that it was not being exhibited to its greatest advantage. Still, there was something about the painting that caught the eye.

'Mr Frogmorton, you must understand, had explained at the beginning of our talk that he knew nothing of art, and had little interest in learning. So, unfortunately, he could tell me very little about the provenance of the piece, nor even whom it portrayed. And that would have been the end of that, were it not for the fact that my friend, chilled by our walk in the storm, took quite unwell and Mr Frogmorton was again generous to a fault, and asked us to stay for a few days, while she recovered her strength.'

'Mr Frogmorton's wife was present?' I interjected. 'He is, I take it, a married man?' I hurried to reassure her I meant no impertinence. 'It is important that we know all the facts, Miss Rhodes, and you have not mentioned her as yet.'

She coloured a little at my question, and I felt myself redden somewhat in response, concerned that she might take my clumsy words as an accusation. Before I could say anything further, however, she laid my mind at rest, both regarding the missing wife and my own potential lack of gallantry.

'Lady Alexandra was visiting her sister when we arrived, Dr Watson, though there were servants in residence. She returned towards dinner time, as it happens, or we could not have remained overnight.' She smiled in my direction, which was reassuring, but then spoiled the effect a touch by concluding, 'I know that some people look askance at two young women travelling alone and unchaperoned, but Mr Frogmorton could not have been more of a gentleman, I assure you, and his wife was wonderful in her solicitude for our misfortune, and was particularly attentive to my poor friend.'

Holmes gave the smallest of starts, as though wakening from a daydream, and, fearing his interest was waning, I thought it best to steer the conversation back to the painting.

'I am sure she was,' I said, returning her smile. 'I must admit to being impressed by the manner in which you were trusted to buy for so prominent a gallery at such a young age, Miss Rhodes.' I was aware of Holmes watching us closely, and congratulated myself on re-engaging his flagging interest. 'Have you always been interested in art then?' I asked, finally.

The question appeared to discommode her for some reason I could not imagine. 'Since I was a young girl, Doctor,' she replied coldly after a pause then fell silent, her mood, it seemed to me, suddenly changed. Holmes, as one might have expected, noticed nothing amiss, and resumed his questioning as though I had never spoken and she never replied.

'You were explaining, I think, that the painting caught your eye due to its prominent placement, Miss Rhodes, rather than any inherent artistic value? But presumably once you examined it more closely, there was some element in its construction, some portion of its makeup, which caused you to consider it afresh? Why else, after all, would you have chosen it alone of all the paintings in Hamblin Hall to purchase for London's newest and most fashionable gallery?'

Miss Rhodes visibly brightened as Holmes spoke, which was not, in my experience, the common reaction to one of his interrogations. There was an eagerness in the way in which she nodded her agreement, and a note of satisfaction in her voice as she described her time at Hamblin Hall, and explained that she had taken on the task of cleaning up the painting as a project with which to pass the time while her companion recuperated.

'You would never have believed it, Mr Holmes! From underneath that dust and grime there emerged an enchanting image of England's martyred King at prayer. The colours were as fresh as the day it was painted, vibrantly green and red, and the brushwork... well I could not have been more surprised to discover something so beautiful in a Hottentot village! I almost feared that Willoughby would insist on keeping it, in the end!'

'Quite so,' Holmes agreed. 'The artwork was striking, then. Was there anything else you noticed about it? Any element other than its quality which stood out as unusual?'

'Nothing, Mr Holmes. It was memorable only in its loveliness.'

'It could not – and I hesitate to ask this and do so only for completeness' sake – have been a forgery?'

'No!' Miss Rhodes was vehement in her denial. 'As I said, I cleaned it myself, and in doing so became more intimately acquainted with the painting than is common even in a gallery such as this. The painting I purchased and which was originally hung in these rooms was a seventeenth-century portrait of a living king, not some cheap imitation from two centuries later!'

'A real treasure then, would you say?' Holmes's voice betrayed no sign that this particular choice of words held any special meaning. It may be that it did not. In any case, Miss Rhodes nodded her agreement.

'A piece worth treasuring, I should say, Mr Holmes. To discover it had been stolen and replaced with a poor imitation was a blow, but it caused me even greater pain to realise that none of our visitors even noticed the switch.' She shook her head, sorrowfully. 'One tends to think of the London public – certainly those who visit our gallery – as cultured and educated, but that anyone could mistake that forgery for Hamblin's original...' She trailed off disconsolately.

'Yet you did not yourself notice the substitution, Miss Rhodes?'

'I had been out of town for the past week, Mr Holmes, and I can assure you that there had been no substitution before I left. Whatever occurred did so after I departed.'

'Of course,' said Holmes. 'The painter, then, this Hamblin,' he continued. 'Could you perhaps tell me a little of him? Of his life and his work.'

'If you think it will help,' she replied.

Holmes beamed at her with approval. 'It will help enormously, I assure you. The more specifics that Dr Watson and I know, the better.'

'Though forgotten now,' Miss Rhodes began, as though addressing a lecture hall, 'Sir Horace Hamblin was a prodigy of his age: a polymath, an artist, writer, mathematician and scientist, with interests in every area of the scientific and artistic life, from translating Latin poetry to the mathematics of cryptography. An unapologetic and notorious Cavalier and secret Catholic, Hamblin was a close personal friend of King Charles, until they had a mysterious falling-out during the Civil War that led to a cooling of their friendship. Hamblin created this single painting of the King at some point in the 1640s, before he was himself killed by Roundheads in November 1647.

'Legend has it that, following the King's escape from captivity on November the eleventh of that year, a company of Parliamentarian soldiers was sent to search the estates of known Royalist sympathisers. In due course they rode up to Hamblin Hall but Hamblin had been forewarned by his tenants, and they found the Hall barred to them. The Roundheads camped outside for days, wary of his reputation locally as a man prone to unholy scientific experiments and content to wait him out.

'Eventually, however, pride overcame fear and they smashed in the door. When they marched inside, they discovered that Hamblin had wired up a convoluted series of levers and pulleys, reaching from the front entrance up the main staircase as well as left and right into the neighbouring rooms. The first man to enter, the captain of the Roundhead forces in the area, was killed by an arrow fired via a thin wire attached to a tensed bowstring. Four more Roundheads allegedly fell to one or other of Hamblin's many booby traps before he was captured and hanged from a tree in his own grounds.

'His memory is much revered in the local area, even to this day, because he had every opportunity to flee before the Roundheads arrived and chose not to do so, through loyalty to his friend, the King.'

The thought appeared to disturb and sadden Miss Rhodes, and she fell silent. Holmes, however, was unmoved by either the death of this most loyal of subjects or by the distress felt by the more modern young lady currently seated beside him. He frowned at her silence and prompted her to continue. 'So much for Hamblin the man,' he said. 'But what of Hamblin the artist? Did he paint any other works?'

'If he did, then no trace has remained of them. There are a handful of engravings and charcoal sketches from his university days which are, I believe, held somewhere at Oxford, but other than that he seems entirely to have eschewed art for science.'

'That is unusual,' Holmes murmured to himself and for once, when I asked him to explain himself, he deigned to do so.

'The artistic temperament is not one which can simply be turned on and off, as though a tap, Watson. You recall the matter of the French sculptor, Seneche, and the Duc d'Amboise in seventy-seven? Or closer to home, the Scotsman Liddell, who included the names of his victims in each of his paintings? Each man caught because he could not bear to stop creating. And yet Sir Horace appears to have been interested in art as a young man, and to have painted his King years later, but to have done nothing, *created* nothing, during the decades in between.'

'Perhaps he came to painting late in life,' I suggested. 'Had he not been executed in such a gruesome fashion, perhaps he would have gone on to produce any number of paintings in the future?'

'Perhaps,' Holmes admitted. 'Anything is possible.'

Miss Rhodes was still standing, waiting to be of assistance, while Holmes fell into a brown study, staring with unseeing eyes into the middle distance. Behind Miss Rhodes I could just make out a break in the heavy London sky through a picture window and I found myself wondering if it might stop raining soon. I was about to remark on this to Miss Rhodes when Holmes suddenly started to life and asked whether she had purchased any other artworks during her stay at Hamblin Hall.

At this, Miss Rhodes brightened considerably. 'Why yes, I did. We have one other portrait from the Hall in the Gallery collection, though it is not currently on display. If you would care to wait here, Mr Holmes, I will go and arrange to have it brought up.'

She left on her errand, and I turned to Holmes with some annoyance. 'You might make some effort to be pleasant to Miss Rhodes, Holmes!'

Holmes, however, gave no indication that he had heard me. Instead, he walked over to the window and stood, inspecting the street outside, until Miss Rhodes reappeared.

'Mr Holmes,' she called. 'I have had the painting brought up and placed in one of the unused rooms, if you and Dr Watson would care to follow me.'

We followed her downstairs and into a small side-room. Like all the rooms in the Gallery it was spacious and well lit, with a large window dominating the far wall, though otherwise featureless. The object of our curiosity had been set up on an easel directly in front of the door, with a white cloth covering it. Miss Rhodes preceded us in and pulled the cloth off with a flick of her wrist.

'Mr Holmes, Dr Watson,' she began, 'I am pleased to introduce you to Sir Augustine Hamblin, fifth of that name and grandfather to Horace Hamblin. The identity of the artist is unknown, I'm afraid, but it is a striking work, is it not?'

I agreed, though I know almost as little about art as my friend Holmes. To my eye, there was little to distinguish this depiction of an elderly, heavy-set gentleman from any other, but Holmes obviously felt differently, for he immediately strode up to the painting and, with his magnifying glass never more than an inch from the canvas, examined it in great detail.

Miss Rhodes and I shared a look as Holmes leaned in ever closer, muttering softly to himself.

'The light in this room is not ideal – that's the reason it's never been used for display – but even so, I think you must admit that it is a striking piece.'

'This is Horace Hamblin's grandfather, you said?' I asked.

'Yes. Six generations of eldest sons in the Hamblin family were named Augustine, until Horace was born and broke the run. Evidently his father – this Augustine's eldest son – decided he didn't care for the name, even though it was his own.'

'Another oddity about Horace Hamblin,' I said, though it did not seem important. 'Is there anything else you can tell us about either Hamblin?' Holmes had often impressed upon me that even seemingly inconsequential facts could prove vital to our understanding, and besides, I was keen to talk further with Miss Rhodes.

'Nothing about the elder man, I'm afraid. But Horace Hamblin was the eldest of seven sons, all of whom died during the Civil War. He and one of his brothers were particularly close to the King, and are even rumoured to have sheltered him while he was on the run from Cromwell's troops. Perhaps I could–'

'Miss Rhodes!' Holmes's voice cut through our conversation like a thrown dagger. 'There is something not quite right about this painting.'

Miss Rhodes and I hurried to join Holmes. Before she or I could say a word, he handed her his magnifying glass and pointed one long finger at a point where the canvas met the ornate gilt frame in which the painting was enclosed. I could see nothing amiss, but Miss Rhodes gasped at my side, and I knew that there was something that I was not seeing.

'Look here, Watson, for pity's sake!' Holmes exclaimed, seeing the confusion on my face. He prodded the painting hard and I expected Miss Rhodes to caution him to take better care, but she said nothing, only stood in the grey light of the storm clouds outside, her face pale with shock.

'What are you talking about, Holmes?!' I snapped. Holmes could be irritating at times, and the painting looked exactly as I expected a depiction of a dissolute rake of centuries past to look. Wordlessly, he handed me the glass and indicated a specific small section of the frame.

Through the magnifying effect of the glass in my hand I could see several tiny holes in the wood of the frame, which I attributed to woodworm or some such insect. The painting had been hanging, all but ignored, in an old country house for centuries, after all.

I said as much to Holmes, admitting myself baffled as to the reason for his concern.

'Woodworm do not create perfectly straight holes, Watson! They twist and move as they burrow their way into wood, forming crooked lines, not straight. Only a small drill could possibly have created the holes in that frame, and the only reason to add "wormholes" to the frame is to make the painting it encloses seem older than it truly is.'

'Because it is a forgery!' I interrupted in sudden understanding.

'Bravo, Watson! A capital deduction! Yes, a forgery. But not of the same standard as the first forgery, you'll note. The portrait of King Charles was so poorly done as to be spotted almost as soon as it was moved; this, on the other hand...'

His voice tailed off, but Miss Rhodes – who had until that point been standing in silent shock – completed the thought for him, '...is a work of art in its own right. The attention to detail is exceptional, the brushwork exquisite...'

In turn, she too fell silent and it was left to me to ask the obvious question. 'Why should the two be of such differing quality? Can there be two groups at work?'

'Both busily forging paintings taken from the same obscure country home, then swapping them for originals handily held at the National Portrait Gallery? I think not, Watson. No, the solution to that minor puzzle is obvious. What concerns me far more is that we are no closer to solving the greater question.'

'Obvious?'

Holmes's air of intellectual superiority was justified, of course, but nonetheless grating for all that. My irritation must have shown on my face, for he swiftly continued, 'Less complex, then. The paintings vary in quality because of the time taken in their creation.' He turned to Miss Rhodes. 'I believe you said that the portrait of the King was about to be removed from display and lent to the Royal household, from where it could not possibly have been exchanged? In such a case, with little time to waste, the replacement was of necessity hurried and consequently of a poorer standard than that of Sir Augustine which, one presumes, was longer in the planning and manufacture, sitting as it did securely in storage.'

Explained thus it was indeed obvious. I admitted as much to Holmes, but he had already dismissed the matter from his mind and was preparing to leave. As he swept down the stairs towards the entrance, I reassured Miss Rhodes that we would be sure to keep her informed of any developments, bade her a hasty goodbye and hurried after him. By the time I caught up, he had already hailed a cab.

Once we were under way, I took stock of our situation before I spoke to my companion. His earlier condescension still rankled a little, and I preferred to have all the facts of our case safely marshalled before making any observations.

We had discovered two forged paintings at the National Portrait Gallery, of two distinct subjects, by two different artists, separated in time by almost a century. Our only potential suspect was dead, and what had begun as a possible threat against Her Majesty had transformed into something altogether more strange. Considerably less serious, it was true, but more puzzling for all that.

Holmes's voice broke into my musings. He too had evidently been considering our situation, and I was gratified to discover his thoughts paralleled mine to some degree. 'A pretty puzzle, Watson, wouldn't you say? Lacking the drama of an attack on the Royal person admittedly, but none the worse for that. Tomorrow we shall take the train to the village of Hamblin, I think. It will be a relief to get out of the city and away from this interminable rain!'

Earlier in our acquaintance I would have been more surprised by the note of pleasure in his voice, but the years had taught me that nothing so invigorated Holmes as a mystery. So it was that I followed my friend through the door of 221b Baker Street in an unexpectedly positive frame of mind.

Eight

By morning, the weather had improved enormously, with the previous day's clouds and rain replaced by unseasonably clement skies. We breakfasted early and, as soon as Holmes had sent a runner to update Inspector Lestrade on our progress, set off for Waterloo in fine humour. Holmes, indeed, could even be heard briefly humming an air to himself as the hansom rattled through the bright, quiet streets.

The train too was less busy due to the early hour, and we were able to find an otherwise empty carriage into which we settled just as the engine in front thundered into life and we began our journey towards Hamblin.

Before long, the sun shining strongly down through the train windows combined with the heat of the carriage to make me drowsy and I found my head gently drooping against my chest as I dozed my way through the English countryside. Holmes, of course, remained alert throughout the journey, consulting some notes he had copied the night before from one of the many files he kept at Baker Street.

'Now this is interesting, Watson,' he announced loudly at one point, jerking me awake. 'The fortunes of the Hamblin family have taken something of a fall since Sir Horace occupied the Hall. Large sums squandered by a succession of wastrel elder sons, and a considerable loss in an unspecified South Seas venture in the thirties have left the family coffers almost bare.' He flicked through the papers on the seat beside him, and pulled out a large sheet of paper, folded into quarters. Using some coins he had in his pocket to hold down the corners, he unfolded the document and spread it out before us. It was the Hamblin family tree, roughly copied out in pencil. 'You see?' he asked, jabbing a long finger at the paper. 'The current – and last – genuine Hamblin is Lady Alexandra, married in 1873 to one Willoughby Frogmorton, about whom I am afraid I know nothing.'

I failed to see what was so important. Even the great Sherlock Holmes could not hope to know everything. 'What point are you making, Holmes?' I asked.

Sherlock Holmes held his hands out in front of him in mock amazement. 'Once again you surprise me, Watson. For many years you and I have worked together, on a variety of different cases. You have had ample time to observe my methods, and every opportunity to put them into practice. And yet, here we find ourselves. You see everything, but remain incapable of even the most basic of deductions from those observations. I know *nothing* about Willoughby Frogmorton. Nothing at all. What does that tell you?'

'That he has committed no crime?' I ventured.

'More than that, Watson, far more than that! It means that Mr Frogmorton has done nothing of interest in public life. He has won no awards, gained no fortune, been mentioned in no reports, achieved not even the most fleeting of fame.'

'Which leads you to believe…?'

'Again, nothing at all.' Holmes spoke calmly but his eyes glowed with the pleasure of new ideas. 'It does, however, lead me to wonder why the scion of a family with roots back as far as the Conqueror should marry a man with no titles, money or family of his own. Look at the lady's lineage! An uninterrupted sequence of marriages between members of the gentry, until Lady Alexandra. That does not strike you as interesting?'

'Not particularly, no. Times are changing, Holmes. The twentieth century beckons, with all that is likely to entail. But even were it not, people have always married for love, you know.' My protests were perfunctory, I have to admit, for I had suffered through Holmes's views on love and marriage on more than one occasion in the past, and feared a repeat.

But to my surprise, 'Perhaps,' was the only further comment Holmes would make on the subject. He returned to his papers, and I to my interrupted dozing.

Hamblin Hall was just visible through the trees from the road, slumped at the peak of the long ridge that dominated the local skyline. As we travelled there in the tiny village of Hamblin's only cab, through scrubby marshland then along a long rutted dirt track, the building became more sharply focused, though that was not entirely to its benefit.

From the outside, it was plain that upkeep had been allowed to fall away in recent years. The shape of a stylish and carefully constructed ornamental garden could still be made out amongst the tangle of overgrown rose bushes, wind-tilted statuary and scum-coated fountains and ponds, but only in the manner in which the outline of a sleeper may yet be seen on bed sheets for a brief time after he has risen for the day. What had once clearly been a handsome Tudor dwelling had also been allowed to decay over the centuries. The reddish-brown brickwork was cracked in a multitude of places, and one of the tall chimney stacks which bracketed the front entrance had lost its ornamental crown, though an even larger one to the rear retained its own. The chipped paint of the front door and a thin layer of grey dirt on the upper windows signified financial difficulties so clearly that even Holmes did not feel the need to labour the point.

We had discussed our plan of approach in the cab, and as we stood in the chill air before the entrance, Holmes quickly recapped lest there should be any confusion. 'I see no need to do anything beyond explaining our purpose and examining such paintings as we may. With luck, Willoughby Frogmorton will be at home, and we can take the opportunity to examine him at the same time.'

I glanced querulously at Holmes, but he said nothing more on the subject. With a shrug, I knocked hard at the door and stood back, but nobody answered, even after I repeated the action more forcefully. I fancied that I saw a figure move behind the grime of an upstairs window but it could as easily have been a cat. I was about to suggest that we try the rear of the house when the door finally opened and a maid appeared. Holmes explained that we hoped to speak to the master of the house, if he was available, and the maid asked us to step inside.

Inside, a long staircase split to the left and right and continued in either direction in a sweep to the first floor, framing the entrance hall on three sides. Visible to our right as we stood opposite the stairs was what I took to be a library, while through the open door to our left a large drawing room could be seen. I had expected to be shown into the latter, but the little maid directed us towards the library, and asked us to wait while she made our presence known to the master of the house.

It was a well-lit room, with several large sash windows, and a large fireplace. Bookcases lined all four walls, with here and there glass-covered display cases breaking up the monotony of oak shelves. I took a seat in one of the deep leather armchairs, which were set on either side of the unlit fire, but Holmes would not settle, and instead wandered slowly along the bookcases.

'See here, Watson,' he said after a moment, gesturing at one of them. 'There are as many gaps as books.'

'Sold, you think?' I asked, glancing nervously at the door, as Holmes knelt down behind a chair, then crossed to the far wall to examine the artwork that hung there.

'That would seem a logical supposition,' he said. 'The furniture too is relatively new but not of the best quality and… Aha!'

He pressed a finger to the bottom corner of an unappealing painting of a crying child and tilted it to one side. Underneath was a small rectangle of dark, unfaded wallpaper, covering perhaps half the area of the painting that concealed it.

'A poor-quality daub obscuring the spot where a better, if smaller, item once hung. I would say that Miss Rhodes is not the only buyer to enter Hamblin Hall of late.'

Before I could respond, I heard the door of the library creak behind me. I turned to greet the newcomer.

Willoughby Frogmorton stood an inch or two taller than I, a thin, bronzed man of about fifty, with dark hair receding at the crown, brushed straight back and held in place with pomade. He was dressed in the height of fashion in a cream lounge suit, which fell open to reveal a high waistcoat and the thick line of a gold watch chain. His voice, when he spoke, was soft and smooth, almost unctuous.

'How do you do, gentlemen? I am Willoughby Frogmorton, present inhabitant of this draughty old prison, and husband of the beautiful Lady Alexandra.' He held out a slim hand on which two large gold rings were prominent. 'Delighted to meet you. We do not get many visitors, I'm afraid, which fact makes your presence all the more pleasurable.'

To my surprise, Holmes hesitated for a heartbeat before taking the proffered hand, and then abandoned the plan we had discussed only moments before. When he spoke, his voice had taken on the hint of a Scottish accent. When he proceeded to introduce us as James Soames and his colleague Dr Cameron Munro, and explained that we were compiling a guidebook on the manor houses of the county, I knew enough to play along, and complimented our host on the splendid old building.

Frogmorton was affable and charming, declaring himself happy to show us round the Hall, but there was a falseness about him that I found discomfiting, and which put me immediately on my guard. Perhaps it was simply a reaction to Holmes's unexpected use of false names, or a consequence of his damp handshake, but I pride myself that I recognised early on that Frogmorton was not all he appeared to be.

False name or no, however, he and Holmes immediately established a rapport. To my surprise, my friend gave every sign of being taken with the man, ostentatious jewellery and all. They spoke animatedly of the architecture of the Hall for a solid half hour, with Frogmorton gesturing expansively at this feature and that, and Holmes following in his wake, nodding and making loud noises of appreciation when appropriate. I trailed behind the two of them as they left the library and went back outside, the better for our host to point out the sixteenth-century oriel windows and, unexpectedly, the great size of the chimney. Presumably the latter was more impressive than I imagined, for Holmes cooed over the grimy protrusion to such an extent that I wondered if he had perhaps lost his senses.

Holmes chose that moment to interrupt Frogmorton's description of a crow-stepped gable with an apologetic look and a loud cough. 'I wonder, Mr Frogmorton, if I might trouble you for a glass of water?' he asked. 'The trip from the station was a dusty one, and my throat is terribly parched.'

Frogmorton, to give him his due, was at once full of self-recrimination. He suggested we step back inside while he went off to arrange refreshments from the kitchen, leaving us alone in the library once again.

As soon as he was gone, I rounded on Holmes. 'What on earth is going on?' I began in a forceful whisper. 'Why did you give us those ridiculous names? And why hide the reason for our visit? It's almost as if you know the man!'

'I do.' Holmes's knowledge of the criminal fraternity was second to none, so I was not surprised when he continued, 'I believe Willoughby Frogmorton actually to be Matthew McCartney, an Ulsterman who migrated to Malaya in the sixties, and who was responsible for the collapse of the Eastern Malay Rubber Company in seventy-one. You may recall the case. McCartney convinced the Birmingham-based owners of several rubber plantations in Malaya and Burma that he had invented a new method for forcing the growth of the trees upon which the industry relies. He received extremely large sums in payment for his process, which, needless to say, proved inefficacious. In fact, over ninety per cent of the trees treated with McCartney's formula died within a week, the Company filed for bankruptcy within a month and the principal investor was found drowned in the River Severn soon after, his pockets loaded with stones.

'Unfortunately, McCartney had done nothing that was actually illegal. He was briefly under arrest but disappeared after his release and was thought to have fled to Australia, with an army of angry investors on his heels. Until now.'

'Were you involved with the case?'

'No, not at all. Not least because I would barely have been seventeen at the time! But I fear that the name Sherlock Holmes uttered even casually might have caused McCartney – or Frogmorton, I should say – to believe that I am now, with potentially unfortunate consequences. He may have nothing to do with these forgeries, but I am always wary of coincidence. Better to be cautious for the moment.'

Privately I wondered if we might not perhaps be better making our excuses and returning with the police, but Holmes has been right so many times before that I was willing to trust his judgement. 'Very well, but how does this help us in our actual goal?'

'It is an unfortunate wrinkle, true. I *had* intended to use my name to gain the trust of the law-abiding inhabitant of the Hall, but obviously that is no longer an option. Hence my fascination with his home – flattery is as swift a way to gain a foolish man's trust as any number of good deeds, I have often found. Moving the conversation from the fabric of the Hall to its contents should not be beyond my abilities. I should warn you, though, Watson, that I may be forced to–'

Before Holmes could complete his thought, Frogmorton returned, bearing a tray of drinks.

'Now, gents,' he said, 'where were we?'

As he engaged Holmes in fresh conversation, I considered my

friend's words. Could we have stumbled upon a solution so easily? Could this be our man? And – uppermost in my mind, I admit – what exactly might Holmes be forced to do?

I turned my attention back to the two men just in time to hear Holmes remark that Hamblin Hall was well known for the quality of its artworks. 'I have noticed one or two smaller pieces which charmed me utterly,' he was saying, 'but I believe you have a substantial collection at the Hall. Where are the rest?'

Was it my imagination, or did Frogmorton's eyes flicker at that moment? 'Substantial is an overstatement, I'm afraid, Mr Soames. Perhaps once it was true, but no longer. You must understand, neither my wife nor myself are great art lovers and, between you and me, the upkeep of a stately home – even a small one like Hamblin – is an expensive business.' His smile was wistful but insincere. 'In fact we decided some time ago that it was foolish to hide works of art here, where they would moulder unappreciated, when we could instead give them to people who would love them.'

'And I'm sure the money has come in handy,' Holmes interjected, with just a hint of steel in his voice.

Frogmorton endeavoured not to rise to this jibe, but again his eyes gave him away as they flashed a warning at Holmes. 'Yes indeed. Killing two birds with one stone, as it were. We've moved nearly all of the collection on now, releasing those pictures back into the world. I feel that we have given them life again.' He paused theatrically and tilted his head to one side, as though considering some weighty matter. 'You obviously have a keen eye, though. I'll wager you've not been completely honest with me, Mr *Soames*...'

For a moment I was certain that Holmes's charade had been unmasked, and that Frogmorton had seen through our attempts at legerdemain. I braced myself to hold him until Holmes could send a servant to fetch the local constabulary, but as it happened, I need not have concerned myself.

'...you're really an art collector, aren't you?' he concluded with a thin smile.

'You have me.' Holmes allowed himself to be unmasked – in this minor respect at least – with aplomb, smiling ruefully at Frogmorton, and shaking his head as though not entirely surprised.

Frogmorton on the other hand exhibited only delight, though delight run through with a form of triumphalism that was unattractive in the extreme, even without knowing the man's previous history.

'I knew it!' he exclaimed. 'I knew it from the off. I pride myself on my ability to read my fellow man, and the moment I saw you I thought, this is no architectural historian, not this one.' He turned briefly to me, almost the first attention I had warranted since arriving at the Hall. 'Of you, Dr Munro, I could believe it; you seem designed for dusty tomes and constant note-taking, but you, Mr Soames? No, not you!'

His laughter was loud and protracted, allowing Holmes to expand his part from rue to embarrassment. 'How did you know, might I ask?' he enquired humbly. 'We thought we had been so clever.'

Frogmorton eagerly pounced on this further opportunity for self-congratulation. 'Simplicity itself, my dear fellow. I admit my curiosity was first aroused when the maid informed me that you had arrived in the village cab, without bags. No gentleman would spend days away from home lacking even the bare minimum of clean clothes and toiletries. Then I kept a close eye on the two of you. Dr Munro clearly had no interest in, or knowledge of, the Hall, while your eyes kept flicking about the walls, examining every painting, even while I was describing the most spectacular architectural aspects of the building. For two gentlemen about to write a guidebook, well...

London collectors, I thought, and it seems I was right.' He held his hands out, palm up, and shrugged with false modesty.

Holmes nodded in capitulation. 'However you spotted us, I congratulate you most sincerely, Mr Frogmorton. You are, of course, quite correct; we are not engaged on a research trip for a guidebook. That is simply a cover, naturally, but one which has – until now – served us well. Indeed you are the first person to have seen through our deception, and yes, I congratulate you again on your superior intellect!'

Holmes's flattery was shameless, but Frogmorton appeared to see nothing amiss. Indeed, he had entirely regained his composure and had taken our deception in surprisingly good humour. Where before he had been determined to show James Soames all the best features of his home, now he showed equal fascination in discussing the remnants of the Hall's art collection. He showed no sign of irritation as he asked Holmes if there were a particular painting he had in mind, or if this was more by way of a scouting trip.

Thus encouraged, Holmes could hardly fail to move the conversation from the general to the specific.

'You believe in coming straight to the point, I see,' he said. 'And yes, there is a particular item which I had heard whispers about and which I hoped to see today.' He leant in and gestured to Frogmorton to come closer, as though there were a great secret he wished to impart. For myself, I thought Holmes was overdoing matters, but there was no sign that Frogmorton suspected anything.

When Holmes finally spoke, his voice was so quiet that I could barely make it out. 'I have heard rumours that a second work by Sir Horace Hamblin may exist, and may be stored here, at the Hall!'

There was no doubting the flicker of unease that crossed Frogmorton's face this time. It disappeared as quickly as it arrived, however, and in its stead our host exhibited every sign of incomprehension. 'Sir Horace Hamblin? Presumably some ancestor of Lady Alexandra? Can't say I've heard of him. Are you sure that was the name?'

'Certain, Mr Frogmorton. Sir Horace's striking portrait of King Charles the First hangs in the National Portrait Gallery in London and was, I believe, purchased for that most excellent enterprise only last year–'

'King Charles?' Frogmorton interrupted. 'I can't for the life of me bring to mind such a work at Hamblin Hall. We tend to go more for heavy-jowelled members of the family and various stags at bay.'

I had been watching Frogmorton closely as Holmes spoke, alive for signs of duplicity. When Holmes initially mentioned art, he appeared a man who knew little of the subject, and cared less, but who appreciated the worth of money and suddenly saw an opportunity to make more. Now that the topic had switched to a specific example, however, something had changed. I was sure he was lying, but could see no way in which we could prove the painting had ever been here at all, never mind get the man to allow us to inspect the remainder of the collection.

Holmes, however, seemed to have no such concerns. Gesturing for Frogmorton and me to follow, he bounded out of the library, into the entrance hall and up the main staircase, we trailing in his wake.

Halfway up he pointed to a spot on the wall. He called down to where we stood, at the foot of the staircase. 'It hung there, I would suggest. I noticed this discoloured area earlier and though it is not the only such blemish on the walls of Hamblin Hall...' He pulled a tape measure from his pocket and used it to calculate the dimensions of the darker area. 'This section is the exact same size as Hamblin's painting of King Charles the First,' he concluded.

Frogmorton's aura of calm had received another blow. He tugged at the collar of his shirt and pushed a distracted hand through his hair before he spoke. 'Oh, that was King Charles, was it? I *do* remember selling that dusty old painting, and glad to do so, but I always took it to be one of Lady Alexandra's forebears. It had hung in that spot since the day I arrived, and for centuries prior to that, I shouldn't be surprised. And you say it's valuable? I wish I had never... sold it, now.'

The hesitation was unmistakable, and Holmes pounced on it, though only obliquely at first. 'Perhaps your wife could advise us?' he asked sweetly.

Frogmorton's face flushed and he wiped a hand across his brow. 'She is unavailable, unfortunately. She has been staying with her sister for the past fortnight.' He grimaced as he spoke. 'But you say that the King Charles was by some great-great-and-so-on-grandfather of Lady Alexandra?' He visibly rallied as he spoke, regaining his composure. 'I'm afraid that doesn't entirely help. I couldn't tell you who painted what on the walls of the Hall. As I said, I'm a Philistine when it comes to art, and Alexandra, as with most things, is of little assistance.'

His tone was bitter. Evidently, there was no great love lost in the marriage. While I considered that fact, Holmes walked back down the stairs to us, and spoke again.

'I'm sure it must be very difficult to keep track of all your possessions, Mr Frogmorton. It would require a prodigious feat of memory instantly to recall every single painting in Hamblin Hall. I am surprised that you do not have a catalogue, in fact. In our experience, most stately homes have such a document nowadays. Isn't that so, Munro?' I nodded dumbly, wondering where Holmes intended to take the discussion. I did not have long to wait. As

Holmes reached the foot of the staircase he delivered the final blow. 'Did Jessica Rhodes not think to create one for you when she was in your... employ... last summer? I have heard that she is very meticulous in her work and was a particular... intimate of yours.' Holmes's crudely insinuating words fell with the thick slap of a whip.

The change in Frogmorton was astonishing. Until that moment he had been an excellent host, showing us his home, offering us his hospitality, even overlooking the deception we had carried out in order to gain entrance. Had Holmes not issued his warning, I doubt I would have thought any ill of the man at all.

Now, though, he was transformed. No longer the suave and fashionable householder, his face had turned a deep red, and he turned towards Holmes with a snarl on his lips. 'What do you mean by that, sir! How dare you! Why I... I should... Get out at once!' He made to lay hands on Holmes, but for all his unwillingness to exercise, heavy tobacco consumption and at times Bohemian lifestyle, Sherlock Holmes was a man who could have boxed for England. He batted Frogmorton's hands away with ease then, when his opponent attempted a flailing punch, slipped underneath the blow, threw a thunderous right hook and knocked him to the hallway floor.

As he stood over his defeated opponent, Holmes's face was as composed and analytical as ever. 'I have a confession to make,' he said after a moment's reflection. 'I have another untruth to confess, in fact. I am not the man I claimed to be when first you made us welcome in your home. I can only apologise for our deception.' He turned and indicated me. 'This gentleman is Dr John Watson, my good friend and colleague, and I am Sherlock Holmes.'

For a moment nobody spoke. Holmes looked down at his opponent after making his extraordinary admission, while Frogmorton stared up at him in shock. For myself, I was at a loss as to what to say. Regardless of the circumstances, it is invariably awkward to find oneself unmasked as an imposter.

'Sherlock Holmes, the detective?' Frogmorton asked uncertainly, but with an unmistakable edge of fear. 'But how...?'

'Your skin has the permanent, ingrained bronze of long-term exposure to high temperatures,' Holmes said, this non sequitur apparently in response to Frogmorton's confusion. 'Far more than would be the case for a short visit to such a locale, or even a protracted period spent working in, say, southern Europe. Admittedly, you could have passed your younger years in the Americas or Australia, but on balance India or Malaya are considerably more likely.'

'Malaya,' Frogmorton muttered distractedly. 'Plantations.'

'Please do not misunderstand me. I ask no question and require no confirmation. I not only know of your time in Malaya's rubber plantations, but also exactly what you did there. It is not a pretty story, Mr McCartney.'

He was not easily cowed, I'll say that for Frogmorton (I still could not think of him as McCartney). He pulled himself to his feet and glared at Holmes. 'So that's it, eh? I did nothing illegal, you know. My treatment proved less effective than I'd hoped, but such things happen in business, and science, all the time. There's nothing you can do to me, great detective. I have committed no crime.'

'Quite so.' Holmes was unperturbed, though speaking for myself I could see no fault in Frogmorton's reasoning. 'But I cannot help but wonder whether Lady Alexandra knows of your past... or the full extent of your relationship with Miss Rhodes.'

Frogmorton blanched and took an involuntary step backwards as Holmes's accusations hit him with the force of a blow. I too mentally recoiled at his words, and at the thought of the repellent Frogmorton and the delightful Miss Rhodes engaged in an *affaire de coeur*, as Holmes was clearly suggesting.

Holmes, however, was relentless, driving Frogmorton back across the hallway and towards the open door of the library, one step at a time, with the impact of his words. 'You and she spent last summer in a romantic relationship, did you not, Mr McCartney? I am sure it began innocently enough, just as Miss Rhodes describes it in fact, with she and her companion arriving in the teeth of a storm, and the other young lady falling ill. In such a position it is only natural that you should attempt to entertain your guest while her friend recovers. Did your wife also become attached to your two new acquaintances? No? She looked after the invalid, perhaps, while you and Miss Rhodes became close?'

Frogmorton said nothing, but glowered from beneath thunderous brows. Holmes pressed on without mercy.

'In fact, if I remember correctly, Miss Rhodes remarked on the attentiveness of your wife towards her friend. Was it while she was thus engaged in an act of Christian charity that you inveigled yourself into the affections of the unworldly Miss Rhodes? Well, was it?'

All pretence fell away from Frogmorton now as Holmes slowly walked towards him, his every step punctuated with accusation. Only when his back was against the library fireplace did he bring his retreat to a sudden halt.

'It was not like that at all,' he blustered. From the shaking of his hands to the whitening of his face, it was clear that Holmes's words had pierced him to his very soul, and filled him with the terror of exposure which every guilty man carries within himself. The transformation from the confident dandy we had first met to the fear-stricken wreck that now cowered before us was hard to credit, but symptomatic of a certain type of bullying personality. He held out a hand imploringly. 'You won't tell my wife, will you?'

'No, I think not – if you agree to help us with our enquiries. Nor shall I make your Malayan adventure public knowledge.'

'I couldn't care less what you say about Malaya, Holmes,' Frogmorton replied, with just a hint of his earlier bravado. He stood just a little straighter as he continued, 'My wife knows all about that particular blot on my copybook, and besides, as I already explained, I did nothing illegal. Yes, I might be blackballed from a club or two, and cut in the street by the occasional top-hatted fool, but I will not, I assure you, lose sleep over that. But Alexandra knows nothing of my... dalliance with Miss Rhodes. It would break her heart to know I had been untrue, and I see no reason to drag Miss Rhodes's name through the mud.'

'Cause her to throw you out on the street more like!' I have served in the army, worked as a doctor and aided Sherlock Holmes for many years, and have come to know the worst side of Man, but there was something altogether repellent about the figure in front of me, wheedling and conniving to save himself. Only the sense that he genuinely cared for the young lady whose youthful trust he had so shamefully abused prevented me from taking two steps forward and knocking him straight down the stairs.

Fortunately for Frogmorton, Holmes intervened before I could say – or do – anything further. 'Regardless of your motivations, I will expose you in every respect and to every one if you do not give Watson and myself access to the catalogue Miss Rhodes compiled for you last year. And after viewing the catalogue, we will need to see every painting it lists. Agree to these terms and we will be on our way, and nobody need be any the wiser about your various indiscretions.'

I do not apologise for the pleasure I felt in Frogmorton's slumped and disconsolate figure at that moment. His behaviour had clearly been that of a man without honour, and the involvement of Miss Rhodes, for whom I had a great deal of respect, rendered the entire sorry affair even worse. But Holmes had shattered him completely, and even if his perfidious actions could not be made public for obvious reasons, the nature of Frogmorton's defeat brought me only satisfaction.

I was surprised, therefore, to see him hesitate as Holmes offered him an escape that did not involve the ruin of his marriage and his current comfortable life. 'That may not be possible, I'm afraid. It's not my fault,' he hurried to add. 'Jessi... Miss Rhodes did put together a sort of catalogue – more a ledger really – but for her own use, not mine. She said something about it being an invaluable addition to the records of the Gallery and took it with her when she left.'

Holmes's voice was icily calm. 'So you claim to have no records of the provenance of your collection, is that your contention?'

'Well, no. Or rather, yes. That is my contention, as you put it. But it hardly matters, since there's not much left of the collection now. Most of it went the way of the portrait of King Charles. Sold.' He shrugged. 'Had to have the money. Simple as that.'

'In which case, why should I not reveal your tawdry secrets and, at the very least, free your wife from a duplicitous husband?'

'There is no reason, I suppose. But ask yourself this: what'd be the point? True, my life in England would be in tatters, and more than likely I'd have to leave the country. But what of Lady Alexandra, held up to public ridicule? What of Miss Rhodes, labelled a loose woman? Would you really do such harm to two innocent women, Mr Holmes? Dr Watson?'

Frogmorton's words were unpleasantly self-serving and venal, but he was correct. Holmes looked discomfited and did not reply. Frogmorton, now entirely restored to his former brash good humour, laughed at our long faces, and bowed low from the waist. 'Of course I'm happy to show you the paintings we still have, if that's any help? Not that there's a great deal left!'

Without another word he strode out of the library. After a moment's pause, Holmes and I followed.

Nine

T he rest of the evening was disappointingly unfruitful. Frogmorton had not been lying when he claimed that most of the Hamblin Collection had been sold. We followed him from room to room, examining familiar patches of darker wallpaper and, now and again, an actual painting, though none of them appeared forged, stolen or otherwise noteworthy, at least to my eyes. Each subsequent room lowered our spirits more until, upon returning full-circle to the entrance hall again, Holmes announced that we were leaving. Frogmorton did not pretend sorrow at our departure. He said that he hoped we would never need to meet again and slammed the door behind us.

The journey back to Baker Street was a silent one, and Holmes went straight to his room the moment we were in our quarters, waving a dismissive hand at my questions as he did so.

* * *

The next morning, he was gone before I awoke. A note propped on the mantelpiece informed me that he had received a summons from his brother Mycroft which would brook no delay, and that he would return as soon as he might but certainly before that evening. A scribbled postscript suggested I spend the day in relaxation. 'Try and stay out of trouble,' it concluded.

With no more pressing claim on my time, I tried to take Holmes's advice and after breakfast I settled myself in an armchair with a historical novel. The weather outside remained foul, and I did not envy Holmes his trip outside, but even so a vague tickling at the back of my mind made concentration difficult and I quickly found myself supremely confused by the plethora of abbots, knights and squires who made up the cast of my novel. Throwing the book aside, I bathed and dressed then stood, irresolute, at the window, watching the rain bounce from the gutterings of the building opposite. Recalling the condescending addendum to Holmes's note and his dismissal of the previous evening, I found my mood quickly matching the weather outside. It seemed to me, as I contemplated the brewing storm, that Holmes often left me in the dark, and took altogether too much delight in demonstrating that his mental acuity was superior to my own. Within minutes, I had resolved to do something useful of my own volition but could think of nothing suitable.

It would perhaps be more honest to say that I could think of nothing both suitable *and* attractive. Obviously, Holmes would want to speak to Miss Rhodes as soon as he had completed whatever task Mycroft had in mind, and I strongly suspected that a kind word from one such as myself would be more efficacious than Holmes's more robust questioning. But since Frogmorton's revelations I was nervous of approaching her. As an army doctor I have, of course, been exposed to the more sordid side of life, but even so the recent events at Hamblin were enough to force me to reconsider my view of Miss Rhodes. I am by no means a prude, but if I had understood Holmes's accusations correctly, my initial view of Jessica Rhodes might well need to be revisited. Dark indeed was my mood as I considered the situation.

In the end, lack of alternatives forced my hand, and within the half hour I found myself sheltering from the downpour under the entrance portico of the National Portrait Gallery. Had I known the day that was to follow would be one of the most terrible in my long friendship with Sherlock Holmes, I might well have turned on my heel and returned to my book.

Miss Rhodes was directing the relocation of some sculpture when I found her, striking through the name of each piece on a list she held as it was moved to her satisfaction. She had her back to me and failed to notice my entrance for several minutes, time which I spent observing the way in which she managed the team of men who comprised her workforce. A woman in a position of authority was unusual, but the effective and efficient way she directed operations brought it home to me again that this was indeed an unusual woman who should, perhaps, be judged differently to the common herd. Eventually I realised that I was in effect spying on her and, embarrassed, I coughed loudly in order to catch her attention.

'Dr Watson! What a pleasant surprise!'

As soon as she spoke, any doubts I might have harboured about her role at Hamblin Hall evaporated. There was an openness and honesty about her which did not allow for suspicion of wrongdoing. Whatever had occurred at Hamblin Hall that summer, I was again certain that Miss Rhodes was entirely innocent of blame.

With this reassuring conviction in mind, I bade her good morning, and asked if I might have a moment of her time, in private. She smiled her agreement and led me to her office.

The room fell somewhere between a cubby-hole and a box-room, being considerably smaller than Petrie's office, yet with enough room for the sort of curios and artefacts which spoke of a lively and enquiring mind. A small window at the far end illuminated a battered desk on which were piled stacks of notes, catalogues and journals. A single chair and a small side table completed the furnishings.

'Have you made progress with your case, then?' she asked as soon as we were comfortably ensconced within.

I had hoped to avoid discussion of certain of the specifics of our activities the previous day, but, thus pressed, I confirmed that progress had been made, following our trip to Hamblin Hall. 'In fact,' I concluded, 'it is possible that you can be of assistance to us, if you would not object to answering one or two questions.'

'Why, I would be delighted to help you in any way I can, Dr Watson! Though I'm not sure I can, really. I was only a guest at the Hall for a short period, after all.'

I was certain that her desire to help was not feigned, and that her eagerness was genuine, but she had begun with a clear untruth, which emboldened me sufficiently to ask the difficult question that needed to be asked.

'I am afraid, Miss Rhodes, that my first question is one that will seem ungentlemanly to you, appearing as it does to cast doubts upon your recollection of certain events.' I swallowed hard, my throat suddenly dry. 'It has been… brought to the attention of Sherlock Holmes and myself that you were more than just a fleeting visitor to Hamblin Hall last year. We have learned, in fact, that you spent enough time at the Hall to become an invaluable aide and confidante to Mr Frogmorton, and may even have compiled a sales ledger for him?'

I was aware of the creeping note of pomposity in my voice, which made my respect for Miss Rhodes all the greater as she met my accusations with a quiet and becoming dignity. I had feared she would deny everything, leaving me no choice but to call her a liar, but instead she showed no outward sign of distress other than an almost imperceptible quickening of breath. Before saying another word, she opened a drawer in the desk and pulled out a thin, paper-covered notebook of the sort sold in every stationer in the land. She laid it down in front of me.

'I should have known that there was no point in dissimulation with Sherlock Holmes, Dr Watson. Yes, I did become more than simply a houseguest while at Hamblin Hall. I don't even know why I pretended otherwise.

'I was happy to help Mr Frogmorton in any way I could, you see, after he had been so kind to my friend and me. His wife was often away, my friend slept a great deal and as a result we were thrown together more than would otherwise have been the case. So yes, in answer to your question – we did become confidantes, I suppose. And when I had made my own purchases from the Hamblin Collection it seemed only courteous to offer to help him sell the remainder, as he had often mentioned he wished to do. I sent a telegram or two to art dealers and collectors of my acquaintance, supervised a clean-up of some of the better pieces, and helped Mr Frogmorton obtain good prices for each painting.' She pushed the notebook towards me. 'And this is the ledger to which you referred. I should warn you, however, that it is not a catalogue of the Hamblin Collection, but rather my own personal reminders book, in which I am in the practice of noting every work of art that passes through my hands. Every sale made at Hamblin is in there, however.'

Her voice throughout this speech was measured and calm. There was no question in her mind of any wrongdoing, that much was clear. As I took the notebook she asked whether we had discovered more forgeries at Hamblin Hall.

I could see no reason not to tell her the truth. 'No, unfortunately we did not. The coincidence of two forged paintings from a single source may turn out to be exactly that – a coincidence.' Seeing her face fall, I hurriedly went on, 'But we have hopes that your ledger can provide further fuel for our investigation!'

She smiled at that. I flipped open the notebook and cast an eye down the first page. A fine hand had inscribed a year at the top in an ornate calligraphy, and underneath had listed over a dozen paintings, each described in detail, with a location and a specific date noted beneath. 'These dates are those upon which you worked on the paintings, broken down by year?' I asked and, receiving confirmation by way of a short nod, continued to flick through the little book. For such a young woman, Miss Rhodes evidently had a great deal of experience in and knowledge of her chosen field, and as the date which headed each page grew closer and closer to the current year, the number of paintings on each page increased. I turned one page dated some two years previously, in every expectation of reaching Hamblin Hall within a page or two. But instead, the next page was headed 1896 – the current year – with nothing in between. It was as though her country sojourn had never taken place.

I showed her the successive pages. It seemed to me that she hesitated for the briefest of moments, then shook her head, her confusion and distress plain for all to see. 'There should be two pages here, Dr Watson. Two pages that cover my entire time at Hamblin and record every sale in which I was involved.' She handed the notebook back, and I turned it over in my hands. I knew how Holmes would approach the problem, and I could see no reason why I should not apply his methods. Moving over to a light on the wall, I held the book up, turning it first one way then the other, allowing the flame to illuminate the pages. There was something…

'Quick, Miss Rhodes,' I exclaimed, 'come here!'

I held the notebook out in front of her, and gently pulled the two halves of the cover away from each other. 'If you look carefully at the inner spine of the book, it's possible to just make out an irregularity where pages have been removed. Cut out, in fact, I'd say.'

She blanched. 'But this means that someone has been in my office. Someone has…' Her voice trailed off. 'I don't understand, Dr Watson. Why would anyone be interested in my notes? *Who* would be interested in them? And what has this to do with the King Charles and Augustine Hamblin forgeries? Should we not inform Mr Petrie?'

Pleased though I was with my discovery, I had no answers to these questions. It seemed likely that someone wanted to hinder Holmes's investigations, but other than that, I was at a loss. Miss Rhodes's distress was clear to see, but there was no light she could shed on the vandalism we had discovered, nor anyone she could bring to mind who might have reason to carry out such an act. I was keen to continue our conversation and, remembering the criminal Lestrade had mentioned earlier, I rather impulsively asked whether she knew any albinos, though with little expectation of a positive reply. Consequently, I was not disappointed when she shook her head, a look of confusion on her face.

'An albino? No, I'm afraid not. I don't believe I have ever seen such a man, in fact. Why do you ask?'

'It is nothing to concern yourself about, my dear,' I hastened to reassure her. 'Just a stray thought. Would you mind if I borrowed your notebook? Holmes will want to examine it, I suspect, though I doubt if even he can conjure a list of names from pages that do not exist.'

We sat for a moment or two, each of us silently considering the impossible situation we found ourselves in until, with a start and a small sound of surprise, Miss Rhodes looked up and exclaimed that she knew something that might help.

'I do know the location of one item that was contained in those pages, Dr Watson! It was a very minor part of the Hamblin Collection, a miniature depicting Jacob and Esau, the twin sons of the Biblical Isaac, but it had a certain charm that I thought might be of interest to the Gallery. Unfortunately, though, when I brought it to London, it was judged to be too small for effective display here, but I was able by sheer chance to sell it on Mr Frogmorton's behalf to a local collector of my acquaintance. It is only one sale amongst many, but it is at least something, is it not?'

I was inclined to think it a very small something indeed, but even so it was better than nothing at all, and I was grateful to note down the details of the purchaser, a Miss Eugenie Marr, of 11 Craven Street, London. The address was close by, and I initially considered investigating straight away. But I knew that Holmes would wish to be involved and, besides, I feared I might overlook something of vital import that my companion would undoubtedly notice. I took my leave of Miss Rhodes, therefore, and resolved to check our lodgings for Holmes before proceeding any further along this fresh investigative path.

Our rooms were in darkness when I arrived at Baker Street, and I very nearly told the hansom driver to continue on, but I had intended to pick up my revolver in any case, and there was always the possibility that Holmes, even if he himself were not present, might have left a note. I paid the cabman and, running through the unceasing rain, dashed indoors.

The sitting room was cold and dim and heavy with the stench of stale pipe smoke. I moved towards the windows and tugged at the closed curtains, intending to allow in some light and air, but before I could do so, a voice spoke from the shadows.

'Leave the curtains closed, Watson, if you don't mind, and the lamps unlit. I would rather not advertise our presence just at the moment.'

Holmes emerged from behind the door, staring at me in the gloom with a fierce intensity. In his hand he held my revolver.

'Holmes! What's happened?' My natural surprise quickly gave way to concern as I moved closer and realised that there was a splash of dried blood on his forehead and abrasions on his cheek. 'How did you come by these injuries? And the revolver…'

Holmes waved my help away with a grimace. 'The revolver is simply a precaution. Now, I have a great deal to tell you, Watson, and little time to do so. Save your medical ministrations for later and take a seat, there's a good fellow.'

I did as I was bidden, but not before soaking a cloth in water and handing it to him. 'At least clean your face, Holmes. No matter what tale you have to tell, it will not be delayed by that.'

Holmes shrugged and grudgingly dabbed away the blood on his face. 'Very well,' he said as he completed this rudimentary toilet. 'And now that I have done as you asked, will you sit still and listen?'

'Of course, Holmes,' I said, and settled back in my seat, intrigued to hear what had occurred.

'Mycroft had a report which he wished to show me,' Holmes began. 'Not knowing I had moved on from that element of the case, he believed the Brotherhood of Ireland remained of paramount interest to me, and that the discovery of the bodies of several prominent members of the group was something I would wish to know about. It appears that there has been a cull amongst the republicans – by a rival gang perhaps – leaving a round dozen men dead, each executed with a single bullet to the head and their bodies burned on waste ground near Streatham. A message *pour encourager les autres*, in Mycroft's estimation.'

'Was your mysterious Major one of the dead men?'

'Impossible to say, such was the degree of damage caused by the flames. In any case, whatever happened is of no concern to us at present. The case has evolved far beyond simple vandalism, or even the vainglorious sloganeering of a horde of drunken Irishmen, and so I thanked Mycroft for the thought, and hurried back here. I have been meaning to check my records for mention of albino criminals, but nothing I did not already know came to light. In one volume, there is a clipping regarding an Eastern European albino who arrived in London five years previously, but it cannot be the same man. This albino is rumoured to be an exiled prince and a pleasure-loving dilettante, far more likely to be glimpsed at a Society ball than at a robbery.

'All in all, it had been a wasted morning. Finding you absent from Baker Street, I presumed that you had taken a cab to the Gallery to speak to Miss Rhodes, and resolved to follow, hoping to intervene before you asked any particularly foolish questions, but I had no sooner stepped out of the front door than I was almost run down by a four-horse carriage. Fortunately, I had noticed the stationary carriage out of the corner of my eye as I stepped onto the road, and the sound of the driver's whip cracking was sufficient to alert me. I was able to dive out of the way, though not, as you can see, without some damage to my face as I struck the ground. The carriage did not stop, but turned in the road, then hurtled away down the street before finally taking the corner into Marylebone Road while my senses remained scrambled.'

I believe I was as astonished by Holmes's composure as by the assault itself. 'Holmes, this is monstrous! An attack in broad daylight!' Holmes did not respond, so I continued. 'You might have been killed!'

'That was assuredly the intention. I did catch a glimpse of the driver before I was forced to throw myself aside, however.'

'And?'

'And there was nothing to see. He wore a hat pulled down low, and dark glasses, and covered the bottom half of his face with a scarf. Even his hands were gloved. Beyond the fact that he was of below average height, left-handed, fond of extremely poor-quality mutton pie and unfamiliar with the area, I could tell very little about the man.'

'Mutton pie?' I queried. 'The height of a man, even sitting, can be ascertained, and presumably he held the whip in his left hand and the reins in his right, but how could you know his eating habits?'

'A greasy mark on his overcoat, upon which clung several strands of the stringy meat used in cheap mutton pies across London. Another, similar but drier, stain on his lapel suggested that he was in the habit of eating such delicacies.'

'And his familiarity or otherwise with Baker Street?'

'The carriage turned in the street and returned whence it came, along Baker Street and as far as Marylebone Road before turning. Someone more familiar with the area would not have needed to retrace his steps, and would have known that a switch into any of the smaller, and considerably nearer, side streets would allow the vehicle to be safely out of sight far more quickly. Instead, had I not been quite so winded, I would have had plenty of time to observe its escape.'

'A man so completely hidden surely has something to hide. The albino himself, do you think?'

'Possibly, Watson. It would certainly fit with the admittedly small amount of evidence we have.'

'Perhaps he believes that your meeting with Mycroft concerned his own activities? That we are closer to England's Treasure than is in fact the case?'

'Perhaps.' Holmes was non-committal. He passed me my revolver. 'Keep this close to hand for now, as a precaution.'

Suddenly I remembered that I too had information to impart. I dropped the gun into my overcoat pocket, before telling Holmes about the missing notebook pages, and the single customer Miss Rhodes had identified. He examined the book in the dim light for a moment, and I was pleased to see that he could garner little more from it than I had myself.

'Carefully cut out, not torn, Watson, you agree?' he said, holding the book wide open. 'The knife had a small nick in its blade, and has left a nub of paper behind. The vandal did not wish his theft to be known, clearly. But he was working with at least a modicum of haste, hence the overlooked paper stub.'

'Hardly surprising, given the location of the notebook, Holmes,' I interjected. 'Perhaps the miscreant had limited time in which to remove the pages? If his intention was to hinder our investigations then perhaps he had no choice, but nonetheless it was a risky business, cutting the book up in Miss Rhodes's very office.'

'I think you may have wandered from the path of strict accuracy now, Watson, and after such a promising beginning, too. The main aim of the theft was surely to provide information to the thief, and only tangentially to prevent our own access to that information. He must have known that we would find out soon enough by other means to whom the Hamblin pictures were sold – as indeed we have.'

'In one instance only, Holmes!' I protested, but I knew from experience that there was no point in arguing, and that Holmes would, in due course, turn out to be in the right.

'One instance may well prove to be enough, Watson,' he said, smiling. 'It takes but a single worm to catch the fish, so long as the line is sufficiently well cast.'

He strode across to the window and threw open the curtains. 'Enough of this skulking in the shadows, Watson. Let us pay a visit to your lady collector, shall we?'

I almost insisted that we first contact Lestrade and inform him of recent events, but Holmes was already halfway down the stairs and, besides, I knew he would do no such thing. The sole result of such a suggestion would be Holmes lecturing me all the way to Craven Street on the incompetence of the police in general and Lestrade in particular.

I held my tongue, and picked up my hat and coat.

Ten

&

Craven Street was a pleasant street lined with tall buildings, which crossed the smaller Craven Passage at right angles, and was bookended by the Strand at one end, and a busy playhouse at the other. There was nobody in sight as we stepped from the hansom and made our way to our destination, which was a handsome family home of three storeys, with large windows to either side of the front door. It seemed plain that Miss Marr was a woman of substantial means.

As we approached, we could see that the door to Number 11 lay very slightly ajar.

I knocked and received no answer, then stood back on the step, hesitant to enter someone's home uninvited. Holmes, however, had no such compunction and immediately crouched down, placing one palm flat against the rug positioned just inside the door.

'Soaked, even more than one might expect given the recent downpour, and–' He pushed the door further open, exposing more of the rug. 'See for yourself, Watson. The rest of this rug is completely dry, and the line of moisture is an exact and straight one. This door has lain ajar for more than this morning, possibly several days, and has not been moved an inch since it was first left open. Tread carefully, Watson.'

Thus forewarned, I pulled the revolver from my pocket and, holding it in front of me, led the way into the silent house.

The hallway was short, with two doors leading off from it on the left side, and stairs at the end leading to the first floor. Decoration was sparse – a small occasional table upon which stood three photographs in rigidly aligned silver frames and a bare hat stand just inside the door were the whole of the furnishings – but two very tasteful paintings brightened the plain walls.

I crossed to the first door, intent on trying the handle, but Holmes touched my arm and pointed instead to the end of the corridor, where the second door sat ajar. As we approached I realised I could hear the sound of rustling paper from within. Painfully aware of the warning telegraphed by our shoes on the wooden floor, we positioned ourselves on either side of the doorway and after a silently mouthed count to three, pushed it fully open and, as one, moved into the room beyond.

A cat leapt from the large oak desk that dominated the space, upsetting a stack of paper onto the floor, and shot past our ankles. I watched as it ran along the hall, through the open front door and out into the street.

'Watson!' Holmes's insistent voice brought my wandering attention back to the room – and to the body that lay stretched out on the floor, behind the desk.

That this was Eugenie Marr, the lady we were seeking, was not certain, but there was no doubt that she was dead. A dark purple line at her throat and the redness of broken capillaries in her eyes, combined with scratch marks on her neck where she had struggled to escape the stranglehold of the choking cord, indicated strangulation by garrotte. I knelt by the corpse and carefully manipulated the jaw, neck and arms, feeling for the familiar stiffness. The advanced stage of rigor mortis placed the death at some point the day before, perhaps longer. I turned to Holmes, but he had already dismissed the victim from his thoughts and was busy rifling through the papers on her desk. I almost remonstrated with him for his indifference, but I might as well have lectured the desk, so instead I joined him in his search.

The desk, as with everything else in the room, bar the documents disturbed by the fleeing cat, was neat to the point of mania, with every element perfectly squared off against the next. Evidently, Miss Marr valued precision and order. I had seen similar cases of obsessive, monomaniacal behaviour described in the medical literature. I made this observation to Holmes, but of course he had already noticed it.

'Did you not note that the photographs in the hall stood at exactly ninety degrees from one another? The lady clearly suffered from some form of neurosis.' He shrugged. 'I doubt that that will prove of any consequence to our case, except to confirm that the miniature she purchased has been stolen.'

He pointed to a small section of the desk, which lay empty. 'The portrait sat there, if I am not mistaken,' he said.

It was true that this small square was the only area on the entire desk not covered by tidy stacks of files and books, but even so it was a leap to assume that the miniature had until recently sat there.

Holmes obviously noticed my look of doubt. 'Observe, Watson, how the files on each side of the bare area have been knocked askew, as though someone carelessly reached over and removed something. Someone less meticulous than the victim, for she would certainly have restacked the files afterwards.' He indicated the body on the floor. 'Expensive items have been left untouched; you will have noted the silver photograph frames still safe in the hall. It beggars belief to think that our murderer turned thief for anything other than a very specific item. And I need not remind you that people have already died in the matter we are currently investigating.'

'Very well,' I said. 'But what exactly are we looking for, if the miniature itself is gone?'

'I won't know until we find it, Watson. Correspondence from the Gallery, catalogues from art auctions, a handy list of other artworks Miss Marr was interested in... anything which might provide us with a direction in which to proceed.'

As he spoke, he picked up, opened and examined each file within his reach, before dropping it onto the floor behind him, for all the world like some mechanical sorting machine. Occasionally he would pause for a heartbeat as some item from the victim's life briefly caught his eye, before being rejected and discarded as so much waste paper. Still rankling at his unemotional response to the poor woman's murder, I said as much to Holmes.

'Waste–!' Whatever spark my words had ignited in that most exceptional of brains was enough to cause Holmes to drop the sheaf of documents in his hand and dive beneath the desk. A moment later he reappeared, clutching a wicker wastepaper basket in his hand, which he dropped unceremoniously between us.

'Everything on this desk is related to the victim's work: unimaginative and poorly considered thoughts on the Trinity in the main, with yards of inaccurate translations from the Hebrew.' He pointed to a large crucifix on the wall, and to a small pile of books carefully stacked at one corner of the desk. 'Bibles in Latin, Greek and English. And you will recall that the miniature she purchased was of the twin sons of Isaac, son of Abraham. A religious woman, Watson, working on some obscure and essentially pointless ecclesiastical treatise. This desk represents her life, the very core of her being, but what we seek is something other than that, something upon which she would place a far lesser value.'

With a single sweep of his arm he tumbled everything off the desk onto the floor, then tipped the wastepaper basket upside down onto the now empty surface.

'And here, unless I am mistaken, we have it.' He pushed a discarded church newsletter to one side and picked out a plain white envelope, from within which he pulled a single sheet of folded notepaper. Handing me the envelope, upon which I read Miss Marr's name and address in a precise, printed script, he unfolded the note and read it aloud.

2 Nelson Street

Camden, London

Dear Madam,

Please forgive the intrusion, but I hope to appeal to your Christian nature with regard to an item that I believe has recently come into your possession. I refer to a small miniature of Jacob and Esau, which I am informed you purchased last year.

I represent a small continental art gallery and have been tasked with sourcing items for an exhibition of late sixteenth-century miniatures. I believe that the example you possess would fit admirably into the planned collection, and would be obliged if you would consider selling to me.

Please reply at your earliest convenience. I await positive news with great anticipation.

Yours,

Elias Boggs, esq

He refolded the letter and slipped it inside his coat. 'Printed in the same set of block capitals as the envelope, on reasonably good-quality paper, literate enough but with an occasional lapse into possible error. "Consider selling to me" is an unusual construction, wouldn't you say, Watson?'

'A foreigner, perhaps?' I was sure Holmes and I were thinking the same thing.

'Or someone taking dictation from such a person. Elias Boggs is not a name that rings with the exotic tang of the Eastern European states, though I am reminded of a confidence man of some distinction of that name. In any event, apparently Miss Marr did not wish to sell, hence the discarded note, and so Mr Boggs – or his employer – was forced to collect in person.'

'What if she replied and then disposed of the original letter?' I did not believe this for a second, but felt that the possibility needed to be considered before it could be dismissed.

'I think not. A woman with Miss Marr's particular neurosis would make a carbon copy of any reply, and would attach the original to that, for her own records. No,' Holmes declared decisively, 'the lady was murdered for the miniature, and no other reason.'

'Where to now, then?' I asked. 'After we have alerted the police to Miss Marr's demise, that is.'

'To Camden Town – and with any luck the fate of the unfortunate Miss Marr will keep Lestrade occupied and out of our hair for the foreseeable future.' Holmes gave one of his most hearty laughs, as though someone had said something enormously humorous, but I confess to feeling only a terrible coldness as I looked down at the poor woman's corpse.

Eleven

'**E** ain't 'ere! 'E's at the Bailey! There ain't nothin' more I can tell ya!'

Mrs Elias Boggs was a small woman, with the lines of a hard life etched deeply on her prematurely aged face. Though almost certainly not yet thirty, she looked two decades older, and for all her noisy bravado at our enquiry after her husband, I could see an uncertainty and fear behind her eyes that spoke even more loudly of a lifetime of bullying and abuse. As with Miss Marr, I felt a sadness creep over me as I observed her.

Holmes, of course, felt no such emotion, but instead placed a boot on the base of the door, and a hand beside Mrs Boggs's head at the top and gave both a hearty push. The door swung open and before anyone could react, Holmes was inside the single room in which the entire Boggs family resided. With little option otherwise except to stand on the doorstep while Mrs Boggs glared at me in impotent fury, I followed with a murmured 'Do excuse me.'

Mrs Boggs's room was a good size, with a large window through which sufficient light passed to illuminate the interior, and a second much smaller box room – barely a cupboard, in fact – to one side, from which a baby's cry could be heard. Mrs Boggs pushed past Holmes and me and scooped up an unhappy infant from a wooden crib, which had been crammed into the available space. I briefly considered offering my services as a physician to the child, but he was a healthy enough boy and settled into contented gurgling the instant he was restored to his mother's arms.

Holmes for his part was as unmoved by this sight as by any commonplace human activity, and moved about the main room, closely examining the few sticks of furniture – a small cupboard with some cheap plates displayed in a cabinet above it, and a serviceable desk which served both as dinner table and general work surface – before turning back to Mrs Boggs with a question on his lips.

'You have come into some money, Mrs Boggs?' The question was asked with no apparent agenda, but Mrs Boggs stiffened instinctively, nonetheless.

'No, can't say as I 'ave!'

'No? A writing desk, and new crockery, and yet you say you have not had a windfall? Well, perhaps I am mistaken. Forgive me the impertinence.'

He gave a tiny bow and made as though to turn towards the door, then suddenly swept back round so that he loomed over our hostess.

'Why is your husband at the Old Bailey, Mrs Boggs? Quickly now, why is he at the Old Bailey?'

Holmes's tone was hectoring and bullying, designed to get as much information out of Mrs Boggs as possible, before her natural caution and inbred fear of authority overcame her and she either stopped talking completely, or began to bend the truth to her own ends. I had seen him use the same tactic before, and this occasion was no less successful than previously.

'Well, it's affray, if you must know,' replied Mrs Boggs defiantly. 'Not that it's any of your business, anyways.'

'Affray? Is that all?'

"Course I'm sure! I should know what my husband's been charged with, shouldn't I?' She stopped suddenly and a look of low cunning settled on her face. 'Wait a minute though! If you pair is police, 'ow comes you don' already know that?'

Holmes drew himself to his full height. 'I did not say we were policemen, madam. I would never be so unfair to myself, and I fear even Dr Watson here would be justly offended at such a description. I said we were *helping* the police. *I* am Sherlock Holmes.'

Holmes has always claimed that the fame he has gained as a detective is an onerous imposition, without which he would be both happier and more effective. That said, I have noticed that he is rarely averse to eliciting a reaction, merely by use of his name. In this case, however, he would have been better to remember that below a certain social level, *The Strand* is little known and, consequently, neither are consulting detectives. Mrs Boggs clearly knew nothing of Holmes, and proved this by poking one finger into his chest as she spoke.

'And I'm Mary Boggs, but that's neither 'ere nor there, mister whoever you are. If you ain't police, you got no right to force your way into my 'ome, nor to come sneaking about after Boggs 'isself. 'E's up at the Bailey this afternoon on an affray, and that's all I intends telling you. Now get out of my 'ouse!'

I have had cause to note in the past that Holmes could be charm personified with the fairer sex, if the occasion demanded. Now though he had met his match. For all his attempts to soothe Mrs Boggs and steer the conversation away from our imminent expulsion from the house, the best he managed before we were manhandled into the street was to prise from Mrs Boggs the bare fact that she knew of no sales ledgers, and that the only painting in the local area was one of the Queen which hung in the local church hall.

With this last announcement ringing in our ears, we found ourselves back on the pavement, with the main door of the Boggses' residence slamming behind us.

'A lady of strong views, wouldn't you say, Watson?' Holmes was in no way abashed by our dismissal, nor downhearted by our failure to find any sign of the missing miniature. In fact, he was smiling as he signalled to a passing cab. 'Strong arms too, for that matter.'

It has been said that a prisoner may be tried, sentenced, condemned and hanged without once stepping outside the walls of the Old Bailey, and it is undeniable that any criminal approaching the formidable gated entrance must surely hesitate and falter.

Holmes and I were no strangers to the building, however, and had nothing to fear. We passed through the gate quickly and headed quickly down to the area where we knew Boggs would be being held. If there was a greater than usual bustle of uniformed guards pushing past us, I assumed that today was simply busier than normal, and reminded myself that the main criminal court of the British Empire would, by sheer weight of numbers, never be as other courts. Holmes, though, stopped in his tracks and pulled me towards him, as the sound of shouting reached us from a corridor at right angles to that which we were currently traversing. He grabbed the arm of a guard.

'What is going on?' he asked. 'I have rarely seen the Bailey in such a state of turmoil.'

The guard glared at Holmes angrily. 'Get out of my way! We've a prisoner escaped and two guards grievously injured. I've no time to spare for idle lollygaggers!' With that, he tugged his arm free and hurried away down the corridor.

'Escaped—' Holmes murmured softly. He seemed unperturbed that, for the second time in an hour, he had been brushed aside by someone from whom he required information. For my part, I was burning with indignation at the guard's words. I would have remarked on this to Holmes, but he had already turned and headed down the corridor, in the direction of the greatest volume of shouting.

I caught up with him just as he entered a long passageway that I knew contained cells for holding miscreants awaiting their moment before the judges. All was as it should have been, with the exception of a crowd gathered round one open cell near the end of the passage. It was from this group that raised voices most volubly emanated.

I broke into a run, coming alongside Holmes just as his long-legged stride took him to the door of the open cell. Two guards lay on the stone floor, each still and unmoving.

'Let me through,' I said, 'I am a doctor.'

The crowd parted at my words and I was able to examine the men. The first had a long but shallow gash that extended from his forehead down to his throat. He would have a nasty scar for the rest of his life, but other than that he would suffer no long-term damage. His compatriot would also live, I thought, though his breathing was ragged and shallow. A bump the size of a hen's egg on the back of his head was the only injury I could see so I made him as comfortable as possible and told his fellows that he should be left so until the Bailey doctor came to carry out a more thorough examination. There was nothing else I could do, and I was keenly aware that Holmes was beckoning to me from the very end of the passageway, where he stood, a lamp in his hand, before a doorway leading to a set of descending black steps.

'Both men will survive,' I told him, gesturing back to the wounded duo. 'Have you discovered what happened?'

Holmes's eyes were wide with interest as he turned to me. 'Our bird has flown, Watson. Or rather our bird has been taken. Nobody knows how or by whom, but I am told that the two guards were found, just as you see them, only a few minutes ago, and Boggs's cell was empty. Nobody untoward passed back into the main body of the Bailey, and this is the only exit in this direction. Given the short amount of time available, and the size of the gang involved, Boggs must have been taken through here.' He pointed down the stairway into the darkness then, before I could ask, said 'There was more than one weapon used, Watson, a knife and a blunt instrument, likely a cudgel. Two weapons, two attackers – at a minimum. Add in the mastermind and we have a gang of at least three people. Now, come on! We may have little time!'

Again, his long stride took him away from me, and as the staircase twisted in a corkscrew into the ground, I quickly lost sight of him, though I could always hear his footsteps ahead of me. I increased my pace, taking the stairs two at a time, in spite of the increasingly dim light and the damp stone underfoot. Even so, Holmes remained hidden from view, and I was starting to despair of ever catching him up when I suddenly felt his arm thrust against my chest, bringing me to a precipitous stop. Before I could say a word, he covered my mouth with his hand and pointed further ahead with the other.

The lighting in the lowest section of the Bailey was poor, consisting primarily of the covered lamp in Holmes's free hand and, some distance ahead, through an open doorway at the end of a long corridor, a glimpse of yellow flame against the otherwise pervasive grey. Beyond that, I could make nothing out.

'What am I looking for, Holmes?' I whispered. 'The flame?'

'Quietly, Watson, if you value your life. Hearing you thundering down the staircase some distance behind me, I decided to press on ahead when I reached the bottom. Luckily, I spotted the light ahead, and covered my own lamp, otherwise I would certainly have been observed.'

'Observed?'

'Indeed, Watson. The corridor before us ends at an open archway, beyond which lies a wide, circular room. There are four men standing within and, on the floor, another man, tied at the hands and feet. Mr Boggs, I presume.'

He ushered me forward and followed behind, as we crept towards the glowing light ahead. At the archway it was my turn to put a hand out to stop Holmes. He placed the lamp he carried at his feet so as not to betray our presence while I leaned round the frame and peered into the room. The sight that greeted me was one that I will not easily scrub from my memory.

As Holmes had intimated, there were five men in the room: four standing around a large hole in the floor, and the other lying alongside it, bound at hand and foot. Each of the men carried a weapon of some sort. In fact it would be more accurate to say that only three men stood around the ominous hole, for the fourth and final member of the motley crowd stood a little apart, in the shadows cast by a large lantern which sat on the stone floor. A dampness in the air caused streams of condensed water to run down the walls and pool on the ground. From somewhere nearby I could hear a steady rumble, as though someone were pushing a heavy boulder across a gravel path. I ducked back into the outer corridor, and related everything I had seen to Holmes. His face almost glowed with pleasure as he slid past me and treated himself to a longer look of his own at the strange tableau arranged beyond the arch. I had seen that look before and knew that it betokened Holmes's belief that we were near a conclusion.

'The Albino, Watson,' he suddenly hissed, the excitement unmistakable in his voice. 'Quick, look for yourself!'

The mysterious fourth man had stepped from his shadowed corner, exposing a shock of shoulder-length white hair and a pair of dark glasses. More surprising by far than the mere accident of hair colouring, however, was the manner of his attire. I could not say exactly what I had expected, but the Albino confounded any expectation I might conceivably have had. A black tailcoat, waistcoat and trousers, with a white shirt and bow tie, was complemented by a top hat and gold-topped cane, for all the world as if dinner was about to be served. The effect was startling, as though a peacock had been trapped in a dank cave. This peacock, though, was a dangerous bird, as he was shortly to prove.

As Holmes and I stood in darkness and observed, the Albino crossed to the recumbent Elias Boggs and indicated to one of his men to drag the unfortunate prisoner to his feet. Only once he and Boggs were at equal heights, if not on equal footing, did he address him.

'Boggs, Boggs, what are we to do with you?' His voice was soft and inflected with the smallest hint of an accent, but I could not have narrowed down his country of origin on that basis had I been given a thousand years in which to do so. He seemed dismayed more than angry as he continued in the same gentle tone. 'You came so highly recommended, and yet you have proven such a disappointment. But never mind. Let us speak of other things.

'Do you see what flows beneath us, Boggs? Can you hear the passage of the water?' He laughed, and his laughter was hard and cold, quite unlike his speaking voice. 'I say *water*, but that is, I am afraid, a misleading description for the rancid sludge which comprises the Fleet River. It has long been covered over, you see, Boggs. Covered over and boxed in for decades, a dumping ground for all the filth and offal of London. Can you see it, Boggs?'

Evidently Boggs could not, for the Albino pulled him forward and held him over the hole in the floor, which, belatedly, I recognised as a manhole positioned above the underground river, which flowed in part underneath the Old Bailey. The Albino had not lied about it. The Fleet has been notorious for over a century as the filthiest body of water in the capital and now Boggs dangled above it, only the Albino's impressive strength preventing him from falling to a grotesque and unpleasant death.

The Albino lowered his captive back to the floor and stood over him, shaking his head, I fancied, with regret. 'Unfortunately, you have proven considerably less competent than I expected. You have a reputation amongst a certain type of person for meticulousness in your work, you know. *Elias Boggs, that's your man. He knows how to recover things that are lost.* This is what I was told when I asked in certain quarters for a trustworthy fellow to make preliminary approaches on my behalf. *Respectable, he is, and educated.* This too I was told. And yet nobody thought to mention the drinking. This is why I am so disappointed.'

He held up a hand for silence as Boggs tried to speak. 'No, no, Boggs. You have had your time. I gave you a list of names and tasked you to purchase a painting from each. The English do not trust foreigners, and I was informed that you were a man of learning, who could play the part of my intermediary with ease. Instead, you react to an initial rejection with violence, and thus jeopardise *everything*!' He paused for a moment, to regain his temper. 'Do not misunderstand me, I do not grudge a working man his gin. Every man has his vice, and so long as he does not allow his vice to corrupt his work, then all is well. But when his vice intrudes, when it interferes with his working life – when it interferes with *my* working life – then there is a problem. Then I do grudge it very much indeed.'

The Albino reached inside his pocket and pulled out a small, golden cigarette case, from which he extracted a short cigarette. He stood for a full minute, smoking it completely, before flicking the detritus through the manhole and into the Fleet. His men stood perfectly still, almost at attention, as he did so.

'Where was I? Ah yes, Boggs. I do grudge you your vice when it corrupts my own plans. You knew that the code we seek requires all six elements to be in play if it is to have any meaning at all and yet, because of your drunken animal actions, we risk exposure and, in the end, a failure to acquire the treasure we seek. All because of you, Boggs. The woman is dead, Sherlock Holmes has the scent in his nostrils, and I am forced to come and find you in this dirty little hole. I do not care for that, Boggs. I do not care for it at all.'

Apparently finished with Boggs, the Albino straightened up and brushed something from the sleeve of his jacket. 'I'm bored with Mr Boggs now,' he announced to nobody in particular. 'Do remove him from my sight, please.'

Two of the Albino's men grabbed Boggs as though he were a sack of potatoes and manhandled him towards the hole in the floor. With no time for any more well-thought-out action, I pulled out my revolver just as Holmes threw himself forward. We hardly need have bothered though, for before I could take a step after my friend, a flood of bodies broke over us both, as guards from the Bailey finally figured out where the prisoners must have fled and belatedly reached us.

An over-enthusiastic guard sent Holmes reeling, kicking over the lamp and depositing him on the cold stone floor, while I was buffeted back against the wall and sustained a nasty blow to the back of my head.

Now lit only by the light of the lantern, the cavernous room became a place of shadows and smoke, its walls splashed with orange light that flickered and danced in every passing air current. Black-clad guards fought hand to hand with the Albino's men: desperate men who knew that the near murder of the guards upstairs could mean death at the hangman's hands unless they contrived to escape. Holmes was visible in the middle of the fray, fists tight against his chin, only occasionally striking out with his long reach, but effective every time. His opponent reeled from another solid blow to the stomach then, with a groan audible even in the furore that surrounded us, tumbled to the ground.

My memory of the next few moments is confused. I was still dizzy from the blow I'd taken, and in the inconsistent light figures and actions took on an unreal quality, as though I had opened my eyes underwater, or just woken from a vivid dream. I can clearly picture the Albino stepping back into a patch of darkness near one wall and disappearing, but other than that, everything is fragmentary and unclear.

I saw one guard, stabbed through the arm, snap the blade off and continue to fight with the remainder still jutting from his bicep. My eyes, however, were primarily on the two men yet struggling to pitch Boggs into the Fleet. I stepped into the fray and almost immediately had to duck beneath a wild swing, then fend off a guard who momentarily mistook me for one of the gang. My vision swam for a moment then cleared, and I had an instant in which to take aim and fire at the first, and largest, of the men holding our quarry. He spun away as my view was occluded once more, and when it cleared I saw that he was gone, and only one man now held Boggs prisoner. The distance from the two men to the manhole was considerably smaller than that between me and them. I was aware that I had no time to lose, and but one chance to succeed, as I stopped in my tracks and raised my revolver. I stood there for what felt like hours, though it was certainly only a matter of seconds, waiting for an opportunity to fire without risk to Boggs.

When it came, I was ready. I already held the gun at the correct height, but as Boggs and his captor came into my sights, I slid it to the left a little and squeezed the trigger. Instantly I saw that my aim had been true, as the man staggered backwards as though punched hard in the chest. Too far backwards, as it turned out, for his heel caught the edge of the manhole and, without taking his hands from Boggs, the two men tumbled into the darkness and were lost to this world. I rushed forward but it was too late. I could see nothing in the blackness and hear nothing but the steady, scraping sound of the hidden water below.

Twelve

ℰℐ

The Albino escaped, leaving no clue behind. His men fought like tigers and died, to a man, ensuring he evaded capture, and though the Old Bailey guards searched the bodies, they found nothing useful. Boggs himself, of course, was gone; I stood carefully at the edge of the manhole and lowered a lamp down but the darkness beneath swallowed the feeble light and all I could make out were shades of brown and black. The smell, too, was enough to overwhelm the senses. I stepped back before dizziness made me over-balance and join Boggs in his hellish grave.

Holmes meanwhile was arguing with Inspector Lestrade, who had arrived in the wake of the battle, looking for the Albino. Holmes had a cut on his forehead, which was bleeding into his eyes, and Lestrade was insisting he have it seen to before doing anything else.

Holmes had other ideas. 'It is imperative that we speak with Mrs Boggs immediately, Inspector! We have already been delayed for almost two hours by your cretinous colleagues!'

'In due course, Mr Holmes, in due course. I've sent a constable to the address you provided, with instructions to stay with the lady until we arrive. As soon as we get your head bandaged you can speak to her.'

'That will be too late!' Holmes was furious, his grey eyes wide with anger, his jaw rigid as he strove to control his temper. 'It may have been too late before you even arrived here, Lestrade, but it will certainly be so if we delay any longer. Do you imagine that a man capable of ordering one of his men thrown into *that*–' he pointed towards two constables who were carefully lowering the manhole cover back into place, '–would baulk for a second at killing a defenceless woman? If she yet lives, then a few coins may loosen her lips a little, especially now that her husband is dead, but any further delay will certainly render the possibility moot, in which case we may as well stay here.'

I had long since learned not to be shocked by Holmes's occasional descent into callousness, recognising that in every case what seemed cold-blooded disregard was simply pragmatism. Holmes, I knew, was not without compassion, but he rarely allowed it to hinder an investigation. Lestrade, too, knew Holmes's moods of old.

'Very well, Mr Holmes,' he said. 'Press this handkerchief to the cut, at least, and we'll be on our way, though I'm sure Mrs Boggs will already be enjoying a cup of tea in police custody.'

As soon as we reached the street, it was obvious that something was amiss. Crowds of people milled about in front of the Boggses' home, held back by a single harassed constable.

'Frost! Constable Frost!' Lestrade jumped to the ground while the vehicle was still moving and pushed his way through the crowd, all the while shouting to his subordinate. We followed in the wake he created, until we stood before the front door, which spun on a single hinge. I was reminded of Miss Marr's door sitting open in the rain, and felt a heaviness build in the pit of my stomach. I was suddenly sure that an already bloody day was about to become even bloodier.

By contrast, Constable Frost's relief was palpable as he quickly but concisely gave his report to Lestrade. 'There's a woman's body inside, first door on the right, sir. Looks like she's been attacked by a madman, sir. The kid is with a neighbour. Place is a bit of a mess, sir, but it's impossible to tell if it was always that way, or if there was a robbery.'

'It's unlikely Mrs Boggs had much worth stealing, Constable,' Lestrade said wearily, as we pushed past Frost.

Inside, what had been tattered but clean had been transformed into filthy wreckage. What little furniture the Boggses had owned had been turned over and smashed to splinters, mattresses ripped apart, a cupboard turned to kindling, the door to the box room destroyed and even the baby's cot stove in on one side. Mrs Boggs had been savagely beaten until her face was all but unrecognisable. She sat propped against a wall as though still living, but there was no chance of that. I found a rough blanket in a corner and pulled it over her body.

'The death blow was struck with a heavy, rounded object, directly to the back of the head, possibly while she was on her hands and knees,' I said sorrowfully.

'Like the cane you said you saw the Albino holding, Doctor?' asked Lestrade.

'Perhaps. It's definitely a possibility, but I would need to examine the head of the cane more closely before I could say for sure. You think that the Albino got here before us, and killed Mrs Boggs to silence her?'

'Then why destroy the room?' Holmes interrupted flatly. 'Mr Boggs worked for the Albino, that much was made clear at the Bailey. His job was to retrieve the miniature from its purchaser and bring it to his master, but for whatever reason he muddled the job and the lady in question ended up dead. Even so, Boggs must have given the miniature to the Albino. So I ask again, why destroy the room?'

Lestrade was hesitant. 'He believed Boggs had further information?'

'Or he has a terrible temper when angered?' Though the Albino had been outwardly calm when ordering the execution of Mr Boggs under the Bailey, I had known cases of similarly emotionally controlled individuals who, under certain unfortunate stimuli, were capable of the most terrible feats of violence and cruelty.

Holmes shrugged at the suggestion but I, who knew him better than anyone, could tell that he considered the idea to have little merit. 'That is not unknown,' he said eventually. 'Jack Vincent, who robbed the Bank of England in seventy-four, for instance, was such an individual, and he was not unique.' He turned to Lestrade. 'Even more reason to exercise caution when dealing with this man, Inspector. His cold-blooded ruthlessness was amply demonstrated by the manner in which he disposed of Mr Boggs, but the murder of Mrs Boggs argues for a great inner rage. A combination of the two could prove very dangerous indeed.'

In response, Lestrade called over Constable Frost and gave him a series of instructions. 'Frost will remain at the front of the building for the moment, Mr Holmes, while we wait for more officers to arrive, but in the meantime, will you be wanting to look at anything in the room?'

He need not have bothered to ask, for Holmes was already crouched down on the floor, raking through the grate of the fireplace. He reached inside and pulled out a handful of partially burned scraps of paper, each of which he examined, before discarding. 'Bits of bills and inconsequential scribbles only,' he complained, 'burned recently and with no great regard for their complete destruction. I wonder–'

He picked up one of the larger scraps and looked at it again. 'The same word copied over and over, Watson, do you see? In block capitals too. Our man was practising.'

'Were we in any doubt that Boggs wrote the letter to Miss Marr, Holmes?' I asked, with some irritation. It occasionally seemed to me that Holmes liked to flaunt his abilities when anyone from Scotland Yard was present, and I – painfully aware that the trail of bodies we had followed that day had led us into a dead end – had no patience for such frivolities.

I should have had more faith.

'Yes, yes, Watson, that much is a given!' Holmes was impatient too, and made no effort to hide the fact. 'But who's to say that Boggs had but one correspondent? There is a large quantity of ash here, far greater than one would expect from these few pages. Other, more interesting, correspondence has been destroyed here. Replies, perhaps.'

'Which is all very well, Mr Holmes,' Lestrade interjected, 'but what good does that do us? Without the destroyed letters, have you any suggestions regarding our next course of action?'

'No,' admitted Holmes ruefully. He straightened up and cast an analytical eye over the ruin of the room. 'If we do not discover something here, then we may find ourselves in difficulties in future.' He glanced down at the scraps in his hand. 'But no man can think of everything and it may be that…'

His voice trailed off as he paced around the room, tapping on walls and running his fingers along the gaps between floorboards. This continued for several minutes, until every possible hiding place must surely have been exhausted, and he stood once more in the centre of the room, his face a mask of frustration. I had seen that look many times before and knew the black mood it presaged. Sherlock Holmes did not react positively to failure, even temporary failure, and as I watched his eyes flicker across the room, I hoped for my friend's sake that some connection could be made which would move us forward.

As though he could read my thoughts, Holmes slowly smiled. He walked over to the little box room where the baby's crib lay and pulled the tiny bed into the main living area. Reaching past the shattered side he slipped his fingers beneath the thin mattress – in reality just a worn and much folded blanket – and flipped it out onto the floor. Then, with a cry of triumph, he emerged grasping a sheaf of crumpled paper.

'Never waste anything; that is the invariable rule of the industrious poor! What may not satisfy as a letter intended for a genteel lady will do well as insulation for a baby's bed, Lestrade!'

Propping the cot against the wall, he unfolded the papers. There were three in total. The first was a reply from a Mr Howard Smith of Bayswater, regretting that he had no interest in selling 'the item described'. The others were letters of approximately the same construction as that sent to Eugenie Marr, though addressed to what were presumably other collectors. The nearest – that of Colonel Andrew de la Mare – was not too far distant.

'Can you take us to this address at once, Lestrade?' asked Holmes, his mood changing in an instant. 'With some luck, the Albino does not know that Colonel de la Mare of Mayfair is in possession of–' he consulted the letter, '–an oil painting of Sir James Hamilton of Finnart, nor that a Mr Sebastian Rudge is the current owner of a portrait of Anne Boleyn in a gilt-edged frame. For the first time, we may manage to get ahead of our quarry!'

Thirteen

I felt as though we had spent the day bisecting and dissecting London, criss-crossing the city socially and geographically, rising and falling on a tidal swell of poverty and ambition. From Eugenie Marr, via Mr Boggs at the Old Bailey, to his wife in Camden Town, the hours of daylight had witnessed a savage race in which each mile was marked by a fresh corpse. I was heartsick and morose as the police carriage bounced along Camden's pitted roads, in marked contrast to Holmes, who sat forward in his seat like a predator poised to attack.

To pass the time, and to take my mind off recent events, I surveyed the passing scenery through the open window. Camden was dark and grim in the fading light, and though the rain had held off for the past hour or two, the walls we sped past were wet with moisture and furred with mould. Here and there children played in the streets, their thin, pale faces briefly uplifted in our wake, before returning to whatever amusement they had found, strangely silent in their merriment. I found the entire spectacle disheartening in the extreme, and was not much consoled when, as we passed through Primrose Hill, the terraced houses began to improve in aspect, and the guttersnipes of the streets were replaced by sober men hurrying home from work.

'Come now, Watson, it is no fault of the industrious man that he lives in such close proximity to the destitute, any more than it is the fault of the poor man that he lives cheek by jowl with wealth and prosperity. They did not kill anyone, after all.'

Holmes gave a laugh of sheer pleasure at the look on our faces. The possibility of catching up with the Albino had done wonders for my friend's mood, and if I resented his laughter at that moment, I welcomed his improved humour.

'Everything you think is written plain as day on your face, Watson. When we left Mrs Boggs you were downcast, obviously considering the several deaths we have encountered today, and their cause. Your expression changed to a frown as we passed through the nearby streets, suggesting something had additionally disturbed you. I might have assumed that it was poverty itself that upset you but the frown became more pronounced in the past few minutes as we moved into a more salubrious part of the city. Thus you have been comparing the relative wealth of the people of Primrose Hill with those of Camden Town, and finding the latter wanting. Simplicity itself, Watson.'

'He has you there, Doctor,' Lestrade chimed in. 'You've had a face like thunder since we got in the carriage.'

I could deny nothing Holmes had said, and so satisfied myself with a half-smile and a non-committal grunt of agreement. Fortunately, we had arrived at the Mayfair address Holmes had discovered, and so I was spared the need to say anything further.

We were relieved to discover that nothing was amiss. Colonel de la Mare, a perfectly gruff, red-faced example of the species 'Retired Indian Army Officer', did remember receiving a letter asking if he had any interest in selling a portrait of Sir James Hamilton of Finnart – better known as 'the bastard of Arran', as our host told us with ill-disguised glee, though I admit I had never heard of the man. But he had only recently bought it and so dismissed the matter without another thought. After some pressing from Holmes, he also described a white-haired man who had turned up on his doorstep the previous week, claiming to be an insurance agent, and asking if there were any valuable artworks in the house.

'A suave sort of cove, if you know what I mean? Smooth as silk and oily as a pimp's hair, eh? Soon showed him the door. Fancy he was a foreigner too, eh?'

Lestrade nodded encouragingly, and took the Colonel to one side for a statement, while Holmes and I examined the painting in question, which was displayed over the mantelpiece.

'The Albino, following up Boggs's letter with a personal visit?' I asked.

'Assuredly,' Holmes replied. 'Clearly he was not confident that Boggs would succeed.' He pulled out a magnifying glass, which he twisted and turned as he leant ever closer to the painted surface.

I took the opportunity to make my own examination of the painting. It depicted a sword-wielding knight on horseback, the beast rearing somewhat wildly, set against a rugged landscape dominated by a fortified castle in the background and a stretch of grey water to the fore. While the man's armour was medieval, even an individual as unfamiliar with art as I could tell that the painting itself was from a later period. I said as much to Holmes, who grunted non-committally before deigning to give me a polite answer.

'Yes, Watson. I'd judge it was painted some time around the

1620s.' He peered closer. 'No doubt commissioned by a romantic descendant of Sir James.'

'And the castle? A real structure or an artistic conceit?' At this point our host appeared at my elbow. He seemed glad to be able to discuss his new acquisition, even in such unorthodox circumstances.

'That's Blackness Castle, on the south shore of the Firth of Forth, Dr Watson. Hamilton fortified it while holding the position of King's Master of Works.' He seemed about to expand on his subject, but was halted by my companion, who straightened and announced that there was nothing to suggest that this painting was a forgery. 'There is nothing whatsoever to commend this painting over any other, in fact,' he insisted. 'A somewhat unusual subject, but other than that, quite unremarkable.'

Having arranged to have the painting moved to Scotland Yard for safekeeping, we left for the second address on our list, the house of Howard Smith in Bayswater. Mr Smith turned out to be a schoolteacher of amiable disposition, who was happy to show us a line drawing of the Magi at the Nativity, which he had bought from the Hamblin Estate. Unlike the other artworks we had seen, this was a small pencil drawing, showing the wise men paying homage to the Christ child. Though it was obviously a preliminary sketch for a larger work, and everything bar the main figures was indistinct and unfinished, the face of each man had been depicted in life-like detail, drawing the eye as the artist no doubt intended.

Smith confirmed that the sketch was a rough draft for a larger painting, commissioned by the Bishop of Ely in 1462 for display in his residence. 'I could not, of course, afford the actual painting, even if it had been for sale, but still, I think this pleasing in its own right.' We hastened to agree, before Holmes made enquiries as to any recent activity regarding its sale. No, Smith said, nobody had visited him in connection with the sketch, though yes, he had received a letter offering to purchase it. He had written back to explain that he was much attached to it and was not, consequently, minded to sell at present. He was, however, happy to lend it to the police, on the understanding it would be returned unharmed within the fortnight. Holmes again identified the sketch as an original, and we left for the final address on our list, the home of Mr Sebastian Rudge.

From the moment we alighted from the carriage and walked through the imposing gates of Mr Sebastian Rudge's home in Hampstead, it was obvious that we had arrived too late. A policeman stood by the open front door, blocking our passage until Lestrade was called to vouch for us. Inside, more policemen milled about and I confess I felt a knot in my stomach as I gave thought to the possibility of another murder on a day already replete with horrors.

Imagine my relief, then, when Lestrade spoke to one of the more senior police officers present then relayed to us the news that though there had indeed been a robbery, nobody had been harmed.

'Both Mr and Mrs Rudge were out to dinner when the robbery occurred. Woodrush, the butler, says that a man knocked at the door around an hour and a half ago. The gentleman, according to the butler, wore a woollen hood over his face, with eye and mouth holes cut out. He pulled out a gun and, calling on his confederates waiting outside, ordered all of the servants into the master bedroom, where they were bound and gagged. It seems that they were roughly handled too. They would still be there, but a footman worked himself free and raised the alarm.'

Holmes nodded, distractedly. 'What an enterprising fellow.' He let his eyes wander around the immaculate drawing room. 'May I speak to the butler?' he asked, finally.

Lestrade signalled to the nearest constable, who turned on his heel and disappeared into the rear of the house. He reappeared within a few moments, leading a small man in a dishevelled butler's uniform. The newcomer was short and grey-haired, though that hair mainly congregated around his ears and the back of his neck, with paradoxically bushy eyebrows and moustache. His expression was morose, as befitted one who had contrived to allow his master to be robbed, and when Holmes offered him a cigarette he lit it with shaking fingers. I did not expect that we would discover much of interest from such a downcast and dispirited specimen.

Holmes, however, was clearly more sanguine. 'Good evening, Mr Woodrush,' he said, with great bonhomie. 'My name is Sherlock Holmes and, with your help and that of my colleague Dr Watson, I am sure I will be able to recover your master's lost painting.'

He beamed at the butler, but if he was expecting a lifting of his spirits, he was to be sorely disappointed. Instead, the little man stubbed out his cigarette, and in a surprisingly strong voice, said, 'I'm afraid I don't understand, sir. The sergeant told us that nothing had actually been stolen. He said the miscreants were forced to leave their ill-gotten hoard a street or two away and everything taken was recovered. Is that not right, sir?'

Holmes's face reddened as I had rarely seen before, and it took me a moment to realise that he was *embarrassed*. He glared at Lestrade, but before he could explode in fury at being made to appear a fool, the Inspector rounded on the nearest constable.

'Did nobody think to tell me that all the stolen goods had already been recovered?' he shouted. 'Where's the man in charge here? He and I need to have a word!' He glanced down at the seated Holmes. 'My apologies, Mr Holmes. If you'll excuse me, there's a sergeant somewhere in this house who is about to have a very unpleasant experience.' With a final irritated glare at the room in general, he stalked out and could be heard shouting imprecations as he made his way in pursuit of some unfortunate officer.

Holmes, conversely, had had his equilibrium restored by Lestrade's display.

'It seems that that is exactly the case, Mr Woodrush. I'm sure that Mr Rudge will be delighted. But perhaps you could tell my colleague and me exactly what occurred earlier this evening?'

'There is not a great deal to tell, I'm afraid, sir. Mr Rudge left for dinner at five-thirty exactly, and not ten minutes passed but there was a knock at the door. Thinking that Mrs Rudge had forgotten something and sent the driver back to collect it, I hurried to answer the knock – only to find the masked gentleman I described to the police standing outside.'

'And he–?'

'Well, sir, he had a gun in his hand, and half a dozen big lads at his back, so I did what he said. Backed up into the house, called the staff together and sat tight while they ransacked the place.'

'Ransacked?' I knew that Holmes preferred me not to interrupt his interrogations, but looking round the immaculately appointed house, the idea that it had been ransacked was too ludicrous to be allowed to pass unremarked. 'If it was, the maid has been very busy, I'd say.'

'Of course "ransacked", Watson,' Holmes replied, testily. '*Several* paintings were taken, obviously. Haven't you been listening? Why else bring six burly assistants? For that matter, have you ever previously heard of a single object, no matter how large, being described as a hoard?'

Woodrush hurried to confirm Holmes's deductions. 'The thieves made off with every painting, sketch and drawing in the house, Dr

Watson. They were very specific about what they wanted, in fact, and touched nothing but those items. I said as much to the Inspector. They even removed a photographic image of Mrs Rudge's mother, and the architectural plans for a possible extension to the rear of the house.'

'Even a photograph?' Holmes asked, with interest. 'Are you certain?'

'Certain, sir. They took all sorts. The leader asked about a lambing painting or something, but I told him I had no idea what he was talking about; the master owns no painting that shows a lambing scene, as far as I am aware. I couldn't really tell what he was saying, to be honest, sir, between the mask and the foreign accent. He must've believed me, for he said he had no time to waste and that they should take everything. Which they did. They piled it all up in a large four-wheeler outside, then one man drove it away while the rest of the gang, including the leader, left over the back wall.'

'A foreign accent, Holmes!' I exclaimed. 'That must have been the Albino!'

Holmes's voice was thoughtful in reply. 'A definite possibility, Watson. And a fine, straightforward task for Lestrade and his men. Find the Albino, and find the treasure.'

Without another word he began to criss-cross the room, examining every surface at close quarters and even, briefly, crawling about on the floor. Once or twice he gave a pleased snort as something of interest caught his eye, and at one point he teased a long black hair from where it had lodged in a crack in the wooden mantelpiece.

'Mrs Rudge's hair, what colour is it?' he called across to Woodrush.

'A darkish brown colour, sir,' the butler replied.

Suddenly uninterested in further examinations, Holmes stood and bade Woodrush good night, then strode into the rear of the house without another word. I shrugged my own apologetic goodbye to the old man and rushed to follow him.

By the time I caught up, he was haranguing Lestrade in the larder. 'In the name of sanity, Lestrade, you allowed the driver to escape?'

Holmes had cornered the Inspector at the back of the room, trapping him between a large cheese and a partially eaten steak and kidney pie. Seeing me standing in the doorway, the relief on Lestrade's face was unmistakable. 'Dr Watson, will you please inform Mr Holmes that the primary aim of the police force in a robbery such as this is to ensure the safe return of stolen property. It is not to chase a single thief into areas where, to be frank, the police are not welcome. And besides,' he concluded darkly, 'constables at the scene did attempt to apprehend the driver, but he assaulted several of them before making his escape. One of the constables may not survive the night.'

'Unfortunate,' said Holmes, with feeling. 'The driver could have helped us a great deal. Still, this has been a most informative end to a rather frustrating day.'

To my mind, a day in which we had been too late to prevent three separate murders, and which had been bookended by a theft and a robbery – neither of which we had solved – deserved a more forceful epithet than 'frustrating', but there was nothing to be gained by labouring the point with Holmes. Long experience had taught me that his priorities were frequently not those of other men.

Lestrade too had long since realised that this was the price Holmes's friends paid for his astonishing abilities, and said nothing to reproach him, even though his disregard for the Inspector's injured men must have wounded him. He and I, each in our own way, recognised that something was deficient in Holmes, something indefinable but unmistakably lacking. And yet he was a compassionate man, as I had seen on many occasions, one capable of being roused to genuine fury by injustice and cruelty. At other times, though, as now, he could appear cold to the point of callous indifference.

We watched as Holmes made his way past us then, as though waking from a light sleep, hurried in his wake.

I caught up with him in the drive, where he stood, smoking, and staring intently at the front of the house. 'He was obviously not inside, of course, Watson,' he said. 'If he had been, he would at the very least have prevented his men spiriting away a photograph and a set of blueprints, wouldn't you say?'

It had been a long day, and particularly after Holmes's recent behaviour, I was in no mood to play his games. 'Who, Holmes?'

He looked at me with genuine surprise. 'Why, the Albino, of course! He can hardly have been inside the house, for the simple reasons I have just stated, so it was clearly not he to whom the butler opened the door, mask or no. But he does not strike me as the type to leave an important operation in the hands of idiots. It is a pretty conundrum, Watson.'

'Elias Boggs didn't strike me as exactly a scholar, Holmes,' I protested. 'And yet the Albino employed him. Maybe these fellows were cut from the same cloth.'

'You heard him speaking to Boggs, Watson. Our pink-eyed friend took advice from the local criminal fraternity before employing him. Once bitten, twice shy, I think you'll find. No, these men were not fools like the late Mr Boggs.' He frowned. 'Did you note that Woodrush claimed the intruder enquired about a picture of lambing, of all mundane subjects? Is it too great a stretch, especially with the additional confusion of an unfamiliar accent, to suggest that the words spoken were not "lambing" but "Anne Boleyn"? The speaker was evidently not the Albino himself, who would have recognised the late Queen, I hazard, but a countryman, perhaps, one less knowledgeable on the subject of the British Royal family than he. The Albino told his underling which painting to look for by name, but did not describe the subject in sufficient detail.' He flicked his cigarette away into the darkness. 'But what urgent business kept the Albino himself away?'

'Perhaps he is on the trail of another artwork?' I suggested. A sudden, chilling thought struck me. 'If that is the case, could Miss Rhodes be in danger? Might the Albino not decide to get the information he needs regarding the remainder of the Hamblin Collection directly from the source?' Unconsciously, I closed my hand around the revolver in my pocket.

'Do not concern yourself, Watson. For one thing, it is extremely unlikely that the Albino is currently engaged in any such robbery. We have only recently visited the locations of the other paintings involved in this peculiar mystery, and there was no sign of him at either. Perhaps he is engaged in *planning* such a robbery, but Lestrade left several of his men at each house for that very reason, hoping to catch the villain in the act. Miss Rhodes is in no danger, I assure you, my dear fellow.'

The relief I felt was palpable. I began to thank Holmes, but he had already dismissed the matter from his mind, and had moved on to entirely new conjectures. 'In any case, you are quite correct, Watson. The strongest probability is that the Albino excused himself from this robbery in order to take part in another, more difficult one. In his absence, the thieves were unable to identify the correct artwork beyond doubt and so removed everything, thus burdening themselves overmuch and making their swift capture far more likely.'

'Fortunately for us.'

'Fortunate, indeed, Watson. And once we have added Mr Rudge's portrait of Anne to our own modest collection, we will have more than half of the solution.'

'Half of the—? What solution, Holmes?'

'Did you not listen to the Albino at all, beneath the Bailey? "All six elements", he said. What else could these elements be but paintings? And now we have five of them in our possession, they are sure to give up the secret of England's Treasure!'

Holmes's face glowed with delight as he considered the task ahead and the possibility of a solution, but as we made our way back indoors to wait for the return of Sebastian Rudge, I could not share his good spirits. It barely seemed possible that a case which had begun with a vandalised painting could have turned so deadly, and in spite of Holmes's reassurances I worried that Miss Rhodes could yet be in danger.

As is often the case after a day of traumatic experiences, those that followed were mundane and passed without incident. The five paintings we had amassed – the King Charles, Augustine Hamblin, Anne Boleyn, Sir James Hamilton and the Magi – had been shipped to Lestrade's office in Scotland Yard (Baker Street being considered too insecure a location), but the combined intellectual might of Sherlock Holmes and a coterie of learned art experts had failed to make any progress in solving whatever riddle they held – if, indeed, there was a riddle at all.

Holmes had examined the paintings and their frames, analysed their paints and pencils, and scrutinised their histories, but after almost a week he was no nearer an answer than he had been when he had begun. In subject, tone and type they were wholly dissimilar, to the extent that I wondered whether there was any connection between them whatsoever, but Holmes was steadfast in his belief that the six elements of which the Albino had spoken were six artworks, and that the miniature of the Biblical twins stolen from Eugenie Marr was the missing item.

For a fourth day, therefore, I breakfasted alone. Every morning since the events at the Old Bailey, Holmes had risen early and left for Scotland Yard before I was awake. On the first day I had followed in the early afternoon, but it was made abundantly clear to me that my input was unlikely to be helpful, and so I had spent the last three evenings in idleness, sitting alone in Baker Street after closing my surgery for the day. Holmes had left me in no doubt there was nothing I could usefully contribute, his mood deteriorating as one unsuccessful day followed another, and the breakthrough he had believed imminent at Sebastian Rudge's home faded into the mist.

I tried to read the newspaper, which was much occupied with the sort of atrocity that would usually have greatly interested Holmes. A body, minus head, hands and feet, had been found in the middle of Brook Street. The police, predictably, were baffled, and were likely to remain so for the foreseeable future, as Holmes worked on the Hamblin case instead. Elsewhere, it seemed that the price of coal was likely to rise, a building had been destroyed by arson, and Arthur Morrison's new novel was gaining sterling reviews. I cut out the articles on the murder and the arson for Holmes's files, and dropped the newspaper to the floor.

With nothing better to occupy my time, I decided to write up my notes on the case to date. I laid a pencil and a sheet of paper on the table, and popped my head around the door to ask the estimable Mrs Hudson if she could rustle up a pot of tea. That done, I took my seat and set out what we had discovered so far. It was not, in truth, a long list.

On the positive side, we had in our possession five paintings that we believed were key to solving the mystery of England's Treasure. On the negative, one of those five paintings, that of Augustine Hamblin, was a forgery (we also had a forgery of the Charles the First portrait, but that was hardly likely to be much use to us), and we still had no real idea what England's Treasure might be. Every person who could conceivably have helped us was either dead or a fugitive, and Holmes had made no progress in four days. It was a dispiriting situation, but we had been in worse and emerged triumphant and I saw no reason to doubt that this would be the same, in the end. Stressing the positive, therefore, I took a second sheet of paper and wrote down a description of each of the paintings we possessed, then noted beneath each any thoughts I had on the subject.

I could think of nothing whatsoever to write about Augustine Hamblin or Sir James Hamilton, but under the heading KING CHARLES WITH PRIEST, I scribbled 'executed in 1649, strong Catholic sympathies.' Shamefully, that was the sum of my knowledge of the late monarch, and so I moved on to the next painting, reminding myself to come back to Charles later.

THE MAGI IN THE STABLE AT BETHLEHEM, I wrote on the next line, then crossed to Holmes's reference volumes to look up the names of the three wise men, though again I was sure that I had known them all as a child. I eventually discovered that 'Melchior, Balthazar and Caspar' were the most common names associated with the Magi, so I pencilled them in. I then spent several predictably fruitless minutes trying out various anagrams of the names, without success.

Finally I listed the portrait we had been loaned by Sebastian Rudge under the heading ANNE BOLEYN. Here, I was on much firmer ground. I had studied the Tudors in my schooldays and retained an interest in the period even after moving on to university and, as a consequence, I was able to fill in quite a lot of detail about the subject. I covered the page with notes about Anne's life and death, pleased that the various important dates in her life came to me easily, and without recourse to any reference volume. I even added, with a smile, the information that the Queen had kept a greyhound, had been rumoured by Catholic propagandists to have had six fingers on one hand, and was believed to haunt Hever Castle. Perhaps England's Treasure was guarded by a ghost, I thought, and smiled at my own whimsy.

None of this was immediately helpful, however. Try as I might, I could see no links between the individual paintings. Religion perhaps played a part in some way, but other than that general point, I had to admit myself defeated. There seemed no way in which these five works could be brought together to make a set. I wondered if perhaps the missing sixth painting, the miniature of Jacob and Esau stolen from the murdered Miss Marr, was the crucial key.

Fourteen

W hen Holmes returned that evening, I was still in place at the table. I had covered sheet after sheet of foolscap with my jottings, filling pages with my increasingly implausible theories. The litter of crumpled paper on the floor was testament to my success, or lack thereof.

Holmes barely registered my presence, stumbling past me as though dazed before slumping into his favourite chair with a groan. He pulled his smoking materials towards himself, but sank back and allowed his eyes to close without so much as filling the pipe's bowl. I had rarely seen him so exhausted and was on the verge of expressing my concern when he unexpectedly spoke.

'There is nothing so completely enervating, Watson, as inactivity. I have stood for the past ten hours before the same set of five static images, moving nothing but my eyes, and what is the reward for my diligence? An ache in my head and neck sufficient to render me in grave need of tobacco.'

His eyes flipped open and with a sudden, if transitory, burst of energy he filled and lit his pipe, before allowing himself to sink once more into his chair.

'No luck then, Holmes?' I asked.

'Luck is a crutch for the foolish, Watson, designed to provide an outside agency which the weak-minded may blame for their misfortune,' he replied testily. 'But no, I have made no progress. I have examined each artwork from every conceivable angle but discovered no commonality whatsoever. There is a slight religious thread running through the grouping, so at first I wondered if perhaps England's Treasure was a relic of some kind. A fragment of the Holy Cross, or the blood of Saint George? But if so, what do a Scottish knight, an executed Queen and a corpulent sixteenth-century aristocrat contribute to the puzzle?

'Looked at from a different angle, it is possible to construct an argument that an animal theme unites the collection. Sir James astride his horse, the Magi at the stable in Bethlehem, the falcon on Queen Anne's coat of arms... but even if such a theme existed, how would it help us?

'Then again, the thought occurred that the Magi, Anne and Charles are all royalty – could the Crown Jewels of England be the prize after all? Well, perhaps, but how could these paintings lead us to them? No, I thought, that is both too plain and too subtle; it is not that.

'I placed the paintings side by side, and one atop the other, but nothing came to mind. I examined the ridges of paint themselves, but they were just ridges. I even had the frames removed and checked for hidden writing. Nothing. There is nothing there.

'I am not yet defeated, Watson, but I am disheartened; I cannot deny it. I believed that possession of all the paintings – or rather, *nearly* all of the paintings – would be almost the entirety of the battle, but I confess to a puzzlement that is vexing in the extreme. I actually briefly considered the possibility that this entire case has been a practical joke on Lestrade's part: revenge for my continual besting of Scotland Yard.'

He half smiled at his own self-pity and sat a little straighter in his chair. 'But what of you, Watson? How have you been filling your days?'

'I can do you one better,' I said, matching his laugh. 'Earlier on today I gave credence to the idea that a ghost might be involved!'

'Really, Watson,' Holmes responded acerbically, 'there are limits to the realms of fantasy I am willing to entertain even in extremis, and the supernatural, I can assure you, is a step beyond those limits.'

'I wasn't being entirely serious, Holmes,' I protested. I leaned over and handed him the sheet of paper on which I had listed the various paintings. 'I was simply collating all I knew about the subject of each composition, including the fact that Queen Anne's ghost is rumoured to pace the halls of Hever Castle. She *was* likely born there, of course, and the family lived there for her entire life. In fact, I have heard… Holmes, are you even listening to me?'

Clearly he was not, for he failed to acknowledge my question but instead continued to stare at the sheet of paper I had handed him. I tried to regain his attention by coughing in a pointed manner, but Holmes barely acknowledged the attempt. We sat like that, unspeaking in the dim light, for several minutes. Finally, Holmes broke the silence.

'Why do you imagine a good – if secret – Catholic like Horace Hamblin included a portrait of the infamous Protestant Queen Anne in this most exclusive of collections?'

I was pleased that he had asked a question which I had already mulled over that afternoon. 'I did wonder at that myself, Holmes, but I think you may be about to head down the wrong path entirely.

It may seem strange that a secretly devout Catholic should own a likeness of a Queen famed for her Protestant beliefs, but I believe I can explain.

'I did a little reading in one of your Civil War histories, and it seems that hanging the image of famous Protestant royalty – especially those who could make a claim to martyrdom – was an excellent way of deflecting suspicion of Catholicism and distracting the attention of Parliament's more rabid zealots. Presumably Hamblin used Queen Anne in this manner.'

Holmes, to my surprise, was dismissive. 'No, Watson, no! I do sometimes wonder if I am wasting my time in allowing you to observe me at work. At times you seem to be making reasonable progress, to be flexing your brain at last, but then you say something so asinine that... Well, never mind.

'Of course Hamblin kept the Boleyn portrait on prominent display! To do otherwise would have been to invite suspicion and investigation. But I was not referring to the painting's inclusion in the Hamblin Collection in general, but to its placement in this small subset of the larger whole. Whatever these paintings represent or hide, it was Hamblin himself who chose them, and it is more than passing strange that of all the many items he had from which to choose, he chose an image of a woman despised by those of his sect.'

I admit I had been stung by Holmes's rejection. 'And?' I asked, with some ire. 'I take it you have a theory?'

'*And* therefore the reason for her inclusion must have been unique.' He leapt to his feet and paced up and down before the fire, punctuating his words with stabs of his pipe. 'There is something about Anne Boleyn which is unusual in the extreme, or at least distinctive enough that she was the only example Hamblin could possibly utilise. Or should I rather say *the only example he had to hand*? No? You do not recall what you wrote? You should, Watson, you should, for it is a breakthrough in the case – and all the more pleasurable for its source. Perhaps you have been listening and observing after all!'

Holmes puffed mightily on his pipe, and leaned back against the mantelpiece, blowing smoke rings into the air as he waited for me to speak. With no idea what he was referring to, however, I maintained my silence, knowing that he could not bear not to explain. I did not have long to wait.

'I have, myself, been considering the question of the uniqueness of Anne for four days, without a glimmer of success,' Holmes said, without further preamble. 'I was almost at the point of assuming my initial theory incorrect, and entirely giving up on this line of enquiry. And yet when I return home, disconsolate and disheartened, what do I find? Dr John Watson has scribbled the answer down as a passing thought!'

Holmes still held the sheet of paper I had given him, and now he read aloud from it.

'Anne Boleyn was rumoured by Catholic propagandists to have had six fingers on one hand.'

He paused for comment, but still I could not grasp what he saw which I did not.

'Can it be that still you do not understand? Six fingers, Watson! It is a number, to go alongside the three wise men, Charles the First and the Firth of Forth!'

'The Firth of–? What are you talking about, Holmes?' I was lost.

'The Firth of Forth, Watson!' He shook his head in irritation. 'The backdrop to the portrait of Sir James Hamilton. I had been thinking that the subject was the pertinent thing, perhaps even the castle, but in fact the setting is the key.' He looked thoughtful for a moment. 'I admit that, as yet, I have not identified the numerals to be read in Augustine Hamblin's portrait, but now that I am certain there is one to be found, I confidently expect that to be child's play!'

'A number?' I understood that Holmes had found the missing link between the paintings, but as to the logic behind it, or the use to which it could be put, I remained in the dark.

'Numbers, Watson, plural! Six paintings, six numbers!' Holmes's enthusiasm was infectious, and I found myself smiling as he explained himself. 'One to six, at that, so an order rather than a code in itself. Charles in the primary position, followed by the missing miniature of the Old Testament twins, and then the three wise men, Sir James at the Firth of Forth, the portrait of Sir Augustine – for where else can he go? – and finally Queen Anne.'

'All very well, Holmes, but what does it mean?' I asked.

'At the moment, I am unsure, I admit. But we have one, three, four, five and six from a total of six. If we cannot winkle out the mystery from there, then we are not the men I took us to be. I am convinced that these artworks conceal a code which can be used to discover England's Treasure.'

Holmes's eyes sparkled with sheer delight in the game. This was his natural and most beloved milieu: an intellectual puzzle with the highest possible stakes. Only absorbed in such activity was Holmes truly alive; without it, as he had himself remarked more than once, he might as well be dead.

As I observed him, I was reminded of previous occasions when the trail had grown cold, and all seemed lost, only for Holmes to save the day at the last moment. Then, as now, his entire frame appeared suffused with nervous energy. He leapt to his feet and strode to the window, which he threw open, allowing the cold night air into the house, clearing the room of stale tobacco smoke just as his own tired mind had been cleared by his deductions. The rain had finally stopped for good earlier that afternoon, and in its place the air outside was sharp and crisp, with the promise of a fine winter morning to follow. I hoped it was an omen.

'I feel reinvigorated, Watson,' he said, and would have said more, but for the sudden shattering of the window just above his head, followed by a loud bang as a shelf on the back wall was struck by a shot.

Glass fragments showered Holmes as he took two quick steps to the side, away from the window and out of sight of whoever was shooting at him. I slipped out of my chair and crouched behind it, wishing that I had my revolver to hand, but I had left it in my bedroom and in order to obtain it I would need to pass in front of the broken window, leaving myself open to a second shot. I cast my eyes around that portion of the room within reach, but a small pile of journals and newspapers awaiting Holmes's scissors, and an abandoned tea tray holding the remains of my lunch, were all that was visible. Neither offered much promise as a weapon.

Meanwhile, Holmes had not wasted a moment in reflection, but was already on the floor, sliding towards me on his stomach. As he passed, he paused to speak.

'Twice in the last few days I have thought that someone was following me, but on neither occasion was I able definitively to confirm my suspicions. I gave chase to a little fellow the day before yesterday but he evaded me by the river and disappeared. And yesterday I was sure that I saw the same man in the distance, watching me as I entered Scotland Yard. Someone is worried that we are making progress, Watson!'

There was real satisfaction in his voice, but for myself I was troubled that Holmes had not thought to share this information before now. I said as much, but he merely seemed perplexed that I thought it important.

'Really, Watson!' He frowned. 'I was unable to catch the man, so there was nothing to tell. Now listen to me very carefully.' As he spoke, he rolled onto his back and began stuffing the front of his shirt with the collection of newspapers I had noted a moment before, until he was quite rotund. 'I need you to be ready to run for your room as soon as I act. The instant I stand up, you must go and get your revolver, then return here. Keep as low as you possibly can, but speed is of the utmost importance.'

I stared at him in incomprehension. 'What are you doing, Holmes?' I asked as he tipped an empty cup from my luncheon tray and held the latter out above him.

Holmes rolled onto his side to face me. 'I intend to draw the fire of whoever is shooting at us, allowing you time to run to your bedroom in comparative safety, where you may retrieve your revolver and thereby place us on equal military footing with our unknown assailant. I will count to three, then stand up and walk towards the window, holding the tray in front of me. Are you ready? One, two–'

'You can't mean it, Holmes! It's as good as suicide!'

'–three!' True to his word, and ignoring my interruption, Holmes swung himself to his feet in one easy movement and, tray held before his face, walked towards the window. Whatever his plan, I knew that to delay would be both futile and potentially fatal. I leapt to my feet and, leaving my friend behind, ran to my room. I had barely made it through before I heard another thunderous bang from behind me. My fingers closed round the handle of the gun as something in the other room fell heavily to the floor.

'Holmes!'

I re-entered our sitting room expecting to find some unspecified horror. Instead, I was grabbed by strong, unseen hands the instant I left my own room, and spun round and down behind the same chair I had so recently vacated. Holmes threw himself down beside me with a grunt. His hair was dishevelled but otherwise he appeared wholly unharmed.

Wordlessly, he handed me the tray he had been carrying. Sticking straight through it was a thick wooden quarrel with a wickedly sharpened tip. Before I could ask any questions, Holmes removed the revolver from my hand and, in one sudden, whip-like movement, stood up and marched to the broken window, firing three times as he did so. That done, he ducked to one side of the window, and began counting. When he reached one hundred he moved back in front of the window and stood there for a full minute. There were no further shots from the street.

Throughout this extraordinary passage of events, not a word had been spoken, but now he stepped forward and held my revolver out to me. The movement released me from my stupefied state as though I had been mesmerised and was only just waking from a hypnotic trance.

'What on earth—' I began, '—you could have been killed, Holmes!'

'I hardly think that likely, my dear fellow,' he replied, with a small, self-satisfied smile. 'You no doubt recognise a crossbow bolt when you see one?' He pointed to the tray in my hand. 'There was no gun fired at us, only a crossbow, and I was never in any danger from that.'

'A crossbow bolt can kill just as easily as a revolver bullet,' I protested angrily.

'That is certainly true in the general sense, but not, I would hazard, in this. Glance over at the shelf hit by the first shot. You will note that though one or two items have fallen to the floor, the shelf itself is not destroyed, and the bolt itself did not even have the power to stick in the wall. See – here it is on the floor and this small indentation in the wall is the only sign that it struck at all. No, whoever had the crossbow was sufficiently distant, or was using a weapon in such a poor state of repair, that all force had been spent by the time the bolt reached this room. Had it struck me then I am confident that my padding of newspapers would have absorbed the blow with little harm to myself.'

What he said made sense, and I was somewhat mollified, but I was not willing to allow his recklessness to pass without one further remonstrance. 'Even so,' I said, 'all it would have taken was one decent shot to do you terrible damage. A bolt may not have the power to stick into a brick wall and yet still have enough to pierce an eye or strike the temple. It does not take a great deal to kill a man if his opponent should prove lucky, Holmes.'

'There is that word again, Watson, and I say again that luck has no impact upon any action of mine. There was no risk because clearly our assailant is a poor shot. He could not manage to graze me with his first bolt, even though I was standing still, framed against the window. What chance then did he have of hitting a moving target?' He glanced again at the tray I was still holding, and the bolt that had transfixed it. 'I was, I admit, incorrect in that respect.'

'Do you think you hit him with your shots?' I asked.

'I very much doubt it, Watson. I was not aiming at anyone or anything in particular, but simply made the natural assumption that any assassin who went to the trouble of using a weapon as silent – not to mention archaic – as the crossbow would baulk at the sound of a trio of revolver shots, and flee. And so it proved.'

I walked over to the window, still cautious, in spite of Holmes's reassurances. There was nothing to be seen outside, simply Baker

Street in the dark. 'Who do you think it was? The man you saw following you on the last two days?'

'There is nothing to indicate otherwise. Though I confess that I have not, as yet, deduced who that person is.'

I pulled the curtains shut. 'One of the Albino's men, surely? He is the only person involved in this affair with reason to want Sherlock Holmes dead, and we have already seen how merciless and cruel he can be. Plus he did attack you earlier. He nearly ran you down, after all.'

Holmes said nothing at first, but instead toyed with the bolt he had retrieved from beneath the shelf. 'This is nothing but a plain wooden bolt, hand carved from ash. A common enough tree, even in London.' He turned to me. 'But why should the Albino wish me dead? That he wants the paintings we hold is understandable, but killing me would not make obtaining that task any easier, or any more likely. The opposite, in fact.'

'He may fear your deductive skills, Holmes. He would not be the first criminal arrogant enough to believe that only Sherlock Holmes could ever catch him. Remove Holmes, he may think, and he will be home free.'

Holmes carefully righted the bench he had knocked over and which had made such a noise while I was in my room. 'At the moment all we can say for sure is that it is impossible to say for sure.' He smoothed his hair down and at once it was impossible to tell that he had recently been in great physical peril.

'In light of our new insights, perhaps it would be useful for us to return to Scotland Yard?'

Before I could protest that he was treating a second attempt on his life with an unwarranted lack of caution, Sherlock Holmes picked up his hat, coat and scarf and left the room, pausing at the top of the stairs to instruct Mrs Hudson that a glazier was required before sweeping out into the street. With no other obvious course open to me, I followed suit and soon we were ensconced in a hansom making its way to Scotland Yard.

Fifteen

Lestrade, I was pleased to discover, was more interested in the murder attempt on Holmes than any potential breakthrough regarding the paintings. I admit that, for once, I had some sympathy with his priorities.

'Really, Mr Holmes, you would be best advised to place yourself under the protection of the Metropolitan Police until we are able to ascertain just what the Albino is up to, and who else he may have sent after you!'

Lestrade was in many ways a phlegmatic man, but there was no doubting the strength of his emotions. I had insisted in the hansom that we tell the Inspector about both the shooting and the earlier attempt to run Holmes down in the street, and Lestrade had reacted exactly as I would have expected. He had been berating Holmes for several minutes without pause now.

'If you had informed the Yard about the first attempt, we might well have been in a position to make an arrest by now, and would certainly have been better positioned to offer you a degree of protection from further assaults on your person.'

Holmes, I knew, was only suffering this barrage because without Lestrade he had no access to the paintings, which were securely under lock and key in one of the Yard's vaults. He shuffled from one foot to the other, the pressure of biting his tongue almost palpable. In the face of such unexpected contrition, Lestrade's anger had nothing upon which to feed and it quickly dissipated.

As Lestrade tailed off, Holmes reassured him that, in future, Scotland Yard would absolutely be his first port of call should anyone try to kill him.

'In the meantime, however,' he continued, as though the idea had just struck him, 'might the paintings be brought up?' He smiled. 'I have a theory that I would like to put to the test.'

Lestrade, whatever opinion Holmes might hold of him, was no fool, and knew that he had been duped. But he was a policeman first and foremost, and therefore a pragmatist. 'Very well, Mr Holmes, we'll say no more on the subject for now, and I'll have the paintings brought in for you to examine again... but mind what I said, do you hear?'

Satisfied that he had had the last word, Lestrade left to arrange the movement of our small art collection. Holmes watched him depart with a half-smile on his face.

Within half an hour, Lestrade's men had arranged the paintings on five wooden easels in a spacious, well-lit office at the top of the building. Holmes had insisted on as much natural light as possible, and as I watched him stalk from one to the other, a look of monomaniacal concentration on his face, I was strongly reminded of our visit to the restoration company the previous week. In front of each painting Holmes paused and stared, occasionally making a note in a notebook he carried with him, but said nothing and gave no other indication that he was even aware that Lestrade or I existed.

For hours, long into the night and the following morning, Holmes continued his silent appraisal. Lestrade left at midnight, pleading a busy day to come, and I admit that I was dozing in a chair when Holmes suddenly clapped his hands together and gave out a loud exclamation of pleasure.

'Quickly Watson, come and look at this!'

Holmes was standing directly in front of the portrait of King Charles, with one long finger pointing at the monarch and his priest. I could see nothing unusual and said so to Holmes.

'Evidently your sleep has left you muddle-headed, Watson,' he said mockingly. 'What do you think the two men are doing in this picture? Look closely,' he warned.

I bent my head until my nose was all but touching the paint, but still I could see no cause for Holmes's excitement. The painting was exactly as I recalled, showing the King and his priest standing, reading from the Scriptures, with a large mirror in the background, in which the reflection of a bed could be seen. 'They're looking at the Bible, Holmes. What of it?'

'Not a Bible, Watson, though it was once, I imagine. The artistry is exquisite, but I believe that I can see the tiniest thickening in the depth of the paint where the title was changed.'

'Holmes, for pity's sake, what are you talking about? What blemish?'

'On the book, Watson. On the cover, to be precise. Someone has painted over the front of the book, and replaced whatever was there with something new. Can you not make it out?'

I stood back a little and concentrated on the tiny cover of the book that the King and priest were admiring. The angle at which the artist had depicted the duo, and the manner in which the priest held the book, the better to point out some theological passage or other, meant that only a portion of the cover could be seen, but now that I took the time I could see quite clearly that rather than being some indicator of a Biblical volume, the word, or part word, which was emblazoned on the brown leather was 'quin'.

'Five?' I said. 'Not Charles the First, but the number five. Well done, Holmes! You really are making progress now.'

To my surprise Holmes was exasperated, not pleased, by my words.

'I think not, Watson. The other paintings take their numerical position from their subject matter, not from the minutiae of individual items; I doubt that this is any different. And besides, I realised two hours ago that Augustine Hamblin was the *fifth* of that name. Miss Rhodes told us as much when she showed us the piece. *That* is our number five.

'No, Watson, the significance of "quin" is two fold. First, and most obviously, it is the name of an author – and I would suggest that the author in question is Saint Thomas Aquinas. Secondly, and far more importantly, the addition was skilfully done, and not done recently.'

'The addition? You believe that the title on the book was not part of the original painting, but was added at a later date? Our forger has been busy, has he not? But why both make a forgery *and* make a change to the original?'

Holmes shook his head. 'You will recall that Miss Rhodes described the forgery of this painting as inferior, whereas this act of vandalism is so well done that I did not notice it for hours, even under a magnifying glass. Though see here – even a master craftsman can overlook a tiny detail.' He moved the glass slightly so that it magnified the mirror behind the two men. 'The artist remembered to correct the reflection of the cover, but the paint was too thinly spread just at the edge. Do you see? The last letter of the original title can just be made out. An "E", from the conclusion of "HOLY BIBLE" I would say. It was that which caused me to examine the cover itself more closely yet.'

Now that he pointed it out, I could make out a lighter smudge of paint that could well be an E. 'Could this be the work of whoever forged the portrait of Hamblin senior?'

'A better thought, Watson, but still no – this could not have been the work of the same man,' Holmes replied. 'This change was carried out more than two hundred years ago. The paint used to cover up whatever was originally written on the book's cover is an exact match for the paint used on the cover itself. An *exact* match. Almost as though the paint came from the same palette.'

'You are saying that Horace Hamblin both created the original and amended it later? But why?'

Holmes sighed heavily. 'At some point after painting the original, Hamblin went back and amended his work, obviously, adding the name of Thomas Aquinas. The conclusion is inescapable. The name of Aquinas himself is a clue to England's Treasure, if only we can decipher it.'

Holmes's eyes were sparkling and his long face could barely contain the pleasure I knew he felt as pieces of the puzzle fell into place in his mind. He closed his eyes for a moment then flicked them open again as his extraordinary mind made another link in the chain.

'I must speak with Miss Rhodes, of course. She may be able to confirm the presence of a volume of Aquinas's works in the library at Hamblin Hall. And you had better make arrangements to hire a special train, too, Watson. We will want to take all of the paintings with us to the Hall, and the thought of carrying four extremely valuable artworks on a public train – not to mention the excellent forgery of

Augustine Hamblin – is not one that fills me with joy. While you are doing that I will take the opportunity to examine one or two other elements of the paintings. Perhaps I can find further additions.'

I left Holmes focussing his magnifying glass on the Magi's gifts, and set out to find Inspector Lestrade.

Sixteen

❧

Holmes discovered no further additions to the paintings before they were re-packed for transport on the Special. Miss Rhodes, for her part, had been unable to confirm that the Hamblin library contained any of the works of Thomas Aquinas, but she was certain that there was an extensive religious section, so our hopes were high as we boarded the train.

Lestrade was scheduled to give evidence in court in the morning and so promised to meet us at Hamblin later in the day, but Holmes had asked Miss Rhodes to accompany us, which made the journey north far more palatable to me than might otherwise have been the case. As soon as we boarded, Holmes became lost in a brown study, staring unblinking out of the window as the city gave way to country, leaving the two of us to converse in privacy.

This was, in fact, the first time we had spent any extended period in one another's company, and I was delighted to discover that we had more in common than I would have expected. Miss Rhodes's father had been an army surgeon, though some years before my own service, and she had lived for a time near my first surgery in London. We even had one or two shared acquaintances, to my surprise and pleasure. In such manner we passed the entire journey, and – speaking for myself at least – arrived at our destination in fine good humour.

Even the journey from the railway station to Hamblin Hall, bumping our way along a road seemingly composed more of holes than earth, was not enough to deflate me, and though our conversation was curtailed to a degree by the waking presence of Sherlock Holmes, still I think Miss Rhodes felt similarly buoyed. The day was bright and the air clean and sharp, and I was minded to remark that it was good to be alive.

'It is certainly agreeable to be in the countryside for a while,' said Holmes with more feeling than was his wont. He was convinced that the combination of the numeric code that ranked the paintings, and the name 'Aquinas' hidden in the first, would prove enough to decipher the whole puzzle.

I hoped he was right. The past weeks had been grim indeed, our path littered with the dead, and Holmes a target for the Albino's deadly attacks. The sole bright spot had been my meeting with Miss Rhodes, and I was keener than usual for the case to be brought to a satisfactory conclusion, so that we might perhaps get to know one another better. Of course, I said none of this, but simply nodded in agreement and settled myself more comfortably in my seat as the cab pulled up in front of the Hall.

At first, I thought Willoughby Frogmorton would deny us entry. Holmes had asked Miss Rhodes to hang back while we knocked at the door, ostensibly to hold the cab while we made sure there was someone at home. The truth of the matter was made plain as soon as Frogmorton attempted to close the door in our faces.

Holmes put a foot out to block the closure, while at the same time beckoning to the cab driver, who had parked a little way down the drive. At this signal, he brought the carriage right up to the door, and Miss Rhodes stepped out. The change in Frogmorton was immediate. Where before he had claimed that our presence was likely to endanger his marriage, now he threw open the door and hurried us inside.

'Blast you, Holmes,' he snarled as soon as the door was closed. 'My wife, thank God, is not at home, but even so – what possessed you to bring *her* here?'

It was all I could do not to knock the man down. Miss Rhodes coloured, close to tears, and I had already taken a step towards Frogmorton, my fist clenched, when Holmes spoke.

'One more word from you, Mr Frogmorton, and I suspect that my associate will do you a bodily injury.'

Our host was at once apologetic. 'I'm sorry... I did not mean... You must understand... my wife...'

I recalled his unctuous voice with loathing, and wondered anew what Miss Rhodes could ever have seen in him. With his oiled hair and silk cravat he was the epitome of the louche wastrel. Perhaps that was the attraction for an innocent young lady? The thought discomfited me greatly, and I pushed it to one side.

'Miss Rhodes accompanied Dr Watson and myself for two reasons, Frogmorton,' Holmes frowned. 'First, in order to place pressure on you to allow us entry, if needed. And secondly, because she is an art expert with intimate knowledge of Hamblin Hall, its art and its library. I have reason to believe that a book in that very library may be a vital component in the solution to the case I am currently working on.'

Throughout this exchange, Frogmorton's eyes had never left Miss Rhodes's. I was reminded of the snakes I had seen in Afghanistan, lying lazily in the sun, almost indistinguishable from the sand that surrounded them, sizing up their prey and calculating the best moment to strike. I broke the spell by stepping between them, and asking Miss Rhodes if she cared to lead the way to the library, while the puzzled cab driver unloaded our collection of paintings.

Frogmorton proved to know more about the contents of the library than he had the art on the walls and, once he realised that we had no intention of betraying him to his wife, settled down enough to slip once more into the attitude of false bonhomie with which he had greeted us on our initial visit.

'Now, gentlemen, what can I do for you? You mentioned a vital book?'

For all his newfound amity, he had directed his question squarely at Holmes and me, carefully ignoring Miss Rhodes, though whether his motivation was guilt or fear was impossible to say. Whatever the cause, he frowned his displeasure when she answered.

'Mr Holmes and Dr Watson wish to examine any copies of the works of Thomas Aquinas that might be held in the library,' she said. Her voice, though quiet, was clear and steady, but a flicker of revulsion crossed her face as she spoke, and I could tell that the scales had fallen from her eyes with respect to Willoughby Frogmorton.

Again, Frogmorton addressed himself to Holmes. 'Aquinas, you say? There's a collection of sixteenth-century religious volumes just over here.' He gestured to a crowded shelf towards the rear of the room. 'It's a handsome set, but incomplete, so I've never been able to sell it.'

Holmes hurried over to the shelf, with Miss Rhodes and I following close behind. Frogmorton hung back, however, then disappeared through the library door without another word. I admit I was not sorry to see him go.

There were perhaps a dozen books, each bound in brown leather, and stamped with a title and a roman numeral in gold leaf on the spine and front cover. As I ran a finger quickly along the row, it was clear to me that Frogmorton had told the truth. The collection as published had obviously consisted of at least twenty volumes, but this library contained only the first eight, and numbers seventeen to twenty. I cast a quizzical look at Holmes, unsure where to begin and loath to do any damage to the books, but he had no such qualms and began pulling them out, throwing them onto a nearby table. More cautiously, Miss Rhodes and I collected what remained and placed them carefully beside the others.

'Any more?' Holmes asked the room in general. He walked a brisk circuit of the library, examining the contents of each shelf quickly but carefully until he returned to the spot from which he had started, standing directly in front of us. He rubbed his hands together with pleasure. 'Shall we see what we can discover in these dusty tomes?' he asked, but the question was a rhetorical one, for he was already flipping through the thick pages of the first book. I chose another and Miss Rhodes the next, and we sat and examined every page with an intensity which belied the fact that we had no real idea what we were looking for.

The cab driver brought the artworks into the library, then left us to our search. An hour passed, then a second, but we had made no progress.

Outside the sun was setting, bathing our surroundings in a pearl wash which delighted Miss Rhodes, though I believe it was only Holmes's unfailing courtesy towards the fairer sex that prevented him from asking her to leave when she loudly declared her love of the countryside. Eager to avoid any disagreement, I asked whether she cared to take a stroll round the grounds with me. I cannot deny the warmth of feeling I experienced when she smiled her consent and took my arm. We left Holmes holding a book up to the gas light with a scowl on his face. I doubt he realised we were gone.

Walking across the lawn, warm from the sunny day just ending, we talked about everything that came to mind, though not about the treasure we sought. She told me more about her early life as the daughter of an army doctor, and in return I recounted some tales of my younger days. Perhaps it was the pleasure that I felt in her company, or the still perfection of the evening, but for whatever reason, I allowed myself to become distracted and so was not prepared when, coming round the east side of the house, she suddenly cried out and pointed to a stand of trees on the opposite side of the lawn.

For a moment I was unsure of her meaning, before the shifting evening light briefly illuminated a small, dark shape scuttling from the shade of one tree to another, the unmistakable silhouette of a man against the evening sky. It was impossible to discern any facial features at such a distance and in such poor light, but when I shouted a hallo, one of the figures waved a hand in friendly greeting.

'Some sort of farm gang, I expect,' I remarked to Miss Rhodes as we turned the corner. 'I imagine the estate requires a reasonable amount of upkeep.'

She seemed unconvinced. 'I don't recall gangs of men working so late when last I stayed at the Hall,' she said uncertainly. 'But perhaps things have changed since then.'

I was keen that she should not dwell on her previous visit and so suggested we return to the Hall, for there was a growing chill in the air, and I feared she would catch cold. She agreed happily, and so we strolled slowly back to the house, for all the world like two people without a care. Appearances, as I long ago learned, can be deceiving.

The instant we were inside we hurried to the library, where Holmes had not moved from his seat. As we entered and pulled the door shut behind us, he looked up.

'Watson, take a look at this,' he cried, jubilantly. 'Miss Rhodes, too.'

He had singled out a slim volume of Aquinas's writings and spread it out on the table. Like the others we had examined, this was a glorious leather-bound book, debossed with gold leaf.

'This little volume was tucked away at the back of the shelf, Watson,' he said. 'Observe the inscription!'

He handed me the book already open at the correct place. In an ornate hand someone had written 'Horace Hamblin, 14th November 1647'.

'I'm sorry, Holmes,' I said, conscious that again I was unable to match Holmes's brilliance, and more conscious still that Miss Rhodes was again witnessing my intellectual failure, 'but wonderful though this discovery may seem to you, it hardly strikes me as terribly unusual that a library that once belonged to Horace Hamblin should contain a book which at one point also belonged to him.'

'Look at the date, Watson–' Holmes began, but got no further before Miss Rhodes excitedly interrupted. 'The fourteenth of November! The day before Hamblin was killed!'

'Well done, Miss Rhodes,' Holmes exclaimed. 'I hope that spending time in your company sharpens Watson's wits to a similar degree.' He turned to me, with a small smile on his lips to demonstrate that he was speaking in jest. 'You see, Watson, Hamblin died on the following day, and if you glance at the other books in the series, you will note that none of them have a similar date on their flyleaves. There is significance in this marking.'

'Still,' I said, unwilling to cede the point too readily, 'a name and date in a book do not bring us any closer to solving the riddle, do they?'

'Ignore the inscription then, Watson,' said Holmes, curtly. 'Look below that, instead.' He stabbed a long finger at the bottom of the page, where someone had scribbled a string of nonsense letters. I had noticed but dismissed them before, but now I saw that Holmes had copied the letters down on a clean sheet of paper:

WXYUQFSGAGTSRMZ

'You believe there is some meaning in this jumble?' I asked.

'Without doubt. I believe this is a Vigenère cipher encryption, a method by which a phrase can be encoded and then only translated by means of a key, which is made up of the repetition of another word or phrase entirely, mapped against a third set of letters. The trick is to find the key to this, as you rightly say, jumble. Unfortunately, at the moment we do not have that key or any idea how to find it.'

He sighed heavily, the temporary elation of discovery already dissipating.

I cast about for some crumb with which to comfort him. 'The key must be in the paintings, you said so yourself. All we need do is winkle it out. Give me a hand moving them. Perhaps if they are arranged in a row, so that you can study them in order, something may become apparent.'

I was not confident, but having contributed so little to date, and with no other potential action presenting itself, it was the best I could suggest. Holmes and I propped each painting against the back wall, then stood back and examined them.

Nothing resembling a key phrase was evident. Each painting remained stubbornly as it had always been, and none provided any fresh insight.

At that moment, Frogmorton appeared in the library doorway. The expression on his face was a mixture of sheepish embarrassment and defiant annoyance but when he spoke he appeared sincere enough. 'My wife is away until the weekend so I suppose it does no harm to have you people rummaging around. Towards the end of Jessica's previous stay, Alexandra became displeased by our friendship, but since there's not a soul on the estate in her absence bar myself, I suppose the odds of her finding out are pretty long. Anyway, I came to ask if you'd care for refreshments. Tea and whatnot, or something stiffer if you'd prefer?'

Holmes waved the offer away impatiently and returned to his work. He had written the nonsensical letter series from Aquinas's book in large letters on a sheet of paper, and was scribbling what appeared to be random words underneath – 'KING', 'STUART', 'HAMBLIN' – repeating each word until the number of letters in each row matched, before scoring them out in obvious irritation. The current iteration read:

WXYUQFSGAGTSRMZ
CHARLESCHARLESC

With a snarl he crumpled the paper into a ball and threw it across the room.

'This is pure guesswork!' he complained. 'I am no better than a third-rate mesmerist in a fleapit of a theatre, or a Scotland Yard detective at the scene of a murder! "CHARLES" is too obvious a key; Hamblin would have chosen something more complex than that which could be guessed by a mere child!'

I have known Sherlock Holmes for many years, and in many moods, and as he looked up at me, I recognised the driven, obsessive demeanour which had, on more than one occasion in the past, presaged a period of intense study, devoid of rest or sustenance, culminating in the solution to some almost intractable conundrum. There was nothing I could do on such occasions but stand by, ready to provide whatever service Holmes required. In the meantime, I accepted Frogmorton's offer of tea, as did Miss Rhodes. There was no point in being thirsty while we waited for Holmes to uncover some new avenue to explore.

'I should perhaps offer to help Mr Frogmorton, since he has no servants at present,' Miss Rhodes suggested, innocently. I was on the verge of insisting she stay in the library while *I* went to help, when the significance of her words struck home.

'He said he was the only person on the entire estate, didn't he?' I asked the room in general. Miss Rhodes nodded her agreement a bare second before I saw the same look cross her face as, I assumed, had very recently crossed my own.

'He did,' she said, quietly. 'But if that is the case, then who waved to us from the copse of trees in the grounds?'

The conclusion was inescapable. Whoever had been following us throughout our investigations, whoever had tried to run Holmes down, and shot at us through the windows of Baker Street, whoever had killed Mr and Mrs Boggs, and murdered Miss Eugenie Marr, whoever *they* were, they were outside Hamblin Hall right now.

'Holmes!' I cried in horror. 'The Albino has men in the grounds!' I hurried to explain about the 'servants' in the trees, but Holmes was preoccupied, still mired in the problem of the cipher, and dismissive of anything that did not immediately touch upon that puzzle.

'That is fascinating, but worthless, information,' he remarked with ill grace. 'We could not have hoped to keep ahead of them forever, Watson, and at least here we are behind good thick walls.

Lestrade will be with us shortly and, if I am correct in some recent conclusions of mine, we have less to worry about from the Albino than we at one point believed. In the meantime, perhaps I can return to the puzzle of the paintings? I am so close that I can taste it, Watson. It is as though Horace Hamblin is speaking to me across the centuries.'

I looked at my friend, quizzically. 'That may make sense to you, Holmes, but I admit it leaves me baffled. Would you care to explain – and quickly, if possible? For all your talk of good thick walls, we do not know the strength of the Albino's forces nor their intentions, and in the event of an attack I would prefer Miss Rhodes at least to be far from here.' Holmes made a vague noise of agreement, but it was clear his mind was elsewhere, and I would need to be more forceful if I were to get through to him. 'Holmes, the Albino could be at the door any second. We must either create a defensive barrier, or leave while we can!'

As though he had been summoned by my words, the door to the library slowly opened and a dark figure stepped through. It was obviously not the Albino, however, though it was clear that Holmes recognised him.

The newcomer was an average young man in every respect. Almost boyish in appearance, he was approximately five foot eight inches tall, clean shaven, with short brown hair. He wore a plain brown suit with an open collar, and a light overcoat, as befitted the season. The only peculiar things about him were his eyes, which were so dark as to appear violet. Something about that fact nagged at me for a moment, before I realised that the pistol he held was pointed in the direction of Miss Rhodes, who stood closest to the entrance. I slid my hand into my pocket and wrapped my fingers round my revolver, but before I could move, Holmes stepped forward.

'Major Conway,' he said evenly. 'Why, I thought you were dead –
or returned to Ireland, at the very least.'

Seventeen

❧

My own reaction was far less sanguine. 'If you intend to harm Miss Rhodes in any way–' I began, but Conway interrupted before I could complete the thought.

'I am not in the habit of assaulting defenceless women, Dr Watson.' He appeared offended by the suggestion, in fact, and moved his gun around to cover Holmes and me.

With a twitch of the barrel Conway indicated that he desired us to sit. The most minute shake of the head from Holmes convinced me to leave my own revolver in my pocket, and thus we gave no trouble to the Major as we seated ourselves.

Holmes's disappointment with himself was plain to see. 'You have been working for the Albino all along, of course,' he sighed, reaching inside his jacket for his cigarettes. He offered both the Major and myself the case, then lit one for himself. 'I should have wondered at the ease with which I was embraced by the Brotherhood, should I not? An error of judgement on my part.'

Conway spoke for the first time. 'Come, come, Mr Holmes. Don't be so hard on yourself,' he said, in a voice entirely bereft of an Irish lilt, but with more than a hint of the American. 'I had no concept of your identity when we first met, though I was made aware of your true name after your abortive, if entertaining, self-assassination attempt. I myself was relatively newly inserted into the republican movement, truth be told, and was concerned enough for my own concealment, without worrying about yours.'

He smiled agreeably, and blew a large, thick smoke ring towards the ceiling. 'My role was simply to find out what the Brotherhood was up to, to ascertain whether the assault on the Portrait Gallery was in any way linked to our own search for England's Treasure and to act accordingly. Having discovered it was simply another of that group's foolish indulgences I moved on to pastures new, as it were.'

'But not before removing several of the more prominent republicans from the field of play,' Holmes replied. 'The Metropolitan Police have you to thank for the deaths in Streatham, I presume?' Major Conway nodded, and Homes continued. 'I will not weep for those particular deaths, I admit.'

A frown crossed the Major's face and I think he would have spoken, but Holmes was in full spate by now, and nothing short of a revolver shot would have silenced him.

'But what have you been doing since then? Where have you been, Major? A man such as yourself is not a natural recluse, but neither do I imagine yours is a face currently welcome in many of the capital's public houses.'

'No,' Conway replied with a laugh. 'Fair to say it's not. But I've kept myself busy, Mr Holmes, don't you worry. I've been *information gathering*, you might call it. Checking out the lay of the land, as it were, on behalf of my employer.'

'Does he trust you so much then?'

'He flatters me with his confidence, yes. 'Course, it helps that I saved his life only a few days ago. You recall the vault beneath the Old Bailey, and the eager constable who knocked both yourself and the good Doctor to the ground as you prepared to shoot our mutual acquaintance?'

'That was you? I admit I had not made the connection. I should have recognised you in Limehouse, however. I almost did, in fact. You *were* the beggar by the riverside, were you not?'

'I was. My task recently has been keeping an eye on the two of you, and the circumstances lent themselves to my saving the day.' He grinned hugely. 'I did wonder if you had recognised me, down by the docks. I would have told you something to your benefit then, had there been an opportunity. I tried to get Dr Watson's attention just after, but his mind was elsewhere. Yes, sir, I've been following you around London for days, keeping an eye out for danger... but you have me talking away, when I intended by now to be listening to what you gentlemen have to say.'

As Conway spoke, Holmes's face twisted into a scowl. 'We will reveal nothing before your principal arrives, Major.'

It was clear that Holmes was stalling for time. I knew my part of old in such an undertaking. 'Holmes! Enough!' I said with all the passion I could muster. 'You cannot seriously be considering helping these people! This is the man who tried to crush you beneath a hansom cab, who attempted to kill you with a crossbow in your own sitting room, and who – in case you have forgotten – murdered Miss Marr and Mrs Boggs! For God's sake, his forces are outside this building as we speak! Will you make polite conversation with the representative of the very man who may at any moment order an armed attack on us?'

Holmes looked around for an ashtray and, seeing none, walked over to the window and flicked what remained of his cigarette outside. 'Really, Watson, you should know better than that,' he said as he strolled back to his chair. 'If one of the Albino's men could so effortlessly walk into this library and confront us with a gun, do you imagine that they would bother with a full-scale attack? From the manner in which Major Conway was able to immediately find the library, I would further hazard that he has been here before – or at least scouted the Hall out at some point – and so knows that a frontal assault is entirely unnecessary. There are not even servants enough to keep watch on the many entrances, never mind defend the place from a concerted attack.'

'That's all very well, Holmes,' I replied with what I hoped was a convincing degree of anger, 'but even if it was not Conway himself who attempted to kill you, it was his master, or another of his men.'

'Again, I would say not. You heard the good Major. He is not in the habit of murdering innocent, defenceless women. I believe that Miss Eugenie Marr, at least, would count as such a person.'

'And you believe him?' I asked, making no attempt to keep the growing incredulity from my voice. I understood that Holmes desired as much delay as we could create, but I was becoming confused as to what was bluster and tactics, and what was Holmes's genuine thoughts on the subject of the Albino.

'I do. I would go further, in fact. I am now persuaded that the Albino and his men have played little part in the more unpleasant aspects of this case. The presence of Major Conway was final proof that there is another, darker force at work, one determined to obtain England's Treasure, whatever the cost. That force, I am convinced, operated under the leadership of the Lord of Strange Deaths.'

As he spoke he kept his eyes keenly fixed on Major Conway. He need not have worried. Even a sidelong glance, such as I gave the Major in the shocked moments following Holmes's dramatic announcement, was enough to establish that he knew and despised the name of the Chinese politician we had met the previous week.

'Bravo, Mr Holmes!' said Conway, slowly clapping his hands as he spoke. The tone he employed appeared sincerely congratulatory, with a hint of smug self-satisfaction, as if he himself had made some great discovery, and not Holmes. 'I wondered how much you had figured out. Yes, sir,' he continued, 'the Lord of Strange Deaths has proven a thorn in the flesh of my employer in recent months. It's not for me to go into details of that, but would you mind if I asked how you figured it out? I know for a fact that Scotland Yard never have, and it would pass the time while we wait for my employer.'

Holmes pushed himself to his feet and, pacing up and down in front of the bookshelves, set out his thoughts.

'I have first to admit that I have made several mistakes during the course of this investigation. I dismissed the Brotherhood of Ireland too quickly, without considering the curious nature of their apparent leader. It is clear now that, although the involvement of the Brotherhood itself was tangential at best to the question of England's Treasure, it would have served us well to wonder whether anyone else was similarly investigating the level of their knowledge, given their activities at the National Portrait Gallery, unconnected as it proved to be.

'I can claim no credit for this deduction.' He allowed a thin smile to play briefly on his lips. 'So much, then, for the republicans.

'But, conversely, I was far too ready to accept that the mysterious Albino was the villain of the piece. Lestrade first mentioned him in relation to England's Treasure and from there every particle of evidence appeared to point directly at his guilt. One of his men, Elias Boggs, murdered Miss Eugenie Marr, and we ourselves saw him order Boggs's death in his turn. And as a group, you were attempting to bring together the collection of paintings that is the key to the Treasure, whatever it may be. This much is undisputed fact.

'There is an odour of blood about your employer, Major, and that was the scent we followed, for better or worse. Perhaps I am being too hard on myself. If the evidence of our eyes under the Old Bailey is to be accepted, the death of Miss Marr was repugnant to your employer, but even so, she would not have died but for his actions. There is certainly guilt enough to go around. But whatever the truth in that particular respect, Dr Watson and I witnessed Boggs's death and that, combined with immediately thereafter discovering the slaughtered body of Mrs Boggs, hardened our belief that the Albino's hand lay behind *all* the crimes relating to the Treasure. At the start of this affair I was nearly run over by a hansom cab driver who kept his face hidden. Taking later developments into account, I concluded that an albino was the most likely person to require such concealment.'

'I can assure you, Mr Holmes, that my employer is not given to driving a hansom cab around London, never mind using one to trample a man in the street.' To my surprise, Conway seemed more amused than guilty. Perhaps it was my long exposure to an eccentric companion, but I found it increasingly difficult to dislike him.

Holmes shrugged. 'I realised later, however, that an albino is not the only person who might wish to hide his face, lest he be too easily recognised. A Chinaman, too, would not wish to be too readily identified. That was my first inkling that the Lord was involved.'

'And after that? My employer has a saying he's fond of: a new theory does not gain traction unless considerable evidence is found to strengthen its case.'

Holmes cocked his head to one side, quizzically. 'Your employer is not wrong, Major Conway. Very well then. There were two major points of interest, as well as many more minor, or circumstantial, considerations.

'First, the savagery of the attack on Mrs Boggs and the destruction of her home did not match my observations of your group beneath the Old Bailey. Either you or your principal spared Boggs's guards, even though it would have been more expedient to kill them. And yes, the fate to which you consigned Mr Boggs was a malodorous one, but a relatively quick death nonetheless, and one with a purpose, designed to send a specific message. There was calculation of cause and effect there: calculation leavened by mercy of a sort that was utterly missing from the unnecessarily brutal slaying of Mrs Boggs. Considering that, I was reminded of something else, something the Lord of Strange Deaths said to me only a few days ago: that in China, when a man is executed, a relative is often also killed. The brutality of that killing I saw first-hand in Limehouse.

'Incidentally, Major, I wonder if you might clear something up for my own satisfaction? You never attempted to rob a family by the name of Rudge recently, did you? And your current "gang" contains no one of Oriental extraction, does it? And has at no point recently contained such a person? No? I thought not.' He turned to me, shaking his head. 'You see, Watson, the Chinese who committed suicide while returning the second forgery to the National Portrait Gallery was no traitor to the Lord, after all. That villain murdered the man's family simply to further incriminate the Albino. That is a particularly advanced form of evil, indeed.'

'And the Rudges?' I asked curiously.

'Again, the behaviour of those involved was of a piece with the murders of the two ladies. Men already tied up badly beaten by the intruders, a policeman nearly killed by one of the gang – and a single hair left behind. Not the white hair of the Albino, either, or the brown of Mrs Rudge, but a long, jet-black one, such as you may recall is common amongst the Chinese population of Limehouse.'

Conway had pulled out a scrap of paper and a pencil and was busily taking notes as Holmes spoke. Holmes politely waited for him to finish before he continued. 'And then there was the second attempt on my own life. Someone used a crossbow against me, firing through the window of my rooms in Baker Street. I briefly considered that the choice of weapon was predicated upon a preference for silence. But why should a gang otherwise willing to snatch their prey from within the Old Bailey itself and then execute him on the premises, care a jot for a little sound and fury? It made no sense. Far more likely that there was another explanation.

'The simplest solution was that there was another group with an interest in my investigation into England's Treasure. The leap from there to the realisation that the Lord of Strange Deaths was the mastermind was a lengthy one, admittedly, hence my failure to mention it to my friend Watson here. I was not absolutely certain until you appeared in the doorway just now, but I began to suspect a second hand at play after the discovery of Mrs Boggs's body.'

He turned his full attention on Conway. 'Perhaps we could dispense with the gun, Major? I give you my word that we will make no attempt to escape before we meet your employer, though given that he is standing outside that door, the length of time involved is likely to be short.'

Conway looked from Holmes to the gun he held and to the closed door, then, with a smile, placed it on a table.

'A wavering shadow at the base of the door, combined with the firm belief that he would want to know what was said at first hand,' Holmes said, though Conway had asked no question. 'Perhaps you should invite him in?'

There was no need, however. The door creaked open, framing

the Albino in the dying light coming through the low windows in the entrance hall.

He was certainly a distinctive figure, now that we could see him in a clearer light than that beneath the Bailey. His hair was cut just above his shoulders and was of the purest white, and his eyes, which he blinked somewhat more than the average man, were a pale pink colour. He stood around six foot tall, with broad shoulders and strong legs, the whole perfectly contained in immaculate evening dress, which, it seemed, he habitually wore. In his hands he held a freshly brushed top hat and a gold-topped cane, both of which he now laid down upon a nearby shelf.

'Good evening, gentlemen,' he said. His soft tone reminded me again of our previous meeting, when he had quietly ordered Boggs thrown to a terrible and squalid death. I took a step in front of Miss Rhodes, and slipped my hand into my jacket pocket again. Holmes might be willing to negotiate with the man, but I was less trusting.

'Good evening, Mr–?' Holmes replied on our behalf, but the Albino ignored the question as though it had never been asked.

'I am delighted to make your acquaintance, Mr Holmes. And you, Dr Watson – and the lovely Miss Rhodes, of course. Please make yourselves comfortable while we talk.'

If Conway was the bluff, honest American to the life, then the Albino was the epitome of the decadent European nobleman, then prevalent in the society columns of the popular press. Even allowing for his lack of pigment he exuded an air of artificial weariness and a contrived sensuality, which his soft, almost feminine speech did nothing to improve.

'Major Conway,' he murmured, 'would you be so kind as to obtain refreshments for us all? It has been a busy day and I would appreciate a little tea.'

He pressed his head close to Conway's as he passed, and the two men exchanged whispered words that we could not make out.

Finally the Major left to make arrangements, and the Albino seated himself, pulled out the golden cigarette case we had seen at the Bailey, and lit one of his small cigarettes. I recognised the scent of opium immediately and so, I was sure, would Holmes. Perhaps it would give us an advantage.

Once he had the cigarette lit, the Albino continued. 'I have long been an admirer of the manner in which you have winnowed out the lesser lights amongst the English criminal fraternity, Mr Holmes. Your removal of that vicious madman, Moran, was particularly welcome, I must say, as his attempts on my own life, while fruitless, had begun to prove... irritating. And I do so hate irritation.'

While the man spoke, I looked over at Holmes. He sat unblinking in his chair, with his chin resting lightly on his hand and his eyes never once leaving the Albino. What thoughts were going through his head at that moment I could not have said, but the sense of a hunter finally scenting his prey was unmistakable. The Albino for his part seemed entirely at ease. His courtesy and affability were not what I had expected, but I knew enough about criminals as a class to know that appearances could be deceiving.

I felt Miss Rhodes slip her hand into mine as I observed my friend, and reminded myself that while Holmes might revel in such confrontations, at least one person in this room was terrified. I squeezed her hand quickly, for comfort, and resumed my study of the Albino.

His eyes were half closed as he went on, in a voice that at times fell so quiet as to verge on the inaudible. That aside, there was no sign that the drug had any effect on him. A habitual user, then. 'I wonder, Mr Holmes,' he said, 'how much you have managed to discover. Has

that huge mind of yours worked everything out yet? I do hope that it
has. You see, I know everything but the solution – and while I flatter
myself that I am no idiot, it would be ridiculous to imagine that I am
as capable of problem-solving as the great Sherlock Holmes. Major
Conway says that you were willing to exchange our information
for your own, but that you hesitated to be the first to speak? Quite
understandable. You had no reason to trust me, after all.

'I would like to change that, if possible, Mr Holmes. I would like
to gain your trust, if I can.'

Holmes's tone was doubtful. 'How do you intend to do that, Mr…
I'm sorry, how should we address you? It seems absurd to refer to
you as Mr Albino.'

The Albino smiled in acknowledgement. 'Zenith will suffice. It is
a name I have used before.'

'Very well then. How do you intend to do that, Mr Zenith?'

'Just Zenith,' said the Albino. 'And I hope to gain your trust by
demonstrating that I am not the bogeyman of this tale, and never
have been. You are perhaps aware of something of my alleged past?
Amongst the police forces of six countries it is rumoured that I am
a disgraced prince, the reprobate scion of a minor European royal
family.' He raised his hand to his brow in mock salute. 'I am guilty
as charged, Mr Holmes. A *very* minor royal family, it is true, but
even so…'

His voice trailed off into silence. I wondered if it were the effect
of the drug, but the pause was brief and he quickly resumed his tale.

'In any case, I am no longer recognised by my family, who are
ashamed of the life I have chosen, and of the type of man I am.
They are within their rights, by their lights. I am a thief and a killer,
after all, a drug user and a sybarite. But still, I retain many of my old
allegiances. I am no Fabian, no friend to the working man. No "Robin

Hood". I find the poor rather tiresome, if truth be told. I find most things tiresome, in the end. But I have always believed in loyalty.'

He shrugged. 'You will appreciate, then, that when I was made aware of a certain rumour – one which made mention of another Royal family, a family to whom I am distantly related – I felt it my duty to act, even though my own family had rejected me.'

'England's Treasure,' said Holmes quietly. It was not a question.

'Yes, England's Treasure. Once I was made aware of its existence, if not its substance, I investigated more fully, and discovered a link to a group of obscure paintings. Unfortunately, other parties also became interested, and there has been some recent unpleasantness as a result of our mutual interest.'

'The headless and limbless corpse in Brook Street,' Holmes muttered to himself.

'Amongst others,' Zenith agreed. 'I have been working for the last few months to stay ahead of these other parties, and to make sense of a most intriguing puzzle.'

'One you have been unable to crack. The fact that you have not killed us already would argue not.'

Zenith's heavy-lidded eyes flickered once at that, then were still again. 'I'm pleased to see that you have not mistaken any previous mercy on my part for weakness, Mr Holmes. I do not destroy without cause, and I endeavour never to kill the innocent or the defenceless. But I consider you neither of those things, and I will not hesitate to kill you if that action would serve my needs best.' He flicked an invisible speck of dust from his immaculate trousers, and continued with a new hint of steel in his voice. 'I had hoped to come to bring this matter to a satisfactory conclusion without your assistance… but I am a realist above all, and now I am delighted that I had Conway keep you alive. I would like you to consult for me, Mr Holmes.'

Eighteen

The room fell completely silent as we each considered Zenith's request. For myself, I knew that Holmes would never agree to work for the Albino.

I was not wrong.

'That is unfortunate,' said Holmes, finally. 'I am not in the habit of working for criminals, no matter how charming they may be. Besides, it would be folly on my part to give anyone access to an object about which I know so little.'

Zenith took Holmes's rejection calmly enough. 'That is your final word, Mr Holmes?' he asked.

Holmes nodded.

'We are at an impasse then. I am unable to discover England's Treasure without your help, and if you will not help then you are of no use to me, and potentially could identify me to the police. I fear that your removal will be the only option left open to me if I cannot persuade you to co-operate.'

'I assure you that there is nothing you can say or do which would make me help you,' said Holmes.

Zenith's response was as short and direct as it was repulsive. 'What if I were to threaten to kill Miss Rhodes?'

'How dare you suggest—' I ignored both Miss Rhodes's gentle tug on my arm, and Holmes's more robust attempts to quieten me, as I leapt to my feet. 'Is this the way a prince of royal blood behaves? Like a coward who would threaten a lady!'

I pride myself that I am not a slave to my emotions, whatever Holmes may occasionally claim, but Zenith's words had sickened me to the core. I took a step forward, reaching into my coat pocket as I did so. But my fingers had no more than brushed the metal of my revolver, when Zenith brought me up short.

'Please do not do anything unfortunate, Dr Watson. I hope to form a temporary alliance with Mr Holmes, and your death at my hand would render that prospect remote.'

From nowhere he had conjured a small but deadly-looking pistol, which he held pointed directly at my heart. The languidly complacent drug fiend of a moment before had been replaced with an active intellect and a steady hand, and I was in no doubt that he would kill me if he had to.

As I stood there indecisively, Holmes's voice cut in from behind me. 'Sit down, Watson, there's a good chap,' he said. 'Zenith will do nothing to harm Miss Rhodes.'

Major Conway chose that moment to re-enter the room, bearing a tray that he laid down beside us. Holmes grimaced at the interruption, but waited with reasonably good grace while drinks were poured by Zenith and handed round by his lieutenant. If anyone else was conscious of the incongruity of such civilised activities in so tense a situation, they did not mention it.

Zenith broke the silence after a minute or so. 'Mr Holmes is correct. Of course I would never harm the lady. But I might well hurt you a good deal if needs be, Dr Watson.'

Now it was Holmes's turn to leap to remonstrate with our captor. 'Enough of this, Zenith. I do not believe a civilised man such as you claim to be would ever resort to torture.'

Zenith looked at each of us, then gave a nod to Conway, who came round behind me and, slipping his hand into my pocket, extracted my revolver. 'Sit down, please,' he said.

I sat, but Holmes remained standing. 'Sit down, Mr Holmes,' Zenith repeated, but more forcefully, with none of the languid air, which I suspected he exaggerated for effect. Holmes did not move, but continued to stare down at him.

'Very well,' Zenith said, shaking his head as though disappointed in Holmes's reaction. 'Major Conway, please be so good as to shoot Dr Watson through one kneecap.'

I had no time to react. Conway quickly grabbed the back of my head and pushed me forward so that I stumbled and fell to my knees. I had just enough time to look up and see Zenith covering Holmes and Miss Rhodes with his pistol before I felt the hard metal of my own confiscated revolver pressed down against the back of my left knee. In the instant before Conway pulled the trigger I tensed my muscles and resolved not to give Zenith the satisfaction of crying out.

'Stop!' Holmes's shout echoed off the walls of the library. 'Let me see the letter from Horace Hamblin and it may be that I can point you in the direction of the Treasure.'

I felt rather than saw Conway look up at Zenith, then heard the soft click as he eased the hammer back on the revolver and replaced it in his pocket.

'Nothing personal, Doctor,' he said, as he helped me to my feet. I sat down heavily, doing my level best to control a slight tremor in my hands. I have faced battle before, but the speed of execution and the business-like manner of Conway's actions had left me quite shaken. Miss Rhodes again took my hand. It was enough that she did so. I sat up straighter and glanced up at Holmes, who remained standing before us.

Zenith, meanwhile, was also staring at Holmes. 'Letter?' he asked. 'What makes you think that the information I have was received in the form of a letter?'

Holmes's impatience was palpable. 'While we have been speaking, you have three times moved your hand towards your pocket as though to retrieve some item, then stopped. A letter is the most likely such item.

'Additionally, how else would you know of the Treasure at all? A "rumour" that has survived the centuries intact, and which details six specific paintings that might lead to great wealth, but no other criminal has heard of or thought to come after in all that time? Do not insult my intelligence, Zenith.

'There is obviously a letter, from Hamblin himself, I'd wager, which has remained hidden these many years, until you laid your hands on it. It provides a starting point for any search for England's Treasure, at least, and possibly more. If you allow me to examine it, I will share any deductions I make. In return, and before I do anything, you will set Dr Watson and Miss Rhodes at liberty.'

Part of Holmes's genius, as I have remarked elsewhere, lay in his ability to act a part with utter conviction. Where I could see the concern in his eyes and the fear in the way his shoulders sagged as he awaited Zenith's reply, to the rest of the room he gave every sign of barely repressed annoyance, as of a man holding a winning hand at cards baulked in his desire to lay them down.

He did not have long to wait. 'Miss Rhodes certainly may go, for she is of no use to me as leverage for your continued co-operation. Dr Watson must stay, however.'

Holmes nodded once, briskly. 'That will have to do, I suppose,' he said, in as offhand a tone as he could manage.

Miss Rhodes made some sounds of disagreement, but I took her two hands and reminded her quietly that Holmes and I could not act with full freedom while she was present and in danger. She swallowed hard, and seemed on the verge of tears, but eventually assented, if unhappily, to be escorted to the village by two of Zenith's men. Such was the degree of sudden emotion in the air that even Holmes was affected and briefly allowed Miss Rhodes to kiss him on the cheek as she departed.

As soon as she was safely on her way, Zenith reached into his inner pocket and pulled out an envelope from which he extracted a sheet of folded foolscap, offering it silently to Holmes.

'This is obviously not the original,' Holmes said as he unfolded the paper. 'Both paper and ink are new. But the scrawled handwriting indicates that your agent copied directly from the original, and without removing it from its location.' He looked up quickly. 'There are Chinese characters in the margins. Have they been accurately copied?'

Zenith slowly crossed his legs before he replied. 'Major Conway was impressed to find you had already concluded that the Oriental savage had been searching for England's Treasure. For myself, I was slightly disappointed that it took you so long.'

'Had I known that England's Treasure had a political element, I would have deduced the Lord of Strange Deaths involvement much earlier,' Holmes responded, obviously stung by the criticism. 'As it was, I ruled him out on the basis that mere financial gain would not interest him. Another mistake, but an understandable one, I think.'

He resumed his perusal until, eager to know the letter's contents, I asked him to read it aloud.

'My apologies, Watson,' he replied, 'I should have thought to do so already. The letter is from Horace Hamblin to one Simon Jarvis.'

He held the paper out in front of him and read from it slowly and clearly.

Worthy Simon,

I hope this letter finds you in a better state than that of its sorry author, one who finds himself trapped within his own halls, counting the hours until the forces of the Devil on Earth should arrive at his doors, bearing his death along with them.

He whom I shall not name but who brings this letter to you may be trusted completely. His loyalty is perfect, as I have seen on more occasions than one over the past twelvemonth, and his words have been a constant comfort. Help him as you can to escape what was once an island of saints, my friend, for all that was once the glory of England. And remember, if it were a simple thing to love one's ruler then there would be no virtue in so doing.

I am afraid that we shall not meet again on this Earth, but will be reunited only at the feet of Our Lord, for this is a time of endings, of Revelation, and this is the final letter of the book of my life. England's Treasure is gone and lies hidden for the moment, but that you will already have guessed.

You will be pleased to know that I have kept myself busy to the last. I have improved the painting of the King which you admired, and added touches to five more, not of my hand.

After everything is over perhaps it will please you to come to the Hall and examine them in fine? I am particularly content with the flourishes I have added to the portraits of Sir James Hamilton, Queen Anne and my own grandfather, though less so with the sketch of the wise men and the miniature depicting the twin sons of Isaac, but you will be the best judge of my success, or otherwise.

Now I must go, dear Simon. A rider is in the courtyard with news, and I have some final preparations to make.

Your friend,
Horace Hamblin

Holmes slowly re-folded the letter and slipped it back into the envelope, which he placed carefully on the table. He walked to the window and stood with his back to us, hands clutching the sill, one long finger tapping against the wood. One minute passed, then a second, and still he did not move.

Nor did Zenith, I noticed. He held himself erect in his chair, sweet-smelling smoke curling from his mouth as he finished another of his drugged cigarettes. Major Conway, completing our quartet, gave every sign that he was incapable of boredom and leant against the back wall of the library, staring at Holmes's back.

At least five minutes passed in this manner then, just as Zenith began to show signs of impatience, Holmes finally spoke a single word.

'Genius!' he said.

Zenith sat forward, the cigarette dangling, forgotten, from his fingers. 'You have solved it?' he asked eagerly.

Whatever Holmes intended to say would remain a mystery however. As he turned from the window, a single shot rang out and Major Conway spun round with a cry. The smallest dark mark on his shirt leached steadily across his front in a splash of red. His eyes glazed over even as he slid down the wall until he sat, straight-backed but dead, on the carpeted floor. Even after the manhandling he had meted out to me earlier, I was sorry to see him in such a condition.

Conway had been caught by surprise and consequently had not had time to reach for his gun, but Zenith had been forewarned by his companion's death and had drawn and fired his pistol before the Major reached the ground. Cursing my confiscated revolver, I twisted in my seat to see what was happening, just in time to see a small Oriental man fire a metal crossbow bolt directly into Zenith's shoulder, and another rush forward and crash the butt of his rifle into the Albino's face. He crumpled to the floor, definitely unconscious and possibly dead.

As I have noticed occasionally happens after a flurry of violent action, the next few moments were completely silent and still. Holmes had not moved from his position by the window, and I was frozen in my seat. One Chinaman lay dead from Zenith's shot, while the other two stood on either side of the doorway.

Then, like actors suddenly exposed by the raising of the curtain, everything came to life once more.

I shook my head to clear it and hurried over to aid Zenith. Criminal or not, he needed medical help, and I was obliged by my oath to provide it. The shoulder wound was not as serious as it might have been: the bolt was long and wickedly sharp but unbarbed. It could not safely be removed in the library, but in a hospital it would present little problem. More worryingly, the blow to his face had cracked his cheekbone and probably concussed him. I whispered a quick hope that his skull had not been fractured and arranged him more comfortably where he lay.

Holmes, meanwhile, took two steps across to the fireplace and dropped the letter he held into the flames then stood, arms crossed, as if waiting for something.

The wait was momentary.

Exactly as he had in Limehouse, the Lord of Strange Deaths shuffled into the room, flanked by his giant guards. Behind him scurried a young boy holding a small, padded stool. The Lord stopped in front of Zenith and clapped his hands, prompting the stool to be placed behind him. With a groan, and the assistance of the boy, he lowered himself down to a seated position.

'Have you an answer for me, Sherlock Holmes?'

The unexpectedness of the old man's voice made it stranger than it might otherwise have been, but in any circumstances the high-pitched, scratchy sound would have excited comments. His English was, however, unaccented, if a little old-fashioned.

Holmes turned to face our latest captor. 'I do. I have unravelled the riddle of England's Treasure,' he said, but there was no triumph in his voice. Generally when Holmes had the solution to a case at his fingertips, he was a man transformed. On this occasion, however, there was no such change. If anything his back was more stooped than before, his voice more weary. 'I thought I had been so clever,' he continued, 'but I have not been a tenth as clever as Horace Hamblin. Oh, to have met the man and spoken a while! What a detective he might have made – or a criminal, for that matter!'

He suddenly stopped and looked about himself, like a man seeking direction. Not for the first time that day I was conscious of a peculiar feeling of time slowing down, creating a pocket of calm in which only we existed.

The Lord held up a skeletal hand and murmured, 'I must insist on knowing the answer, Sherlock Holmes. When last we met I told you that England's Treasure should not fall into the hands of a dishonourable man. That remains the case. This abomination—' he pointed a skeletal finger at the unconscious form of Zenith, '—will not live to see another dawn, in any case. I, however, intend to use the Treasure for a very honourable purpose indeed.'

The Lord shifted on his stool slightly, wincing as he did so. 'Since the Treaty of Nanking,' he continued, 'China has been no better than a whipped cur cowering before the boot of its master. No, do not deny it! Britain took Hong Kong from us, Sherlock Holmes, and filled the bodies of our commoners with opium. They humiliated the Emperor and burned the Summer Palaces, stole our people to build America's railways and forced their religion upon us. But no more! No more!'

A harsh, barking cough shook the old man's body as he raged. The boy at his side quickly pulled a stoppered cloth pouch from inside his jacket and handed it to his master, who sipped from it slowly until his coughing fit subsided enough for him to continue in a calmer tone.

'I do not know what England's Treasure might be, but it has been whispered in dark places that it is a priceless gift for one who wishes to see the English brought low. I am such a one, Sherlock Holmes. China *will* be avenged. Now, I ask you again, have you an answer for me?'

'Miss Rhodes should now be safely on a train back to London,' Holmes replied incongruously. 'I have instructed her to order the train stopped at the next available station – some eleven minutes from Hamblin by my measure – and once there to send an urgent telegram to Scotland Yard, informing Lestrade that if he has not left for Hamblin Hall already then he should do so with all possible haste. Fortunately, Mr Zenith was not aware that we travelled down on a Special, booked for our use alone, or that it was waiting to take us back to London again.'

He smiled coldly. The smile, I noticed, did not trouble any part of his face but his lips.

'By my reckoning you have less than an hour to vacate this place before Lestrade and his men are at the door.'

The Lord was not so easily cowed, however. 'Time enough for my purposes,' he said, returning Holmes's smile. 'More than enough, in fact. Do you disagree?'

Holmes stepped to one side and pointed down at the remains of the letter he had disposed of moments before. Already it was merely a sheet of ash in the shape of a letter and as Holmes jabbed it firmly with a poker, it collapsed in on itself and was indistinguishable from the surrounding hot ashes.

'Generally speaking I would agree with you, but on this occasion I am afraid that all the time in the world will be of no benefit to you. You see the paper burning so merrily in the fireplace? That was the map which I discovered and which Mr Zenith was about to take from me. It depicted some area of England – I did not recognise it – and contained a tiny black cross under which, I presume, the Treasure is buried. How unfortunate that I did not have chance to do more than glance at it before it was destroyed. Now nobody will ever know what England's Treasure was.'

The effect on the Lord was startling. With a strangled cry he screeched something in his native tongue to one of the bodyguards, who ran over to the fireplace, then plunged his hands into the very flames. I could smell the burning of his flesh as he attempted, with no chance of success, to scoop up what was left of the letter, but it was ash and flame alone and could not be salvaged. Perhaps most disturbingly, the man made no sound as the fire cooked his arms, and continued to attempt his impossible task until his master called him back. To nobody's surprise the giant took two steps, then tumbled forward onto his face, his entire body in shock. He lay there, twitching but still silent, while the Lord continued to rant in what I assumed was Mandarin.

Though it took several minutes, he finally calmed down enough to speak English again. 'You think you have defeated me, Sherlock Holmes?' he asked. 'Know that you have not. I have sought England's Treasure ever since one of my people purchased a book from the owner of this house and found an ancient letter inside. And yet I have never discovered what the Treasure is, nor where it can be found. If nobody may have it, then I am no worse off than I was before I heard its name, and though I may not use it to China's benefit, no other nation may use it to force England into an unfortunate alliance.'

This long speech appeared to have exhausted the old man, for he held out a hand for balance, which the boy at his side provided. He sat like that until he regained his breath, then barked a command at the two men guarding the doorway. Whatever he said, the effect was troubling.

Each man reached behind his back and pulled forward a lethal-looking crossbow, which they loaded with a bolt apiece. The Lord was helped back to his feet and the boy retrieved the padded stool, while the bowmen ensured Holmes and I made no surprising moves.

I looked over at Holmes as the Lord shuffled his way back to the door. He gave a tiny shrug in response. Were we to be allowed to leave?

At the last moment, the Lord of Strange Deaths paused then issued a final guttural command.

This time there was no doubting his intentions, for the two bowmen stepped smartly forward and prepared to fire at Holmes and me. I had a moment in which to wonder why they did not also kill Zenith, and another to realise that they would do so as soon as they had disposed of the only conscious enemies in the room, before the room exploded in a frenzy of movement.

At my side, Zenith suddenly sat upright and shot his right arm forward until it was completely straight. By means of some mechanical marvel concealed within his sleeve, a tiny Derringer pistol shot into his palm and, without a pause, he fired its single shot into the chest of the first bowman prior to lapsing into unconsciousness once more. The Chinaman staggered back on legs that suddenly would not obey him, then crumpled like a discarded linen sheet to the floor.

On the other side of the room Holmes had taken advantage of the distraction to chop the second bowman across the throat, and followed this with an uppercut as accurate as any in the boxing ring.

If Holmes had expected his opponent to drop, however, he was to be sorely disappointed.

Instead, the man took a step backwards and launched a flying kick at Holmes's head. The height reached was as astonishing as it was unexpected and Holmes only just managed to duck to one side, otherwise the fight would have been over before it properly began.

I would have watched the contest with interest, had I the time to spare, but I realised at about that time that I had been left, unarmed, to face the remaining enormous bodyguard, who pulled a wickedly sharp sword from the belt at his waist and walked slowly towards me.

I quickly knelt and snatched the crossbow from the hand of the dead bowman, but the bolt had dislodged when he fell and was nowhere to be seen. The delay was almost fatal. I barely managed to get back to my feet before a mighty blow from the bodyguard's fist sent me spinning across the room and into a set of mahogany bookcases, which shuddered with the impact as my back and head painfully connected.

I lay stunned on the floor and watched a giant set of feet walk towards me, dimly aware of the sound of Holmes still fighting as consciousness slid away from me. I feebly swung an arm in a lamentable attempt to trip my assailant but he stood just outside my reach and laughed down at me. Still, I had no intention of giving up, and swung at him again, with as much success – but the tips of my fingers as they traversed their arc brushed against something sharp and metallic.

The crossbow bolt had rolled beneath the bottom shelf and wedged itself between the base of the bookcase and the floor. If I moved another six inches closer I might extract it and I would at least have a weapon, but it might as well have been back in Baker Street for all the use it was likely to be, with the giant raising his sword high above his head, ready for the killing blow.

In retrospect, I should have wondered about Frogmorton before he saved my life by running into the room and shooting the bodyguard in the neck. Even that might not have been enough to kill a man of such prodigious size, but as he wobbled I rolled backwards, grasped the crossbow bolt in my right hand then, spinning back round and terrified I would pass out before I completed my task, stabbed the point into the giant's thigh.

The bright geyser of blood from the wound confirmed that I had hit the femoral artery. Within seconds the bodyguard had swayed backwards and within a minute he was sprawled unmoving across a table. The last thing I saw before blackness engulfed me was Holmes kneeling at my side...

Nineteen

ᛡ

There is something primal about battle which causes even the most bitter of enemies to discover common ground in its aftermath. I have seen it on the fields of Afghanistan and in English street brawls, and now I saw it in the drawing room of a Home Counties country house.

I had come to my senses to find myself sitting in an unfamiliar armchair before a roaring fire, with Holmes sitting opposite me in a high-backed wooden seat, a look of concern etched on his face, which disappeared as soon as I opened my eyes fully.

'The Lord of Strange Deaths?' I asked as soon as Holmes had handed me a glass of water and I had moistened my dry throat. My head thumped with all the force of a set of steam pistons and every thought seemed leaden and slow, but I had too many questions to consider resting.

'Gone,' Holmes replied. 'It does not sit well with me, but I was faced with the stark choice of aiding you and Zenith, or chasing after the Lord. I chose the former, and I do not believe I was mistaken. It may interest you to know, however, that when I sent Miss Rhodes to contact Scotland Yard I did mention that the men they should particularly look out for are a group of Orientals.

'Even if the police do catch him, the government will eventually be forced to release him, I imagine. He is an important man in China, and it would not be what Mycroft would call "politically expedient" to detain him.' He shrugged. 'The inconvenience and embarrassment will be marked, though.'

'He did not get what he came for?'

'No, he did not. He left with his tail between his legs, thanks to the sterling efforts of Mr Frogmorton who, for all his past failings, is quite the warrior when roused.'

'He saved my life, Holmes. Where is he? Was he injured?'

'No, he is quite well. In point of fact, he has gone down to the station to await the arrival of Lestrade and Miss Rhodes.'

I winced a little at this snippet of information, but there were more important things on my mind at that moment. My problem was articulating them through the thick fog that still clouded my thoughts.

'Zenith?'

'Present, Dr Watson!'

Zenith stepped into my eye line and gave a bow. His cloak was gone, and there was a rent in the shoulder of his coat through which I could see the white of a bandage, but otherwise he was exactly as he had first appeared in the library.

He settled himself across from me and, without further preamble, turned to Holmes and said, 'The good Doctor is now awake. It is time for you to fulfil your side of our bargain. Tell me about England's Treasure.'

I struggled to rise but a wave of dizziness pushed me back into my seat. 'What are you doing, Holmes?' I asked.

I was aware that Zenith had saved us both, in all likelihood, but even so I could not believe that Sherlock Holmes would aid a criminal to steal what might well be a national treasure.

Zenith raised the glass he was holding in a slow salute. 'You are very tenacious, Doctor, and very dutiful. But Mr Holmes and I have come to an agreement that suits us both and satisfies the honour of all involved. For myself I have no desire whatever to embarrass Her Majesty or any member of her family. But I am a curious man, when all is said and done.'

'We do not have much time before Lestrade arrives,' Holmes interjected. 'If we are to conclude our business before the Inspector claps one or both of us in irons, we should make haste.' His words did not fill me with confidence, but I allowed him to continue without interruption. 'I hope you will trust me, Watson, but perhaps if once I have fulfilled my promise to Zenith, I then tell you of his to me? Then you, with your great fund of solid common sense, can decide what the final outcome should be? Would that be acceptable?'

Shameless flattery, of course, but I have always trusted Holmes and I would have agreed to his terms without cajolement. 'Very well,' I said. 'Go ahead, Holmes.'

He gave me a peculiar look, as though he had expected more of an argument, then began to speak.

'If you will permit me to begin with a small digression, it is strange to me that a case which began with an attack on a powerful man should end in much the same way. It seems an age since Corporal O'Donnell took such a dislike to Lord Salisbury's portrait, and yet from that insignificant beginning we find ourselves now contemplating the disgrace of a king of whom O'Donnell, I suspect, would greatly have approved.'

'Disgrace?' interrupted Zenith. 'Why do you say that?'

'Surely you recognised the quote from Edmund Campion in Hamblin's letter?' Holmes replied. 'No? Very well, let me explain. Campion was a Catholic priest, martyred during the Reformation. Legend has it that, upon being found guilty of treason, he cried *"you condemn all your own ancestors, all our ancient bishops and kings, all that was once the glory of England, the island of saints."* That, I suggest, is a particularly pointed and specific epigram for Hamblin to have included, especially when combined with a lament for the difficulty of loving one's ruler.'

In response, Zenith lit one of his cigarettes, before offering the case to me. I shook my head, as did Holmes, but lit a more conventional cheroot and made myself comfortable. Holmes waited patiently then picked up the portrait of King Charles, which I now saw was one of several paintings stacked by the door. Before taking a seat beside the Albino and myself, he carefully propped the painting up before us.

'Do you have any proof of what you have just said, Mr Holmes?' Zenith asked once Holmes was settled.

Holmes shook his head. 'That England's Treasure is something which would disgrace a king? Other than the Campion quote, nothing as yet. But let me test my hypothesis, and we shall see.' He tapped a long finger on the painting in front of us. 'You recall the errant letter "E" reflected in the mirror, Watson? Of course you do; it was that, after all, which allowed us to make sense of the first part of the puzzle and so brought us here.

'Now consider this. What if that single letter was not missed by the painter at all? What if Hamblin in his brilliance intended that smudge of an E to serve a dual purpose? To signal the replacement of the word "BIBLE" with that of "AQUINAS", of course, but also to serve as the first letter of a six-letter word. The key, Watson, the key to the cipher!'

He moved the portrait of Charles to one side, exposing the next painting, that of the Magi attending Christ in his manger. 'Each painting holds a hidden letter as well as a hidden number. Once you know that it is child's play to recreate the cipher key. Do you see the way that Balthazar holds his hands?' he asked, tracing a finger across the canvas in a series of straight lines and right angles. 'An "H", wouldn't you say? His fingers could never naturally have lain in that manner and Hamblin's amendment is not quite as well done as elsewhere. But this is most definitely his work, Watson. Only *he* had the opportunity and the talent required to make such subtle changes, and the intelligence to create the necessary cipher.'

'So, do you have the complete key?' Zenith asked, a note in his voice betraying – for the first time – the excitement he felt.

Holmes flipped each painting forward as he replied. 'A perfectly straight sword held aloft... the decoration in Augustine Hamblin's ruff... the curl of Anne Boleyn's hair. The miniature of Jacob and Esau in which the second letter is hidden is in your possession, Zenith, but I think I can confidently fill in that particular gap without troubling you to fetch it. There are only so many words containing the letters E, H, I, C and S, after all.'

'Ethics!' I cried, prompting Holmes to smile indulgently.

'Indeed. Now if you will hand me that scrap of paper and my pencil, Zenith, we will see what secrets the cipher holds.'

The Albino did as he asked, prompting a period of feverish scribbling from Holmes.

While he worked, I expressed my sorrow for the loss of Major Conway. Zenith, to his credit, seemed genuinely upset by the death of his lieutenant.

'I had not worked with him long, of course, but he was extremely competent, and rather a good card player,' he said matter-of-factly, but his face amply conveyed his feelings.

Holmes, meanwhile, gave out a small cry of triumph behind me. Before I could push myself from my chair he had bounded over and clapped me heartily on the shoulder.

'I have it, Watson,' he exclaimed. 'We need to find one more book and the riddle of England's Treasure will be complete.'

He pulled a nearby table across and spread a sheet of paper out on it. As previously, the very top of the page contained the odd string of letters that we had found written in Aquinas's book, but underneath Holmes had written 'ETHICS', repeating the letters of the word until they lined up with the nonsense above. The page was, therefore, not very dissimilar to Holmes's earlier attempts. It read, in part,

WXYUQFSGAGTSRMZ
ETHICSETHICSETH

Now, though, a third line could be read beneath these two. SERMON ON TYRANTS, it said, in Holmes's distinctive script.

'A sermon about tyranny by another great Catholic thinker,' he announced triumphantly. 'Savonarola, if memory serves. An interesting choice of hiding place, would you not agree, Zenith? The title alone suggests that Hamblin was no dewy-eyed royalist who believed the King to be a perfect ruler, but was rather a pragmatist determined to help his friend, even while knowing he was in the wrong. Of course, Savonarola was executed for challenging the authority of his rightful lord, the Pope, so the sword is two-edged.'

Zenith was far too impatient to discuss such tangential matters, however. 'You believe the Treasure to be hidden inside a sermon?' he asked, querulously.

'Inside a collection of sermons, perhaps, or a biography of

Savonarola. Something of that nature. Perhaps it is a map, and I was not entirely lying to the Lord of Strange Deaths after all?' He grinned suddenly. 'Wait here, Watson, while I check for a copy in the library.'

He hurried out. Zenith, after one quick glance in my direction, followed hard on his heels, determined that Holmes would have no opportunity to play him false. I was amused by this evidence that the pact Zenith and Holmes had concocted was not founded on as solid a base as they believed. I knew that Holmes would not break his word, but for all his apparent bonhomie and brash self-confidence, Zenith was not so trusting.

The two men were back within minutes.

In his hands, Holmes held a small clothbound book. This thin volume he spread face down on the table then, with the sharp pocketknife he habitually carried, slit the cracked spine down the middle. An index finger inserted into the gash and pulled back ripped the front cover off, exposing a neatly folded sheet of paper which had been secreted inside.

Zenith reached for the document, but Holmes pulled it back quickly. 'I think it best that whatever this may be, it stays in my own hands for now. I would not care to put too much temptation your way, Zenith.'

With the merest hint of a smile, Zenith acquiesced, and retook his seat. For myself, I was considerably recovered and felt confident enough in my condition to walk over to the sideboard and pour myself a drink. Whisky in hand, I returned to my seat, and waited for Holmes's inevitable explanation.

As it turned out, Holmes had a more active role in proceedings in mind for me. As soon as I was seated and had placed my glass down, he handed me the folded paper and asked me to examine it. I half expected Zenith to snatch the document from my hand, but he remained where he was, opium smoke curling from his mouth and partially obscuring his face.

The paper was old but expensive, a buff yellow in colour, and thick and slightly coarse to the touch. I could feel the resistance of untouched centuries in the folds as I carefully levered them apart, nervous of splitting the sheet along the line of a sharp crease. In this manner I managed, over the course of several anxious minutes, to fully unfold the sheet and lay it down upon a table which Holmes carried over for the purpose.

It was neither a letter, nor a map.

Instead, laid out before us for the first time in two hundred and fifty years, was a proclamation that could turn English history on its head.

In a mixture of gloriously golden individual letters and short though ornately scripted sentences, it proclaimed that King Charles agreed to cede the throne of England to the French crown, in return for military help from King Louis the Fourteenth of France against the Parliamentarian New Model Army. The language was unequivocal – and damning.

Howsoever Princes are not bound to give Account of their Actions, but to God alone; yet, for the Satisfaction of the Minds and Affections of our loving Subjects, we have thought it good to set down thus much by Way of Declaration: that we seek to prevent war and discord in this Country most fair and that we are in this unwilling to Gamble as though with Dice with the future of our Realm.

Let no Man put about Falsehoods and Calumnies, but understand that we are no more Ignorant of such vile slanders than we are Ignorant of the Sun and Moon. We are Confident that God is at our side in all things and that Victory over the current Rebels is a Matter of Time alone, but we fear that Destruction stalks the Field and Death follows behind on his Black Horse.

So it is that in all Reason and Honour we call God to record, before whom we stand, that it is our Heart's Desire to pass that Title, of King and Defender of the Faith, to our Royal Brother, Louis of France in sincere recompense for the Gift of his Soldiery at this Time. We shall take ourselves to the Continent where we shall continue our studies and live a Life of Quiet Contemplation.

And now having laid down the Truth and Clearness of our Proceedings, all wise and discreet Men may discern, by Examination of their own Hearts, whether the Happiness of this Nation can be parallel'd, by any of our Neighbour-Countries; and if not, then to acknowledge their own Blessedness, and for the same be thankful to God, the Author of all Goodness.

There was an absolute silence in the room, broken only by the steady tick of a mantel clock.

Holmes, predictably, spoke first.

'That is not precisely what I expected,' he said. 'I had reasoned that the Treasure was not actually a trove of great size, of course, but I had assumed that it *was* something of great value, if comparatively modest dimensions. Originally, I assumed some item of personal jewellery, or a precious gemstone. This, though, is far more interesting.'

He held the document up and tilted it against the light, looking for watermarks or secret writing, I presumed.

'It is a simple enough matter to reconstruct events based on the evidence to hand. Horace Hamblin, loyal supporter and companion of King Charles the First, is visited by his royal friend at some point in the early years of the First Civil War, and is given a great secret – that Charles intends to abdicate his throne in favour of King Louis the Fourteenth of France, in the event that his army is defeated. Such was Charles's belief in the divine right of kings and his distaste for Parliament that he preferred that England fall into foreign but royal Catholic hands, rather than those of his disloyal subjects. Hamblin reacts badly to these confidences – you recall Miss Rhodes mentioned a falling out between the two men early on in the war, Watson? – but he is loyal to the core and cannot completely turn his back on his monarch.

'With that date in mind, we can confidently say that at some point between the initial disagreement and his capture by the Scots in the summer of 1646, the King had Hamblin create the proclamation we have before us, and put it aside for a time of desperate need. The paper has been folded more than once – you can see the fainter fold lines cutting across the ones you so ably undid, Watson – thus it was in Hamblin's hands for some time, I would say.

'In any case, the plan was obviously that should the time come when all looked lost, Hamblin should take the proclamation to Louis' court – or more likely his envoy in England – and exchange the Crown of England for French arms and safe passage for the King to Europe.'

'Why did he not play this card when Charles fell into the Scots' hands, or when the Scots sold him on like a slave to the English in January 1647?' Clearly Zenith had read up on English history.

'I do not like to guess, and it is impossible at this remove to say for certain, but I would say that while kept a prisoner it would not have been possible for Louis to guarantee Charles's safety. Rescue operations can go wrong very quickly, and lead to dead prisoners as easily as dead guards.

'But the King escapes from his Parliamentarian captors for a few weeks in November of 1647, and it is while he is at liberty that Hamblin judges the time right for an appeal to Louis. Perhaps Charles manages to get word to him, and orders his plan put into action? Whatever the case, Hamblin's exit is barred by the troop of belligerent Roundheads camped in his grounds. If he cannot deliver his precious cargo to the King of France, then he must ensure someone else can.

'So it is that he conceives of a most audacious plan. Barring his doors in order to gain enough time to complete his task, he sets out to combine his skills in art and cryptography to create a riddle which only a man he has specifically chosen could ever solve. He subtly amends something in each of six works of art. That done, he carefully secretes the proclamation where it will not be found, except by those he wishes to find it. Finally, he writes a letter to the man he has chosen, Simon Jarvis, providing just enough information for the recipient to find the proclamation and take it to the French court.

'A brave, brave man, Horace Hamblin, in addition to his many other talents. He must have known his own death was imminent, yet he spent the last days of his life constructing a great riddle which he hoped would save the King with whom he had once been so close. Unfortunately, something went wrong, and the letter to Jarvis was never sent, but instead ended up inside a neglected book in a forgotten library, until the Lord of Strange Deaths stumbled across it.'

'By which time, it was long past the time when Hamblin could do the King any good,' I said, a little sadly.

'That is true, Dr Watson,' Zenith said, equally sorrowfully, 'but the true irony is that the result of Hamblin's efforts could be a scandal that would rock the current holders of the British crown. Picture the scene if political agitators should get wind of this. An English King selling his homeland to save his own skin? It would play very well amongst the radicals and malcontents who plague the capital cities of Europe. That is something I would avoid at any cost. It was for that reason that I agreed that once we knew what the Treasure consisted of, we should ask you, a most – if you will forgive the description – solid Englishman to decide its fate.'

It struck me that, for all his exaggerated indolence, there was an iron core and a strong intellect contained within Zenith, which was utterly unconnected to his more commonly displayed persona. I couldn't be sure which aspect was a sham, but I was positive that the Albino was a man to be respected as much as feared.

He took a step back and inclined his head just a notch in my direction. 'What shall we do with England's Treasure, John Watson? The decision is yours.'

I knew what would be the safest decision, but instinctively I also realised that the safest and the best options were not one and the same. 'We should destroy this document immediately, of course,' I said, 'but… it is a thing of beauty, *and* of historical importance. One day it will have no power left, and on that day I should not care to be the one who must admit he had destroyed it through fear.'

Zenith appeared content with my answer. He flicked his cigarette into the fire and prepared to take his leave.

Holmes tapped one finger against his lips, then nodded once, sharply, towards the Albino. 'My brother Mycroft will be able to make the document disappear, but without losing it forever. You have my word on the matter, Zenith.'

Zenith nodded in turn and, as they stood together in front of the fire, I was struck by the resemblance between the two men – the one a tall, spare and dark-haired Englishman, the other an equally gaunt white-haired Continental. One man a negative image of the other, they shook hands. Zenith retrieved his hat and cane, and with a short bow to each of us, exited through the drawing-room window and was quickly lost in the darkness outside.

As Holmes carefully folded King Charles's proclamation and placed it in his inner jacket pocket, I heard the first sounds of carriages arriving at the front of the house, followed by the subdued chatter of many men attempting to remain in ranks as they approached an unfamiliar target in the dark.

'Perhaps you should open the door for the Inspector,' Holmes suggested solemnly, but with a mischievous smile. 'I doubt that he will have brought Miss Rhodes along, but I'm sure he can direct you to her.' His smile widened to a definite grin. 'Should you wish to check on the lady, of course.'

'Really, Holmes!' I protested, but with no conviction, and hurried to welcome Lestrade and his men.

Acknowledgements

As is customary with a first novel, I have a few people to thank for getting me this far. Scott Liddell, Paul Magrs and George Mann have been both the best friends I could hope to have and a constant source of encouragement and good advice. Angela Douglas, Elaine Conway and Ross Douglas read the book in draft and gave me excellent, if overly kind, feedback, and Miranda Jewess was as near to perfect an editor as a fledgling author could hope to have.

Finally, all the love and thanks in the world to my wife Julie, and my children Alex, Cameron and Matthew, who have put up with me cluttering the house with tat for years now, and didn't complain *too* much when I added a pile of books on Victorian London while researching *The Albino's Treasure*.

About the Author

S tuart Douglas is the author of numerous short stories and novellas, and has edited several anthologies, including *Iris Wildthyme and the Celestial Omnibus* and *The Obverse Book of Detectives*. He was a contributor to Titan's *Encounters of Sherlock Holmes* anthology; *Publishers Weekly* described his story as 'reminiscent of the original brilliance that Conan Doyle gave us more than a century ago'. In 2009 he set up Obverse Books with Paul Magrs, which holds the short story rights to Sexton Blake and Fiction Paradox, and is the features editor of the *British Fantasy Society Journal*. He lives in Edinburgh with his wife and three children.

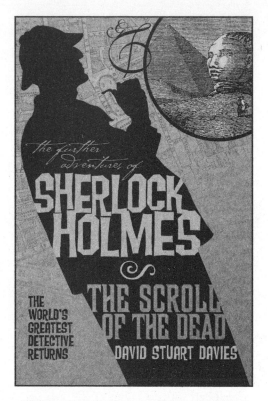

THE FURTHER ADVENTURES
OF SHERLOCK HOLMES

THE SCROLL OF THE DEAD

David Stuart Davies

In this fast-paced adventure, Sherlock Holmes attends a seance to unmask
an impostor posing as a medium. His foe, Sebastian Melmoth is a man hell-
bent on discovering a mysterious Egyptian papyrus that may hold the key
to immortality. It is up to Holmes and Watson to use their deductive skills
to stop him or face disaster.

ISBN: 9781848564930

AVAILABLE NOW!

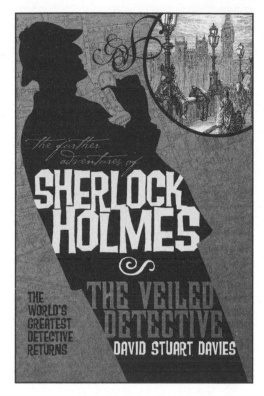

THE FURTHER ADVENTURES
OF SHERLOCK HOLMES
THE VEILED DETECTIVE

David Stuart Davies

It is 1880, and a young Sherlock Holmes arrives in London to pursue a
career as a private detective. He soon attracts the attention of criminal
mastermind Professor James Moriarty, who is driven by his desire to
control this fledgling genius. Enter Dr John H. Watson, soon to make
history as Holmes' famous companion.

ISBN: 9781848564909

AVAILABLE NOW!

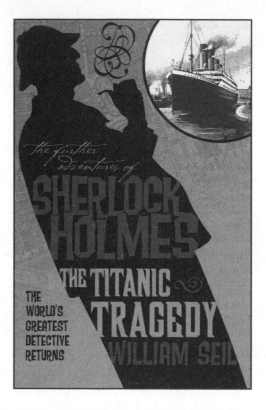

THE FURTHER ADVENTURES
OF SHERLOCK HOLMES

THE TITANIC TRAGEDY

William Seil

Holmes and Watson board the Titanic in 1912, where Holmes is to carry
out a secret government mission. Soon after departure, highly important
submarine plans for the U.S. navy are stolen. Holmes and Watson work
through a list of suspects which includes Colonel James Moriarty, brother
to the late Professor Moriarty—will they find the culprit before tragedy
strikes?

ISBN: 9780857687104

THE FURTHER ADVENTURES
OF SHERLOCK HOLMES

THE WEB WEAVER

Sam Siciliano

A mysterious gypsy places a cruel curse on the guests at a ball. When
a series of terrible misfortunes affects those who attended, Mr. Donald
Wheelwright engages Sherlock Holmes to find out what really happened
that night. Can he save Wheelwright and his beautiful wife Violet from
the devastating curse?

ISBN: 9780857686985

AVAILABLE NOW!

THE FURTHER ADVENTURES OF SHERLOCK HOLMES

THE STAR OF INDIA

Carole Buggé

Holmes and Watson find themselves caught up in a complex chessboard
of a problem, involving a clandestine love affair and the disappearance
of a priceless sapphire. Professor James Moriarty is back to tease and
torment, leading the duo on a chase through the dark and dangerous
back streets of London and beyond.

ISBN: 9780857681218

AVAILABLE NOW!

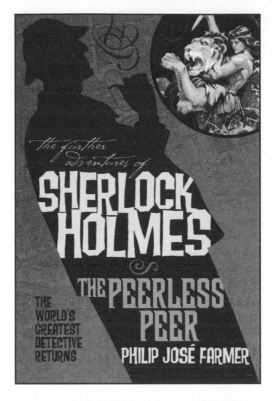

THE FURTHER ADVENTURES
OF SHERLOCK HOLMES

THE PEERLESS PEER

Philip José Farmer

During the Second World War, Mycroft Holmes dispatches his
brother, Sherlock, and Dr. Watson to recover a stolen formula. During
their perilous journey, they are captured by a German zeppelin.
Subsequently forced to abandon ship, the pair parachute into the dark
African jungle where they encounter the lord of the jungle himself…

ISBN: 9780857681201

AVAILABLE NOW!

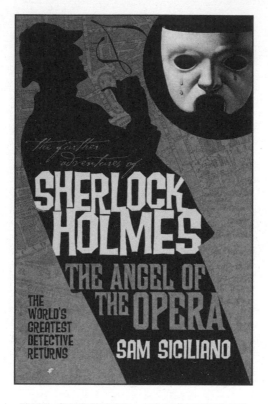

THE FURTHER ADVENTURES
OF SHERLOCK HOLMES

THE ANGEL OF THE OPERA

Sam Siciliano

Paris 1890. Sherlock Holmes is summoned across the English Channel
to the famous Opera House. Once there, he is challenged to discover
the true motivations and secrets of the notorious phantom, who rules its
depths with passion and defiance.

ISBN: 9781848568617

AVAILABLE NOW!

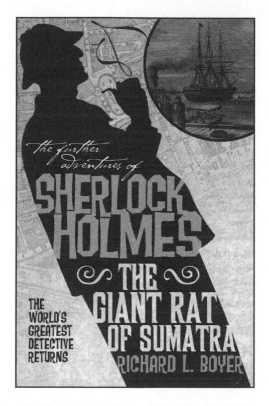

THE FURTHER ADVENTURES
OF SHERLOCK HOLMES

THE GIANT RAT OF SUMATRA

Richard L. Boyer

For many years, Dr. Watson kept the tale of The Giant Rat of
Sumatra a secret. However, before he died, he arranged that
the strange story of the giant rat should be held in the vaults of
a London bank until all the protagonists were dead…

ISBN: 9781848568600

AVAILABLE NOW!

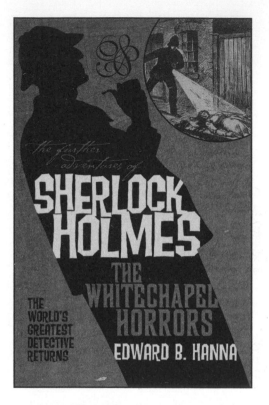

THE FURTHER ADVENTURES
OF SHERLOCK HOLMES

THE WHITECHAPEL HORRORS

Edward B. Hanna

Grotesque murders are being committed on the streets of Whitechapel.
Sherlock Holmes believes he knows the identity of the killer—Jack the
Ripper. But as he delves deeper, Holmes realizes that revealing the
murderer puts much more at stake than just catching a killer…

ISBN: 9781848567498

AVAILABLE NOW!

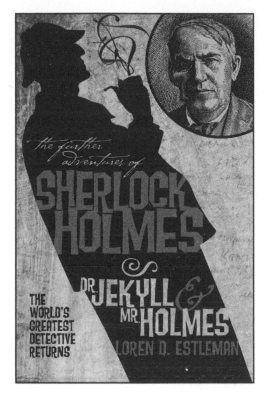

THE FURTHER ADVENTURES
OF SHERLOCK HOLMES

DR. JEKYLL AND MR. HOLMES

Loren D. Estleman

When Sir Danvers Carew is brutally murdered, the Queen herself calls on
Sherlock Holmes to investigate. In the course of his enquiries, the esteemed
detective is struck by the strange link between the highly respectable Dr. Henry
Jekyll and the immoral, debauched Edward Hyde...

ISBN: 9781848567474

AVAILABLE NOW!

THE FURTHER ADVENTURES
OF SHERLOCK HOLMES
SÉANCE FOR A VAMPIRE

Fred Saberhagen

Wealthy British aristocrat Ambrose Altamont hires Sherlock Holmes to
expose two suspect psychics. During the ensuing séance, Altamont's deceased
daughter reappears as a vampire–and Holmes vanishes. Watson has no
choice but to summon the only one who might be able to help–Holmes'
vampire cousin, Prince Dracula.

ISBN: 9781848566774

AVAILABLE NOW!

THE FURTHER ADVENTURES
OF SHERLOCK HOLMES

THE SEVENTH BULLET

Daniel D. Victor

Sherlock Holmes and Dr. Watson travel to New York City to investigate the
assassination of true-life muckraker and author David Graham Phillips. They
soon find themselves caught in a web of deceit, violence and political intrigue,
which only the great Sherlock Holmes can unravel.

ISBN: 9781848566767

AVAILABLE NOW!

THE FURTHER ADVENTURES
OF SHERLOCK HOLMES

THE STALWART COMPANIONS

H. Paul Jeffers

Written by future President Theodore Roosevelt long before The Great
Detective's first encounter with Dr. Watson, Holmes visits America to solve a
most violent and despicable crime. A crime that was to prove the most taxing of
his brilliant career.

ISBN: 9781848565098

AVAILABLE NOW!

THE FURTHER ADVENTURES
OF SHERLOCK HOLMES

THE MAN FROM HELL

Barrie Roberts

The murder of Lord Blackwater propels Holmes and Watson into an
intriguing case that points to the shadowy figure known only as 'The Man
from the Gates of Hell'. A tangled web of deceit, violence and tragedy
unravels as Holmes' deductions bring him closer to those behind the plot.

ISBN: 9781848565081

AVAILABLE NOW!

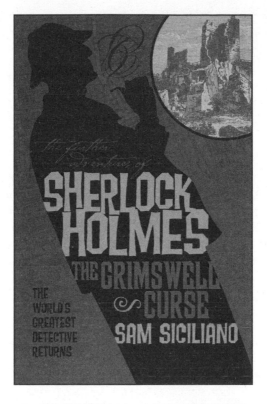

THE FURTHER ADVENTURES
OF SHERLOCK HOLMES

THE GRIMSWELL CURSE

Sam Siciliano

When Rose Grimswell breaks off her engagement to Lord Frederick Digby, the
concerned fiancé calls on Sherlock Holmes, begging him to visit the ancestral
home and discover the reason for her change of heart.

ISBN: 9781781166819

AVAILABLE NOW!

SHERLOCK HOLMES

THE WILL OF THE DEAD

George Mann

A rich elderly man has fallen to his death, and his will is nowhere to
be found. A tragic accident or something more sinister? The dead
man's nephew comes to Baker Street to beg for Sherlock Holmes's
help. Without the will he fears he will be left penniless, the entire
inheritance passing to his cousin. But just as Holmes and Watson start
their investigation, a mysterious new claimant to the estate appears.
Does this prove that the old man was murdered?

Meanwhile Inspector Charles Bainbridge is trying to solve the case of
the "iron men", mechanical steam-powered giants carrying out daring
jewellery robberies. But how do you stop a machine that feels no
pain and needs no rest? He too may need to call on the expertise of
Sherlock Holmes.

"Mann clearly knows his Holmes, knows what works… the book is
all the better for it." CRIME FICTION LOVER

"Mann writes Holmes in a eloquent way, capturing the period of
the piece perfectly… this is a must read." CULT DEN

"An amazing story… Even in the established world of Sherlock
Holmes, George Mann is a strong voice and sets himself apart!"
BOOK PLANK

WWW.TITANBOOKS.COM

THE SPIRIT BOX

George Mann

German zeppelins rain down death and destruction on London, and Dr Watson is grieving for his nephew, killed on the fields of France.

A cryptic summons from Mycroft Holmes reunites Watson with his one-time companion, as Sherlock comes out of retirement, tasked with solving three unexplained deaths. A politician has drowned in the Thames after giving a pro-German speech; a soldier suggests surrender before feeding himself to a tiger; and a suffragette renounces women's liberation and throws herself under a train. Are these apparent suicides something more sinister, something to do with the mysterious Spirit Box? Their investigation leads them to Ravensthorpe House, and the curious Seaton Underwood, a man whose spectrographs are said to capture men's souls…

"**Arthur Conan Doyle was a master storyteller, and it takes comparable talent to give Holmes a second life… Mann is one of the few to get close to the target.**" DAILY MAIL

"**I would highly recommend this… a fun read.**" FANTASY BOOK REVIEW

"**Our only complaint is that it is over too soon.**" STARBURST

"**An entertaining read.**" EUROCRIME

WWW.TITANBOOKS.COM

SHERLOCK HOLMES
THE BREATH OF GOD

Guy Adams

A body is found crushed to death in the London snow. There are no footprints anywhere near it, almost as if the man was killed by the air itself. While pursuing the case, Sherlock Holmes and Dr. Watson find themselves traveling to Scotland to meet with the one person they have been told can help: Aleister Crowley.

As dark powers encircle them, Holmes' rationalist beliefs begin to be questioned. The unbelievable and unholy are on their trail as they gather a group of the most accomplished occult minds in the country: Doctor John Silence, the so-called "Psychic Doctor"; supernatural investigator Thomas Carnacki; runic expert and demonologist Julian Karswell… But will they be enough? As the century draws to a close it seems London is ready to fall and the infernal abyss is growing wide enough to swallow us all.

"A rollicking horror-filled adventure featuring the world's greatest detective… This is highly recommended." DREAD CENTRAL

"Smartly written in the familiar Holmes style, the book has a crisp wit, high adventure, knowing nods to literary fans, and a well plotted mystery." THE DAILY ROTATION

"A tremendous amount of fun." HELLNOTES

WWW.TITANBOOKS.COM

SHERLOCK HOLMES

THE ARMY OF DR MOREAU

Guy Adams

Dead bodies are found on the streets of London with wounds that
can only be explained as the work of ferocious creatures not native
to the city.

Sherlock Holmes is visited by his brother, Mycroft, who is only
too aware that the bodies are the calling card of Dr Moreau, a
vivisectionist who was working for the British Government, following
in the footsteps of Charles Darwin, before his experiments attracted
negative attention and the work was halted. Mycroft believes that
Moreau's experiments continue and he charges his brother with
tracking the rogue scientist down before matters escalate any further.

A brand-new original novel, detailing a thrilling new case for the
acclaimed detective Sherlock Holmes.

"Deftly handled… this is a must read for all fans of adventure and
fantasy literature." FANTASY BOOK REVIEW

"Well worth a read… Adams is a natural fit for the world of
Sherlock Holmes." STARBURST

"Succeeds both as a literary jeu d'esprit and detective story, with a
broad streak of irreverent humour." FINANCIAL TIMES

WWW.TITANBOOKS.COM

THE STUFF OF NIGHTMARES

James Lovegrove

A spate of bombings has hit London, causing untold damage and loss of life. Meanwhile a strangely garbed figure has been spied haunting the rooftops and grimy back alleys of the capital.

Sherlock Holmes believes this strange masked man may hold the key to the attacks. He moves with the extraordinary agility of a latter-day Spring-Heeled Jack. He possesses weaponry and armour of unprecedented sophistication. He is known only by the name Baron Cauchemar, and he appears to be a scourge of crime and villainy. But is he all that he seems? Holmes and his faithful companion Dr Watson are about to embark on one of their strangest and most exhilarating adventures yet.

"[A] tremendously accomplished thriller which leaves the reader in no doubt that they are in the hands of a confident and skilful craftsman." STARBURST

"Dramatic, gripping, exciting and respectful to its source material, I thoroughly enjoyed every surprise and twist as the story unfolded." FANTASY BOOK REVIEW

"This is delicious stuff, marrying the standard notions of Holmesiana with the kind of imagination we expect from Lovegrove." CRIMETIME

WWW.TITANBOOKS.COM

SHERLOCK HOLMES
GODS OF WAR

James Lovegrove

It is 1913, and Dr Watson is visiting Sherlock Holmes at his retirement cottage near Eastbourne when tragedy strikes: the body of a young man, Patrick Mallinson, is found under the cliffs of Beachy Head.

The dead man's father, a wealthy businessman, engages Holmes to prove that his son committed suicide, the result of a failed love affair with an older woman. Yet the woman in question insists that there is more to Patrick's death. She has seen mysterious symbols drawn on his body, and fears that he was under the influence of a malevolent cult. When an attempt is made on Watson's life, it seems that she may be proved right. The threat of war hangs over England, and there is no telling what sinister forces are at work…

WWW.TITANBOOKS.COM

SHERLOCK HOLMES

THE THINKING ENGINE

James Lovegrove

March 1895. Hilary Term at Oxford. Professor Quantock has put
the finishing touches to a wondrous computational device which, he
claims, is capable of analytical thought to rival that of the cleverest
men alive. Indeed, his so-called Thinking Engine seems equal to
Sherlock Holmes himself in its deductive powers.

To prove his point, Quantock programmes his machine to solve a
murder. Sherlock Holmes cannot ignore this challenge, so he and
Watson travel to Oxford, where a battle of wits ensues between the
great detective and his mechanical counterpart as they compete to
see which of them can be first to solve a series of crimes. But as man
and machine vie for supremacy, it becomes clear that the Thinking
Engine has its own agenda.

Holmes and Watson's lives are on the line as a ghost from the past
catches up with them…

AVAILABLE AUGUST 2015

WWW.TITANBOOKS.COM

3 1901 05772 9412